PENGUIN BOOKS

A STONE OF THE HEART

John Brady was born in Dublin. He now lives with his family in Toronto and makes frequent visits to Ireland. His other Minogue books include *Unholy Ground* (1989), *Sic Transit* (1990) and a work in progress, *All Souls*. Brady, a heavily disguised introvert, holds Canadian citizenship but travels on an Irish passport.

D0892193

A STONE
OF THE HEART

John Brady

PENGUIN BOOKS

PENGUIN BOOKS

Published by the Penguin Group
27 Wrights Lane, London W8 5TZ, England
Viking Penguin Inc., 40 West 23rd Street, New York, New York 10010, USA
Penguin Books Australia Ltd, Ringwood, Victoria, Australia
Penguin Books Canada Ltd, 2801 John Street, Markham, Ontario, Canada L3R 1B4
Penguin Books (NZ) Ltd, 182–190 Wairau Road, Auckland 10, New Zealand

Penguin Books Ltd, Registered Offices: Harmondsworth, Middlesex, England

For Hanna, Julia, Elizabeth and my mother, Mary Brady
– and in memory of my father, Christopher Brady

First published by Constable & Company Ltd 1988
Published in Penguin Books 1990
1 3 5 7 9 10 8 6 4 2

Printed and bound in Great Britain by
Cox & Wyman Ltd, Reading

CHAPTER ONE

Too long a sacrifice can make a stone of the heart
W B Yeats, "Easter 1916"

Mary Brosnahan alighted from the train at Pearse Street station. Although she was going to be late for Miss Black—she could see Miss Black's tight little mouth saying 'nine sharp'—Mary was not one for running. Her only sister, Francie, had had a stroke three years ago and Francie was only fifty-three, three years younger than Mary.

Mary pressed into the Friday morning crowd which was flowing toward the top of the stairs. Behind her, the station began to vibrate and thunder with the starting train's efforts to push itself on to the south suburbs of Dublin. Mary had known these same trains for thirty years. Like most other Dubliners starting into the 1980s in their greying city, Mary had insulated herself with a benign cynicism. No matter what they said, the new electric trains were a pipe dream concocted to catch votes. Never happen, not in a million years.

While Mary was on the train she had caught sight of the headline on the *Independent*. Now it appeared to her again in the stacks of papers by the foot of the stairs: "*Kidnapped RUC man found dead.*" Another one, she thought.

Mary's attention was then taken up with negotiating the murderous traffic in Pearse Street. She pressed the button for the pedestrian light and waited. Momentarily, she recalled the headline again and the photograph of something (clothes? a sack?) lying in a ditch, with policemen and soldiers standing around. As the light changed, she scurried through the crowd and made her way toward the back gate of Trinity College.

Mary worked as a skip in the college. Her job was to house-clean the students' rooms and other residences. She had been doing this for fifteen years. She entered the grounds and immediately headed for the passageway between the gymnasium and the science blocks. A bicycle hummed by slowly with its chain rattling. Again Mary recalled the photograph in the *Independent*. This time, she summoned up the memory of the daily glimpses of the Dublin mountains she caught as her train crossed the Liffey by the Custom House. Mary seized on this recollection to quell the feather touch of anxiety she felt coming over her.

She emerged from the passageway to face the broad playing fields lined with trees. Mary did not miss the propriety of the flowers and shrubs held in by the tended beds which followed alongside the path. There was care taken here and things were kept in order—at least that could be said for the place, no matter the likes of Miss Black who ran it. Outside the walls, Dublin had gone to pot in Mary's estimation. Where was the polite and decent city she had grown up in? You'd be run over by cars and you on the footpath even, she had concluded. The clerks in the shops didn't so much as look at you these days. People eating in restaurants and houses being knocked down for shops and offices.

"It's them Johnny-Jump-Ups from outside of Dublin has the place gone to hell. What do you call them, the entrepreneurs and the like. Hucksters and bogmen. They take the money and run," Mick said.

The thing was, it was happening all over the world. Like Father

O'Brien said in the pulpit, things were changing too quickly. We didn't have our priorities right, he said. That's it, Mary thought, we don't have our house in order, we don't have our priorities right.

Mary quickened her pace. She consoled herself that at least it was Friday. Miss Black and her 'nine sharp.' Little dry old Protestant face on her, Mary thought scornfully. What was it one of the other skips said she'd like to ask her . . . ? 'O Miss Black, how's your arse for cracking walnuts?'

Mary imagined the house they'd buy after they retired. It'd be out in Portmarnock with a bit of sea air, near the amenities. A bungalow with a garden for Mick, someplace a person wouldn't be beat up or burgled or run over by traffic. At least it wasn't like up the North, with men shot dead at their doors in front of their families, she thought.

Mary's eye was caught by the sight of a piece of white plastic bag lying in the clump of bushes. Late as she was, Mary was affronted by this. She looked around at the groups of students who passed. None of these youngsters would bother to pick it up of course. Exasperated, Mary stopped and sought a way into the clump which would allow her to get at the bag without getting up to her ankles in muck. She became even more irritated.

Mary walked around the back of the bushes and bent to get into the bag. Bent over, she poked at it with her umbrella, pinning it to the earth. Then she tried to flick it back toward her. She couldn't. The bag was full of something. Mary became angry. She inched in further and looked down at it. It was full of bits of paper. It had to have been some student blind drunk last night who had thrown his notes away. Probably one of them engineers, she surmised, dealing out justice to the anonymous culprit.

Mary picked up the bag. She noticed the sleeve of a coat some six feet away. She hadn't seen it from where she had stood before. She looked at the shrubs nearby. Some of the stalks and branches were showing spots of white where they had been broken. There must have been drink taken last night, she decided. Mary made

3

her way over, her anger now tempered by anxiety and the embarrassment at being in the middle of a bed of shrubs, late for work.

A group of Modern Language students had stepped out of the library to have a smoke and a sit-down in the chairs facing College Park. One of them was ridiculing a psychoanalytic reading of the character of Hamlet when a scream came across the air from behind them. Then another scream.

As they turned, Mary came thrashing out of the bushes with her mouth open and her hat snagged on a bush behind her. She tripped and fell over a waist-high red-leafed bush. Her forearms beat into the ground to save her fall. She scrambled to get up, sliding in the clay again. Mary Brosnahan was quite unconcerned about being late for Miss Black, moving to Portmarnock or fretting about Dublin's lost civic pride. Her chief concern was to get away from that clump of bushes and shrubs, where her pattern of day-to-day life had been wrecked completely for some time to come by finding the corpse with its head bashed in.

That Friday afternoon saw Inspector James Kilmartin, offices in Dublin Castle, in the company of Garda Tom Connors, of Kevin Street Garda Station but seconded for training to the Murder Squad, sitting in a navy blue unmarked Garda car.

Kilmartin and Connors had just stepped out of the side gate of Trinity College. Kilmartin had listened to Mulholland and then Lacey from Garda Forensic while Connors stood with his hands pocketed, his hair tossing almost in rhythm with the flapping ends of the plastic cordon pegged around the site. The two detectives from Forensic took turns pointing to spots in the bushes. Three other men crouched in the bushes as they talked. Kilmartin watched the three as they inched their ways from spot to spot on their hunkers. He considered that they would make reasonable gardeners but that they'd need something better than tweezers and plastic bags.

"No, sir. No sign of whatever gave him the clout," Lacey had said.

"Nothing like a little hatchet or that class of thing?" Kilmartin murmured.

"Divil a bit, sir. He was brought over here all the same. We might do better now when we find out where he was done in."

"Dragged, is it?" Kilmartin asked.

"Carried would probably be it, sir. He's a hefty lad so . . ."

"Did ye take any casts, then?"

"We took two, sir. They were women's shoes."

Kilmartin looked over at Connors and then beyond him to the pallid sky above the Georgian parapets of the college buildings. Connors was staring at the three policemen in the bushes. They reminded him of fowl on the lookout for grains in a farmyard.

Back in the car, Kilmartin sighed.

"Rain, is it, Connors?"

"You'd never know now, sir. It has the look of it."

Kilmartin lapsed into silence. Connors had learned to wait. Two youngsters with skinhead cuts appeared on Connors' side of the car. The two laughed and tapped on the glass. Connors glanced at Kilmartin before rolling down the window.

"How fast does it go?" asked one of them. "A hundred? Do you have a gun? Aren't you a detective? Show us how the radio works. Any bulletproof glass? Give us a bit of the siren."

Kilmartin, a giant to the two and a man who was out of short trousers in Ballina, County Mayo, some forty years earlier, shifted his weight in the passenger seat.

"Who's your man?" said one of the youngsters, eyeing Kilmartin.

"I'm Kojak. The wheelman here is Danno. Book 'em, Danno. Murder one." Kilmartin said.

The youngsters began laughing again. Connors pulled away from the kerb. Kilmartin wasn't as sour as he looked.

"The telly is a divil, isn't it Connors?"

"The kids are nice though. You'd never imagine them turning turk on you in a few years," said Connors.

"God, haven't you the black heart in you today. Arra, you'll be all right. Sure isn't it Friday?"

Connors grinned again. "My Ma told me that people in parts of Dublin eat their young, so she did," Connors said.

"God knows now she might be right," agreed Kilmartin. He thought about putting on his seat-belt but decided he'd have too much trouble reaching in for his cigarettes.

"Any messages?"

"None, sir."

"Off to Pearse Street. We'll talk to the lads on the spot."

"What was the name of the student?" Connors asked.

"A fella by the name of Jarlath Walsh. Jarlath Walsh."

Kilmartin spent no more than twenty minutes listening to the reports from the two Gardai in Pearse Street station. Kilmartin had worked out of Pearse Street and he hated the building. It gave him the willies. It was old and grimy and cramped. Plenty of action there though, too much. A rough start for a Guard just out of the training college in Templemore. He'd be on the beat right in the middle of Dublin. Kilmartin hated it the day he stepped in the door those many years ago. He had hoped to be posted to a fair-sized town in the West, to be near his folks. He had lived and raised a family in Dublin, however.

He told Connors not to make any notes. It might discourage candour and memory. It would look impertinent too. These two Gardai were well senior to Connors though not in rank. They sat on the wooden chairs poking into their notebooks, their sky-blue shirts making Kilmartin think of Spain.

"About fourteen minutes after nine, sir," one of them was saying. No, no rocks nearby. The body was lying on its back. The forensic team was there at half past ten. Yes, there were some marks in the clay around the body, like shoeprints, dug in at the heel, sort of. *That'd be that woman, Brosnahan, leaping around like a madwoman,* Kilmartin thought. *Shouldn't be so hard on her.* Twigs broken and bent back, yes. Nothing in his hands. Sure it was a he straight away? Yes, the lower part of the face was intact. A bit of a moustache. A white plastic supermarket bag, they'd be for the notes and books. *Why did a student have to use*

6

that as a school-bag? Trinity College students not able to afford
school-bags? Four hundred years of Anglo-Irish privilege walled
up in the place and a student couldn't afford a bag for his books?

Kilmartin noticed a growing sense of pessimism leaking into his chest. It wasn't a run of the mill one, one of those unglamorous family squabbles that ended in a death with the whole thing more or less wrapped up in twenty-four hours. The public wouldn't be much thrilled to find out how petty the causes were for most murders. No, they wanted the headlines, a bit of sex involved, a name they knew, maybe an international link. This was shaping up to be none of these, it seemed. More like a lunatic on the loose or some panicky young fella on drugs. Twenty years of age, a student.

The two men had stopped talking and, along with Connors, were looking at Kilmartin.

"Thank you, gentlemen. Will you please give your notebooks to the desk sergeant for safe keeping. I'll be requiring them at a later date perhaps."

The two Gardai stood up and left the room without a word.

"How's the old enemy, Connors?"

"Half past four, sir."

Jesus, Mary and Joseph, Kilmartin thought, the traffic would be like the chariot race in *Ben Hur*.

"*Tempus fugit.* Off to the Castle. You can leave me there."

A photocopy of a handwritten Forensic Bureau report lay in a wire 'In' basket on Kilmartin's desk. Under these pages he found a crisp envelope containing fourteen black and white photographs and nine smaller Polaroid colour snapshots. Kilmartin had given up trying to get used to the luridly colourful violence he found on the snapshots. Somehow he still expected holiday scenes, people with pink eyeballs at parties.

As he looked through the photographs his pessimism drifted into a stoic pragmatism which was to attend his reading of the draft report. Nothing doing in the boy's bag, save the peculiarity of the bag itself for carrying lecture notes. A train ticket from Dun Laoghaire, bits of things that made up a life. A proper hanky

7

(fresh cotton), six pounds and change, glasses, keys, a watch. Snaps of the site looked like wild Borneo. The body was neater than it could have been; a little care in arranging things?

Walsh, Jarlath Walsh. Student. Kilmartin ruminated for several minutes. It would be late this evening before he'd have copies of statements and a who's-who around the life, now gone but reborn in print in a fattening Garda file, of Mr Jarlath Walsh.

Kilmartin phoned the desk. As the detective answered, Kilmartin languidly wrote down the names of the one detective and four uniformed Gardai who were interviewing Walsh's tutor and his pals in the college. It had fallen to the detective to go to Walsh's parents.

"And have Delaney telephone me at home by eleven tonight, like a good man."

Kilmartin looked through the photographs again. There wasn't much blood on or around the head. Dragged? Carried? The flash had been a little close and the skin seemed to glow with a luminescence which made the gaping mouth all the more odd. Kilmartin noted the tips of the upper teeth showing. His gaze roved to the slight opening between the eyelids, the deceptive sign of life. The forehead was darkened and misshapen, flattened.

An acidy space in his stomach widened. That would be his conscience. Kilmartin became exasperated, but he couldn't settle on a reason for it. "Out with it," he said aloud. Well, sure who else would be able for this one? Shag it. He wrote Minogue's name in his notebook, ripped out the page and stapled it to the reports. Shite, no staples. Rather than sit in Dublin's Friday evening traffic, Kilmartin extricated a poor quality cigar from the back of his desk. He eased his buttocks onto one side and allowed himself a fart, a breezer they called them as children. The fart was in some respects less offensive than the cigar. The world at bay, Kilmartin's stoicism eased a little. Trusting his own mistrust, Kilmartin decided he would give his squad until Monday, but he would call Minogue before then. Kilmartin drew on the cigar. Not for the first time, he tried to understand why he wanted Minogue in on this and why that prospect made him nervous.

Because he felt that Minogue was owed something? Maybe he, Kilmartin, was superstitious and wouldn't admit it to himself.

Kilmartin blew a ring across the desk. It was over a year now since the British Ambassador had been blown to smithereens outside the residence in Stepaside. Somehow Minogue had avoided the same fate, by feet, by seconds. Freakish but hardly magical, no.

Even before that, Kilmartin had been conscious of currents in Minogue which marked him apart. Kilmartin believed that his unease with Minogue was the key to Minogue's rank, rather the lack of it. Minogue doubtlessly made his superiors a bit nervous, the same way he made Kilmartin weigh his words or put on the façade of casual conversation. A circumspect man, Minogue, some powerful imminence in him. He was rumoured to have a terrific sense of humour.

Some months after Minogue came back on duty, Kilmartin wondered if Minogue had snapped maybe, or had become depressed. Minogue had not been publicly outraged, he hadn't sought vengeance. He hadn't relentlessly questioned his hospital room visitors about the investigation. Minogue seemed to have liked the lying in bed, the long afternoons reading in the hospital. His tall frame humping the sheets up, his head resting on a farmer's hand, his other hand holding a book. Minogue didn't shave for weeks. His wife, Kathleen, didn't fuss him.

When Kilmartin went to see him one Sunday, Minogue was asleep. Kathleen had fallen asleep in the chair next to the bed. The broadcast of the hurling match could be heard from the transistor radio. Clare and Offaly at it. Why did Kilmartin remember that detail? Something had impressed itself on him, this scene of a sleeping couple, one supposed to be watching over the other.

Kilmartin had begun a note to leave with them, rather than wake them. Just as he finished, the daughter came in, Iseult. A name out of the past, a darkly Celtic presence: jet-black hair, the same as Minogue had had, tall. A long peasanty black dress and a shapeless coat. Fashion, is it? The fine arts stuff sent them all a bit off. Minogue stirred awake. His eyes opened and he was

9

fully awake, just like that. A book slipped off the bed and woke Kathleen. She replaced it. A book by that fellow Victor Hugo, *Les Misérables*. What kind of a shagging book was that to be reading and him barely back from the dead after that bombing? A year ago nearly.

Kilmartin stood and looked out the window. The street might as well be a carpark with the traffic. *Les Misérables*, he thought, stubbing out the cigar. Must have been set in Dublin. "Fucking city," Kilmartin whispered, almost disinterestedly.

CHAPTER TWO

On Sunday morning, Minogue and his wife left after Mass in
Kilmacud at about a quarter to ten. Mrs Minogue, more devout
than any of her family, much favoured the condensed richness of
a quick sermon. She infinitely preferred the apt word to the
hyperbole which the younger priests seemed to be fond of. Father
O'Rourke still gave them the goods though. His sermons lasted
about five minutes and they were deceptively simple. Then, on
with the Mass and the next thing you knew, you were out the
door three quarters of an hour later. That was just about time
for Minogue to be more or less awake.

Their children confused Minogue's silence in the mornings
with bad humour although he rarely had a cross word to say. He
usually said nothing at all if something irritated him. Through
twenty-four years, Kathleen Minogue knew almost all the signs:
his head would go down, his eyebrows would raise a frown on
his forehead. He'd look around for more tea or maybe fiddle with
the cup. It was Minogue's idea to make the walk down the pier

in Dun Laoghaire after Mass on Sunday. The idea was to let their two children get up late and make all the fuss and hullaballoo they wanted. Iseult could be depended on to come in at about one and Daithi before three every Sunday morning. These hours started when both of them started university. Minogue wondered if that was cause and effect.

Kathleen was for putting the hammer down, 'as long as you're in this house, you'll . . . ' kind of thing. Minogue's own anxiety about their children brought him to a delicate equilibrium. He persuaded Kathleen to hold off on her plan, but every now and then he had to renegotiate with her. The idea was not to talk about Mass or coming in late but to come back home by about mid-day Sunday after a walk and read of the papers. Iseult would have dinner on and Daithi would be presentable, no questions asked. It worked.

Kathleen had been making the mistake of going to wake up Daithi on Sunday mornings. When she had opened the bedroom door, not only was the room like the wreck of the *Hesperus*, but there was also an appalling smell of stale boozy breath and a night's release of beer farts. Minogue had then been pointed toward the stairs and encouraged in no uncertain terms to rouse their son, express the joint parental disapproval and air the room. Minogue, who had been on a tear manys a time at Daithi's age but now knew better and feared for his insides, worried about Daithi's crowd. A crowd of engineering students put next to a rake of drink brought on a lot of high jinks.

Minogue climbed into the car and handed the *Sunday Press* to Kathleen. The car rocked as it took Minogue's weight. While Kathleen began scanning the headlines, Minogue fumbled the keys into the ignition.

"Dun Laoghaire, for a walk, will we?" he asked.

"Down the pier is it? Tell him Inspector Kilmartin, that is to say, Jim Kilmartin, called. I'll telephone him at dinner time. Good day to you, now."

In Minogue's Kilmacud home, Daithi put down the phone and

cursed his awakening by a policeman, no less. Daithi's neck was stiff and his bowels were groaning. A part of his mind registered that seeing as he had swallowed about seven pints of stout the night before, some issue would have to come of it and rapidly. Iseult eyed him and murmured over her handmade teacup.

"Well, brother. In the arms of Bacchus last night?"

"What?"

"Did you fill up well last night?"

"And if I did? I'm not the kind of yo-yo to sit around like the artsy-fartsy crowd talking about the state of the world."

"Like me?" Iseult said.

"Like your pals, anyhow."

"Did you hear about the Irish homosexual, brother dear? Preferred women to drink."

"Nothing personal, I suppose. You want me married off like the Ma, is that it? "

"Arra no, stay home and look after your mother," she replied.

"You're cracked, so you are. When'll the parents be home?"

"Half past twelve."

"An Inspector Kilmartin will be calling for the Da on the blower."

"Matt, did you read that someone told Gay Byrne to eff off on the 'Late Late' last night?" Served him right, thought Minogue. Byrne and the rest of them were a crowd of yobboes.

"No, I didn't. What prize will the fella be getting? For his candour I mean," Minogue said.

"Now would you lookit," Kathleen said quickly. "I suppose he got a rise out of this fella. Liam Cullen. You know, that painter who makes a religion out of being from Dublin."

"Well, they're your crowd, Kathleen. Good Auld Dublin," quipped Minogue. He inched the car into the line-up leaving the church carpark.

"Well, Dublin or not, there was no call for making a show of us with the language," Kathleen added.

"They give the name of the young lad killed the other night.

Inside in Trinity College. Jarlath Walsh. He's not a Walsh we know, is he now, Matt?"

"I can't place him, no."

"Not Jackie Walsh in Bray, his lad?"

"No, that's Brendan."

"God, isn't it terrible, a young lad to be murdered like that?" Kathleen said.

Minogue allowed that it was. As Kathleen read on, Minogue's thoughts ran adrift.

Minogue would have liked to buy one of the British newspapers, like the *Observer* or the *Times*. Minogue used to buy the *Sunday Telegraph* years ago, but since the North, the newspaper had come out in the open as a Tory rag. Minogue tried the *Times* and the *Observer*, but they shoved in enough slurs to turn him away from them. The Irish Sunday papers were rags too.

Approaching Monkstown, Minogue awoke to the understanding that he had not remembered driving away from the church. How had they made it to here and him daydreaming? He glanced over at Kathleen. High cheekbones on her, her eyes disappeared when she laughed. Was she fifty this year?

"Do you know something? I'd love to pick up on the French again. I'll get myself a Paris *Match*," Minogue said to his wife.

The car breasted the hill looking down into Dublin Bay. Howth rested across the postcard-blue water, beyond the East Pier.

Kathleen looked over at him. Senile dementia, it had been called in her mother's day. At fifty-two? Clare people are a bit off anyway.

"Would you now, lovey? Maybe you can teach me a bit and we can go on a holiday to France someday."

She's learning, thought Minogue. Far more effective than coming out with 'Matt Minogue, are you going a bit quare?'

Minogue smiled. He parked the car close to Dun Laoghaire train station. Kathleen and he began strolling toward the pier.

"We're practising for Paris now, Mrs Minogue. We're *boulevardiers*," said Minogue.

14

Kilmartin turned aside from the hurling match on the telly that Sunday afternoon. It was a slow game. The playing field was sodden. The players were all splatted in mud from the opening minutes and the greasy leather ball slipped from players' fingers and off the ends of their sticks. Maybe the Canadians had the right idea, Kilmartin mused, put it on ice and call it hockey.

He fingered through his notebook and practised phrases silently. He felt awkward talking with Minogue, especially since Minogue's injury. Kilmartin dialled. Minogue answered. As he waited for Minogue to finish the greeting, those two seconds brought the image of the Commissioner confiding over his glass in The Bailey those months ago: *jobs which will take his interest, challenges. He refused the disability pension and he still another eight years before the pension. No, he's not handicapped at all outwardly. What we need to do, because he's one of our own, is to give him a new hurley stick, a new reason to go back into the game, if you follow my analogy.* That was fine and well, thought Kilmartin in the hissy quiet after Minogue's greeting, but Minogue might translate it as pity. He'd bridle at that to be sure.

"Good day to you, Matt. Tell me, are you following the match on the telly?" asked Kilmartin.

"I'm not, Jimmy, but I might take a look at what the opposition might be like come the final this year."

"Gob now, aren't you Claremen very cocky now? And how do ye know ye'll get by Cork?"

"Well now. I'm surprised at you, Jimmy, and you a Mayoman rooting for the Cork crowd, but the game is the thing I suppose . . . " said Minogue.

"And will the Clare team be wearing shoes on the field this year, Matt?" Kilmartin jibed.

"Well now. The thing is, Jimmy, the lumps of raw meat were left in the usual spots in under the rocks. God in his providence will decide what class of person will come down and how they'll be attired. The ones who carry sticks, we call them hurlers and we don't look to the footwear. Fate and natural selection have decided the rest by now."

15

None of which was true, of course, thought Kilmartin. Minogue's mannerly dissembling was his way of keeping an order. Here was Minogue doing and saying exactly what one might expect, as if he were subtly mimicking the images people had of him, but with no rancour that Kilmartin, at least, could detect. Where was the twist, Kilmartin wondered. How did Minogue get him to think like this?

Kilmartin asked him if he had read the papers. Minogue replied he had. Had he read about the murder of the student in Trinity? He had. On Saturday's paper, it had been: *'Body of student found in suspicious circumstances with foul play suspected.'*

"It was in today's paper, Jim."

"Well. I have a feeling about this one. Nothing has turned up from the lads looking to it right now. I have the feeling it requires the likes of yourself to come at it."

Silence. Kilmartin wondered if Minogue saw charity in this, if Minogue felt he was being deeded a case to keep him interested. Maybe to test the waters and see if his brain was on the ball after last year.

"Well now. It has the makings of a good little detective thriller, Jimmy."

Equivocal silence again. Kilmartin, who had large feet and plenty of nerve, went direct.

"Would it be something you could drop your current duties for?"

Minogue realised it was not a roundabout question. He knew that Kilmartin could requisition him. In case Kilmartin had forgotten the hierarchy, Minogue placed the formal step out for him.

"As soon as Jack Higgins gives the imprimatur, I expect."

"I took the liberty, Matt. Although he says his office will suffer while you'd be away."

Indeed, thought Minogue. The conversation had really quite run away with them both. He smiled at the almost mechanical way the pleasantries and face-saving entered, registered and left the talk. Miss me, he thought and smiled again. There'd be plenty more bits of housebreaking today and tomorrow and the day after, and Detective Superintendent Jack Higgins would still manage.

"All right so, Jimmy," said Minogue.

"I have all the stuff that's coming for the moment up in the Castle. Will you come up about ten tomorrow?"

"I will that, Jimmy."

"To be sure. To be sure. Connors, my aide-de-camp, will go over to Donavan, the State Pathologist, with you. Needs the experience. How about one o'clock and ye can meet here and go off to Donavan?"

"Grand, so."

"And how's the family?" Kilmartin asked.

"The usual. They have me driven mad. Business as usual."

"Remember me to Kathleen, Matt."

So, Minogue thought as he began strolling toward the kitchen. They want to see if I'm the full round of the clock still. He stopped and looked at the copy of Magritte's *Memory* which Iseult had bought him for his birthday. Now why had she done that? She had said that when she saw it, she knew it was for him. That was the way young people talked, that throwaway, confident exaggeration. Still, he liked the picture's coolness and its stillness. It reminded him, for no reason that made sense, of his father playing "The Moon behind the Hill" on the melodeon nearly a half century ago. Minogue had learned that daughters more or less broke their fathers' hearts effortlessly.

By half past two, Connors and Minogue were sitting outside the State Pathologist's office. Donavan was already late.

Connors was thinking about the new side to Kilmartin he had seen but an hour before. When Connors was called in, Minogue was sitting while Kilmartin was propelling himself around the room with small talk. Signs on, Connors concluded, the two men had known each other for a long time. Minogue managed to say little, maintaining a thoughtful if distant expression.

"And Connors will drive over with you, Matt, and sit in with

17

ye, if you don't mind. Connors is new to the department and will benefit from the experience to no end entirely. Am I right?"

"To be sure, Inspector," Connors had said.

On the way over to Donavan's office, Minogue asked him if he was related to the Horsey Connors or the Hurling Connors. Connors replied that he knew of neither.

"Well there's Connors in Kilrush now and they were born with hurley sticks in their teeth. The Horsey Connors are from East Clare and they break the bookies in England regularly. As easy as kiss hands."

"Maybe I should have claimed relations with them, Sergeant, because I have no luck on the ponies at all. There's nags I put money on in Leopardstown and bejases I'd say they're still running."

"Oh, a bad sport to an honest man, the same horses," Minogue murmured. "There was another family of girls in Ennis but I would never ask if you have any kin with those Connors, not at all."

"Well, the ones in Ennis, are they Connors or O'Connors?"

"Oh they're Connors too, but they'd be nothing to you at all, I'm sure. A family of girls that never married."

"The Horsey Connors, the Hurley Connors," Connors mused.

"And the ones in Ennis," Minogue sighed.

"Who were they?"

"Well they were called the Whore Connors, so they were," Minogue said resignedly. "Silly of me to bring them into the conversation."

Minogue didn't smile but began to stare out over the bonnet of the car as if he were deep in thought.

Footsteps on the stairs and Donavan appeared from around the corner.

"Good morrow, men," said the doctor.

The two policemen eyed Donavan. He was a well-known eccentric. He wore a greying beard under owlish eyebrows with a red face bursting out from behind the hair. Donavan was

18

crammed into a three-piece tweed suit tailored in the manner of suits of Minogue's father's day.

The office was a morass of paper and knicknacks. Connors observed bottles containing yellowy lumps of something, immersed in clear liquids. It dawned on him that these polypy lumps might well be pieces of flesh, preserved to be viewed and pondered over. A faint odour like a chemist's shop came to Connors as his eyes slipped out of focus and he swallowed, trying to rid himself of an unpleasant sweetness near his tonsils.

Minogue studied Donavan as the pathologist took off his jacket. A rugby player of old, exactly the kind of man who could fall down the stairs sober and not hurt himself, Minogue thought.

"Matt Minogue, Doctor. And my colleague, Detective Connors."

"And how is the bold Inspector Kilmartin back at the ranch, men?"

"Oh, pulling the divil by the tail, Doctor."

Donavan sat heavily into his seat. He pulled a file from under a brimming ashtray.

"Do ye want the pictures, lads?"

"No thanks, Doctor. We'll defer to your description."

"The mob in Pearse Street handed this over to you as a matter of course? The deceased was a young man in good health. I suspect that he had been killed on Thursday night at about 9 P.M. Well he was dead between eight and twelve hours. There. Isn't pathology wonderful?"

"To be sure, Doctor," said Minogue.

"Well. To cut a long story short. There's no doubt this young man was killed by whoever set about it. There was no trick acting and playing kiss-my-arse-and-kiss-my-elbow with this. This wasn't a brawl that got out of hand. I found a moderately severe contusion on the left side of the head. My feeling is that this was a blow rendered by some object such as an iron bar, perhaps a good quality bicycle pump or the like of that. It would have been enough to put him out. It certainly wouldn't have killed him at all, at all. What did in this unfortunate lad was the stone or

19

whatever was used on his head. It appears to have been applied several times. The person wielding it would of necessity have to have given good swings at it . . . maybe from the height of a man's shoulders. Now, I'm speculating here. However, he was given a *coup de grâce*, if you like, with a lot of force applied toward the end of the episode."

"With the same object?" Minogue interrupted.

"To be exact and evasive at the same time, with an object of the same material, surface area and weight. Perhaps another stone."

Connors looked up from his notes, his mouth a little open.

"Scrapings under the nails, nothing."

No struggle? wrote Connors.

"This young man had had a glass or two of wine and some class of Italian food."

Donavan looked directly at Connors.

"Perhaps the Garda would require to see details . . . ?"

Connors looked up abruptly from the notes and swallowed. Minogue glanced at him.

"Leave it in the file for the moment if you please, Doctor," said Minogue.

"Could have used a bit of exercise. But couldn't we all? Non-smoker. A bit fond of his rashers and eggs. No signs of sexual activity, if you follow me. Teeth all his own. Isn't the National Health great?"

"One blow, then others?" queried Minogue.

"Exactly. The thing is that the head would have to have been lying on a surface with no give in it when these stones or the stone were dropped. That alone would account for the particular shattering effect at the back too, you see. A simple principle really, no great shakes. Think of nutcrackers. One side couldn't be make of rubber or the like."

Donavan arched back in his chair and filled a pipe. The file lay open on the desk. They listened to Connors' diligent pencil scratching. The window was full of green, like a big sponge,

20

waving slowly. Nothing like a willow tree to show the time passing, thought Minogue.

"Bad cess to the fecking thing," Donavan said mildly. He threw the lighter across the desk. "I don't doubt that Nora paid twenty pound for this bloody gas lighter with the flame thrower thing for the pipe. And you think it works because it cost an arm and a leg? Not a bit of it," he muttered.

Minogue carried a box of matches to remind himself that he was a free man. If he chose to smoke, he would. Minogue offered his box of matches.

As he did so, he caught sight of Connors' glassy stare. That's what it was, the 'arm and the leg' bit. Minogue tried hard not to laugh.

"Detective, would you check with headquarters on the radio to see if there are further matters requiring our consideration, if you please? I'll be down presently."

Connors made no delay in leaving.

Donavan, wreathed in Amphora smoke, laughed gently.

"Is your man just after his dinner?"

"He's new to the department, Doctor. He is a very quick and able officer-in-the-making, I believe."

"Gob, he's quick at getting through doors. Ah, Nora says I have a warped sense of humour. God knows, maybe she's right. Do you know, there's nothing to this really. I mean, I put the radio on. There'd be the news, a bit of music, an interview or the like. I'd be pinning back skin or using the saw or dissecting one thing or another. I work on my own you know, me and the tape recorder with Radio Eireann in the background. I don't like working with an assistant. It seems rude, somehow. I'm trying to help the poor divil there in the room with me, but sure he's dead. Still trying to explain things even after the person is dead. But it helps. It's preventive medicine in a sense. Your pal will get used to it. It's not personal. You're in the presence of some final truth."

Minogue thought for an instant of the stories about Donavan. Maybe it was by default that he seemed to enjoy the living so

21

much. Donavan was no fool. He was a philosopher who knew enough to be able to laugh. Good man at a wake. Maybe invite him to mine.

"Anything worth hanging onto, Doctor?"

"Well, this is the preliminary, you understand. It'll be all typed up and a few more tests will be in but that won't make much difference. You have the gist of it."

Both men were silent for a minute. Donavan turned his gaze from the window to Minogue.

"As an aside, er—"

"—Matt—"

"Yes, er, Matt . . . I have the feeling of some kind of intention behind this thing. Some kind of deliberation. Maybe it's the shows on the telly. Still, I think there's something to this one. Don't quote me now. That stuff is not my job at all. I'd expect anything."

Minogue was to remember this remark; not the words themselves, but the speculation on Donavan's face. Have to do some Sherlocking on this one.

Connors was leaning on the boot of the car outside trying to make his attempt at nonchalance outdo his sheepishness.

"Come on now and we'll go back to the Castle. Jimmy Kilmartin says he has a desk for me and odds and ends from the other lads in the Squad who were at it over the weekend."

"To be sure," Connors said spiritedly. He was grateful that Minogue had passed up on that very Irish liking to send a jibe his way.

CHAPTER THREE

On Tuesday morning, Minogue found himself at his new desk in Dublin Castle, HQ of the Garda Murder Squad. 'Found myself' were the words that came to him as he settled into the chair, and those were the words he'd report his day to Kathleen with: 'Well, I found myself at this desk, you see.'

He tried the phone. Glory be to God, it worked. Would he have to start taking seriously the Minister for Post and Telegraph's threat to make the phone system work? He took another sip of tea. Jarlath Brendan Walsh, k/a Jarlath Walsh. He must have had a lot on his plate with a name like that. Saint Jarlath was a Galway saint. Minogue had known but one person before in his life by that name and the fellow had wisely called himself Jer.

A black and white photograph of a group of young men and women at a party looked up at Minogue from his desk. This was a picture of a crowd of young ones at Trinity Ball, taken the previous year. Jarlath Walsh looked out from behind glasses. One of his arms disappeared behind the waist of the girl standing next to him. Others in the picture were up to antics and posing, so they must have been into the gargle. Our man Jarlath looked composed, in place, as an older man might.

Next to this photograph was an assorted set of colour snaps, also taken from his parents' box, doubtlessly kept in the same kind of old shoebox on top of the wardrobe as Kathleen kept hers in. A younger fellow with different glasses, standing beside a grandparent; milking a cow somewhere; holding a certificate; seated, posing, at the piano. "Hardly started living really," Minogue murmured, but not the time or place to be maudlin. Stick to the necessities. Well, one of the necessities was to be realistic: this young fellow looked fairly stuffy, bookish and mannered.

Jarlath Brendan Walsh was the eldest of two children, the other one a girl, Maria, away at boarding school in County Kilkenny or to be up to date, currently in the family residence in Foxrock, grieving. Jarlath Brendan Walsh was a twenty-year-old observing Catholic with modest academic achievements behind him as he worked through his second year in the Faculty of Economic and Social Studies in Trinity College, Dublin, Ireland. Jarlath Brendan Walsh had no known reason to get himself bumped off. "He had everything to live for," Minogue muttered.

Soap operas aside, Master Walsh could look forward to some entitlement. His father was a well-to-do fruit importer. The family lived in a big new McInerny house in Foxrock, a fine summit of achievement for a man from the country. Mustn't get snotty, thought Minogue: *I'm a benighted peasant myself but, God help me, I have a Dublinwoman and a family of Dubliners in tow.*

Minogue's view from his office consisted of a grey stone wall, patched decades ago with brick and mortar, slashed into a lunatic jumble by the thoughtless installation of distorting glass. He tried to stare through the glass but he became a little dizzy. Jarlath Brendan Walsh studied political science (is there such a thing?) and economics. If Jarlath Walsh wasn't dead and if his passing had not led to Minogue sitting at a desk with several fair-sized

24

reports to read, Jarlath Walsh would be rather nondescript. Shouldn't think that: his parents must be in agony.

The door opened. The arrival was surprised to find someone in the room.

She introduced herself as Brid and announced that she would be adding to the file on Walsh. Minogue turned to the four carbon copy leaves when she left. Detectives from Pearse Street station had found a bloodied rock in the alley which ran next to the Pearse Street side of Trinity's walls. Looks like someone lobbed it over the wall after he'd made use of it. The blood matched. More crucially, there were four strands of hair stuck to it. The stone had apparently come from a stockpile of similarly sized and shaped stones which lay in a heap in Front Square. Trinity College had undertaken the Sisyphean task of repairing all of its historic Front Square. Workmen were ripping up the cobbled square and saving the stones so they could be reset. No wonder stone masons had a reputation for being stone-mad.

No prints that meant anything on said stone. Minogue sat back sipping at the sweet tea. The idea of it, a Catholic lad, parents up from the bog, finally emancipated into some status by attending Trinity College, the bastion of the Anglo Irish, and there he was done in by a stone in these ecumenical times, a stone taken from the squares where scholars walked. Would they find the spot where the boy's head had been smashed though? It had to have been a hard surface, likely cobblestones if it had been done inside the front end of the college. It might rain at any time and wash away clues like blood. At least the rock was something.

Minogue finished the tea. He then surprised himself with the enthusiasm he felt as he pushed off out of his chair. He selected from his files as his intentions required and left the office.

In between sessions with students, which Minogue had purposely set for the morning, his mind worked calmly, fitting details. Killed by a rock is not planned killing. Killed inside a university is hasty killing. Something had happened that very evening, something to precipitate things. It wouldn't have been an unconnected event. It may have been done by more than one person. If it was done by one, then he must have been hefty enough to drag a limp body into the bushes. Presence of mind to brush over the tracks. Professional? Not necessarily, just determined, desperate maybe. But still, if it was the latter, whoever it was, kept cool and saw to little things. Analytical, practical. Does that mean educated? Dragging bodies is not easy. Minogue stopped listening to the student friend of Walsh and remembered the *whump*, the glass flying like sand, the car turning slowly. Then he had felt a terrible silence and stillness as he crawled out of the car, knowing all the time what had happened. He had tried to drag the bloodslick body of the detective, the cheery lad, over to the bush. To what end? He was dead, of course. Minogue had passed out then . . .

Minogue had asked to see the president of the Students' Union. Walsh had been a class representative and, as such, should have been known to the president. Minogue looked over his notes in the intervals between students. He had made a point to thank them before starting. Only one of the young men had wept. Minogue rather liked that young man and he wasn't surprised at such a show of feeling. In a sense that boy had graduated much further than the acerbic self-assurance Minogue detected in the rest of them.

None of these students had been with Walsh in the hours before he died. Minogue found out that Walsh's girlfriend, the one in the picture, if they called one another boyfriend or girlfriend anymore, would not be back until tomorrow. Her friends had packed her off, inconsolable, on the Belfast train. Nothing to it, Minogue thought, even if it was a nuisance that they'd got only brief statements out of the girl last Friday. Plenty of kids from the North attended Trinity. Although it could be done, no one was about to phone the Royal Ulster Constabulary up there to interview her on their behalf or keep an eye on her movements. She'd be rested and ready tomorrow.

The door, formerly ajar, swung open. In walked a tall, bearded president of the Students' Union.

"You wanted a word?" said the newly arrived.

'Intense' is the word, thought Minogue, rising to show some equality.

"If you please, Mr, Mr . . . "

"Roche. I'm Mick Roche. My Da's name is Mr Roche. I haven't inherited the title yet. No hurry either."

"Would you sit down please, er, Mick. I won't keep you long."

Roche sat down. His shirt-sleeves were rolled up to his elbows. He smelled of cigarette smoke. His eyes were lightly ringed. No comb had afflicted his hair since rising from his or whoever's bed today. He affected a look of distance and disinterest. He didn't succeed in concealing a keenness and an alertness from Minogue.

"Spelled R-O-C-H-E, is it?" asked Minogue.

"Yes. An agreeable enough name excepting for a prohibition against narcotics of the same name," said Roche without a trace of humour. Practised that one, Minogue thought.

"Well now. I'm Detective Sergeant Minogue. I'd prefer you call me Matt. To tell you the truth, Mick, I have no interest in that side of things at all."

"In the consumption or in the law enforcement end of things, Detective Sergeant?" asked Roche.

"Well neither, actually. It's about one of your representatives, your colleagues Jarlath Walsh, the lad who was murdered."

"Like they say on the telly, I can fill you in on some background, but I knew him superficially really."

Minogue suppressed a smile by diligently writing a word in his notes. He wrote "*superficially*," thinking that this would be a word to bounce back at this president fellow. He'd be smart enough to catch the drift.

"You were in the same class as Jarlath, I understand."

"If you know that, you'll know that there were about two hundred students in that year. It's a general course we all take, then we branch off."

"Am I right in thinking that it is very unusual for a second-year student to hold your office? You must know your onions, Mick."

Roche said nothing, but Minogue detected with a father's acu-

27

ity the pride which Roche tried to conceal. Minogue was so relieved that he almost burst out laughing. This Roche boy is ordinary, he blooms with praise, Minogue thought.

"Incidentally, what would you be studying if you were an ordinary student?"

"For the files, Sergeant?"

"Well no actually. I have a son and a daughter in college. I'm just interested." That sounded corny, Minogue thought.

"Political science."

"Isn't that one of the things Jarlath was taking?"

Roche's eyes suggested the beginnings of a sarcastic answer.

"It is. There are different types of oddities which call themselves political science. Let's say that Jarlath Walsh's studies would be different from mine."

"I don't understand."

"Well he followed up notions they call consensus theory. Stuff like the rise of the party system or the role of the Senate in decision-making. Jarlath didn't understand the notion of class or the influence of economics. He looked at surface things."

"So Jarlath wasn't afraid to speak up, then? I mean you knew his opinions readily in a class of two hundred."

"We were in the same tutorial group. He stuck to his guns even when it didn't make sense. His position was eventually tautological. He ended up with these unopened boxes like 'culture' or 'nationalism' or 'parliamentary democracy' — American stuff, like Coke. Hymns to the *status quo*."

Minogue began to appreciate the deadly gifts that brought Roche to where he was. A liking for the phrase matched with a passion and knowledge he tried to conceal. 'Tautological,' if you please.

"I think I know what you mean. 'The best of all possible worlds,' don't they say?" essayed Minogue.

Roche looked at him and grinned, then nodded his head lightly.

"Exactly, Sergeant. He was the property of his class. Why wouldn't he follow that line."

28

Meaning you don't, because you've seen through it all, Minogue thought.

"Northern Ireland is a rather mysterious set of events for the likes of Jarlath and the parvenus who'd just as soon forget they came from the bog. In one sense they're right when they say that nothing worth learning can be taught . . . "

"Oscar Wilde said a lot of things like that. What do you call them?" Minogue murmured.

"Aphorisms. Conceits. Sophistry."

Must be a holy terror for the lecturers here if he has things like that at the tips of his fingers. Minogue wondered if he had made any ground with the dig about Wilde. A fellow who could remember stuff like that would be a favourite with the girls, no doubt, especially with his grim, illusionless sight of reality. Outside the window, Minogue saw the ordered history of the college, all grey and angled with manicured lawns, worn steps to the chapel, professors waltzing around in gowns.

"You'll know that Jarlath was in the Fine Gael association here, Sergeant. He bought into them calling themselves social democrats, not fascists. I'm more or less an anarchist, on Saturday nights anyway."

Ah, a joke, Minogue recognised.

"Actually I'm a grumbler in the Labour Party. I spend most of my time trying to get grants for students. I have time for rhetoric usually after office hours. If it's friend or foe with this thing of Jarlath, chalk me up as friend. He didn't deserve what happened. He would have changed, I know it, he would have come round. You know what would have brought him around? His girlfriend. Agnes McGuire. She lived in the real world."

"Isn't she the young lady that accompanied him to the Trinity Ball?" inquired Minogue.

"How did you know that?"

"I might well ask you the same thing," Minogue replied.

For the first time, Roche looked ill at ease. His eyes widened, then he regained his composure.

"Wasn't she my girlfriend in first year?" Roche said with a

29

decidedly emphatic irony. A fraction would have conveyed it to Minogue. So they still called them boyfriend and girlfriend, Minogue thought. Isn't that rich. *Touché*, the atmosphere changed. Minogue asked Roche if he remembered any particularly acrimonious debate involving Walsh. They were all acrimonious, Roche replied. Demonstrations? Out of fashion, said Roche. Other issues? Roche replied after a pause:

"Well, I know that he irritated some people who run the Students' Union magazine with his yarns. We, or rather the editorial board, wouldn't run them because they weren't researched. That's putting it mildly really. They were figments of his imagination. Wild swipes at things."

"Such as?"

"Oh I don't remember a lot of it. Misappropriation of money; you know, the executive filling up on free beer at student expense. Or politics."

"Anything on drugs maybe?"

Roche looked directly at Minogue. Minogue thought he was flicking through his list of possible answers.

"No. I wish he had. Might have brought home some news about the real world."

"I don't get it. Drugs bring you reality?" Minogue asked.

"Do you know what heavy drugs are doing to a lot of kids in Dublin? Well, I do. You wouldn't believe it. No one wants to know about it. Stuff like pot is a joke. It's stupid to chase people for that. I know that heavy stuff surfaces here in college a lot more than people think, but Walsh wasn't going to help anyone with his approach. If you ask me, he was setting himself up for a go at journalism after college. Building a rep for himself here."

"I see. That was Jarlath at his, let's say, most tendentious then?"

"Yeah. He'd jump on the bandwagon with rumours about IRA here in Trinity. No one takes those comments seriously. I mean, look around. What would they be doing here with all the boys and girls from the stockbroker belt going to school here? Ask

30

around. He was just trying to start up some stuff so he would be known."

"Something to think about. Thanks, Mick. If I need to see you again, is it O.K. to phone the Students' Union office?"

Roche stood up to leave.

"Well, yeah. But just give your name. Forget the Sergeant stuff."

As he listened to the feet clattering down the stairs, Minogue privately remarked upon titles. Hadn't Master Roche been the one who insisted on it in the conversation?

Minogue gathered his papers but left his impressions scattered. He followed Roche down the bare stairs. He was looking forward to dinner. The Junior Dean had arranged everything. They would eat in the Staff Lunchroom, if you don't mind.

Minogue stepped out onto the cobbles and took in some of the sulphurous air of Dublin. He felt sprightly. He eyed a few girls, students, dressed up to look ugly but in a certain good taste which Minogue couldn't put his finger on. This was the new wave, then. He felt the sharpness of the square in the sounds it held and echoed. A blind man was tapping over the cobblestones. A bicycle tinkled by him. Laughs and footfalls came abruptly over the air. Something ascetic about it, like a Protestant chapel, Minogue mused. Then it struck him that he knew nothing about Protestant chapels.

Professor Griffiths was like a man out of the thirties. A gown over a tweedy suit, stiff collar and red brogues. A face like a horse, hair a bit long. He greeted Minogue by lifting his eyebrows and extending an arm in the direction of a door at the front of the dining hall.

"Upstairs, Mr Minoooog."

He wondered if he was putting on the Bertie Wooster stuff. Minogue ate an indifferent dinner at a well-laid table in company with the college Security Officer and Griffiths. Huge painted figures of dead bishops and scholars looked down at them. Cutlery clanked, food was prompt. Captain Loftus, the Security Officer so-called, kept his army rank in conversation as well as in other

31

forms of intercourse, Minogue realised. Well, in verbal inter-course anyway.

Loftus was a Corkman. He liked to dress well. He was one of the few men Minogue had met in the last few weeks of whom it could be said he looked very upright. Minogue had heard that he had done tours of duty with the UN or peacekeepers before springing into this cushy job in Trinity. A modest beeper poked from his pocket.

By way of taking his attention from the metallic taste of the cabbage, Minogue spoke:

"Well now, Captain Loftus. Has there been stuff like this before?"

Loftus affected puzzlement.

"This boy Walsh, done in," Minogue added. Loftus leaned forward and confided that there hadn't. Griffiths, no doubt day-dreaming about Homer or "The Rape of Lucrece," looked to Loftus and then began stuffing a pipe.

"Is there anything about politics here amongst the student body that'd go to this extent?"

Loftus looked at him without answering. Griffiths, with a peculiar crack in his face which Minogue suddenly realised was a smile, murmured,

"None other than the boy was a member of the Fine Gael association, Sergeant Minogue. Hardly just cause."

"There was talk of drugs,' Minogue said.

"Mr Walsh was a conscientious student, Mr Minogue. His lec-turers thought very highly of him," said Griffiths.

The *politesse* and containment began to grate on Minogue. The fun was gone out of this place very quickly. The boy was dead. These two stuffed shirts were sitting on the fence.

"An interest in journalism?" Minogue tried.

"As much as any other student, Sergeant Minogue," replied Griffiths.

"Captain Loftus. How often do patrols of security guards go by that area where the body was found? On average, at night . . . ?"

32

Loftus looked up to one of the paintings.

"Em, say roughly once every three quarters of an hour after midnight."

"Reliably?"

"Yes. They log in to check-points, a keying system tied to a timer. The college gates were locked. Pretty well impossible to get in over the walls."

"Say, the lowest would be fifteen foot?"

Loftus looked to Griffiths before answering.

"Well, we don't want it known but there are certain parts of the perimeter that can be scaled without assistance. They're in laneways."

Minogue felt resistance. He had been prodding only. This wasn't the place for swipes. He knew well that someone could get over the wall. He had walked the perimeter the previous afternoon. Griffiths and Loftus were reluctant because they couldn't believe someone in Trinity would do this. Loftus didn't want his security and gadgetry to look bad. Griffiths obviously felt the Gardai were barking up the wrong tree. They presumed that some scofflaw from outside the hallowed walls had done it. Minogue looked away to find the eyes of an eighteenth-century judge staring haughtily at him from a painting overhead. The canvas shone dully. And up yours, too, Minogue thought. At least he had managed to resist an atavistic urge to prod these two. Master Walsh was done in in a hurry as he headed for the Nassau Street gate of the college to catch the 63 bus home. It didn't matter too much right now whether the killer attended Trinity or not: he or they knew enough to drag the body away to a safe place and make an escape.

In the afternoon, Minogue used a college telephone to make appointments with four of the five lecturers Walsh had had. By half past four, Minogue had chatted with all but one, Professor Allen. No, they weren't being asked for statements, he explained. Perhaps recall the last time you saw him. Any unusual things, conversations, remarks.

33

The late afternoon was quietly drawing Minogue's energy and interest away. He asked questions mechanically as the feeling grew that even with but one day gone by, he was getting nowhere. He had not realised quite how distant lecturers were from their students. He thought of Iseult and Daithi, how they lived in this kind of world. But, he consoled himself, they had friends. Minogue thanked the lecturer and asked him to direct him to where he might find a Professor Allen.

"He's Psychology," replied the lecturer.

"Yes," Minogue said. He eyed the lecturer's frown.

"Is there something unusual in that?"

"In psychology?" Both laughed lightly.

"No Sergeant. It's not often that a lad enrolled in things like political science and economics would be doing a psychology course. Nothing wrong with it of course. But would his time allow that?"

Minogue dithered.

"You could phone Professor Allen," the lecturer murmured with a faint smile, waking Minogue from his lassitude.

Minogue found Allen's name in the college telephone book. He counted five degrees after Allen's name. Maybe Allen suffered from an excess of modesty in keeping his other dozen degrees to himself?

A secretary said that Allen was not in his office. Could he make an appointment?

"Are you a student?"

"I'm a Sergeant in the Gardai."

Not impressed. Professor Allen made his own appointments personally, she intoned. Minogue should phone tomorrow. She would leave a message with him to say that Sergeant Malone called.

"And tell him that Sergeant Minogue called too, like a good woman," Minogue said. She did not ask for an explanation. Sorry for asking, Minogue thought, are they all Caesars here?

CHAPTER FOUR

The next morning, Minogue awoke before the clock radio. Amongst other things, he had dreamed of Agnes McGuire. She was the spitting image of Lady Lavery on the old paper money, sitting there looking out in such a melancholy way at the bearer of legal tender. Maybe she realised that the money was going to be exchanged for pints in a pub. Minogue lay still in the cream-lit morning bedroom. He had his fortnightly appointment with Herlighy, the psychiatrist, this morning. There were birds galore outside. The radio popped on and Kathleen elbowed up to look at him. Then she lay down and held her arm over her eyes.

The news came on after the electronic fanfare. Two RUC men had been killed last night in Belfast. They were plain clothes officers in an unmarked car, apparently following a van. The van doors had been kicked open from inside and too late the two realised that they had been drawn into the figures, history, head-lines. Nowhere to hide from an M60 machine gun. The van didn't even stop. It didn't need to. Death on the run, a couple of hundred shells fired off in a matter of seconds. Hardly need to aim it.

Kathleen stirred. Belfast was just up the road really, thought Minogue, a million miles away. In Derry, a rocket-propelled grenade had blown in the wall of a garage which housed some city buses. "If it's not American, it's Russian," Minogue murmured. That was psychology, a message, an experiment to show they had got them and it could have been you. Kathleen blessed herself.

"God look down on them and all belonging to them."

And she means it, Minogue knew. At one time she had discounted the death of a British soldier in a gun battle. She had felt there was some fairness in that. He was part of an occupying army. That was back in the early seventies. Minogue agreed with her then, but with a lifetime's practice, had not said so aloud. What could be said now? Gardai had been shot and killed. Whoever had set the mine that day, whoever had tripped the switch had not been indifferent to Detective Sergeant Minogue's fate at all: there was intention there, but *nothing personal. It was the Ambassador we were after.*

Minogue remembered coming home from the hospital. There were neighbours in, tea and cake and whisky. Everything had been taken care of. It was as if he had just been married. Daithi and Iseult were serious and solicitous. Things had changed. There was new china out on the table. There were new bedspreads and sheets and a bottle of Redbreast in the cabinet below. It was only then that Minogue had realised, quite neutrally as he sat in the deck-chair beside the rhubarb, that he had nearly died. He had prepared a list that day which ran to one hundred and eighty-three items:

4. I will not hate my brother Mick for supporting the IRA.

5. I will not cause Kathleen to worry, so I'll accept the transfer out.

12. I will kiss Daithi and Iseult daily, at least once, even in public.

25. I will accompany Kathleen down the pier as often as she requests.

57. I will continue to be a republican in spite of this.

59. I will visit the National Gallery at least once a week and I will see each painting afresh.

114. I will not lean upon the church.

136. I will live in Dublin as long as Kathleen wants to.

147. I will not treat young people as upstarts

160. I will learn to play Ravel's Pavane on the piano.

Minogue lived again.

"They put me on a case. It's a murder investigation."

Herlighy, the psychiatrist, didn't say anything. Minogue resisted saying more. He let the silence last for a minute.

"To see if I'm serviceable, I suppose. To see if I'm the full round of the clock again. I'm to start this afternoon," Minogue added.

"Can you do it, do you feel?" Herlighy asked.

"Yes. I'm not that leery about it really. They've given me a free hand so far as I can make out," Minogue replied.

It was toward the end of the session. Time had passed quickly for Minogue. He was aware of the hidden expectation that he should talk. That went against his habits and it irritated him frequently. Nonetheless he saw the use of being here.

"And the sleep?" Herlighy asked.

"Oh great. The odd time I wake up early but sure that's normal. If I can use that word. I understand it's not in vogue."

Herlighy smiled briefly.

"You deserve a lot of credit for that, Matt, that you're doing so much," Herlighy said slowly.

Minogue laughed to hide his embarrassment and pleasure.

"Ah sure, time and tide, you know."

"Well, I'm sure you know how much resistance there is to getting proper advice as you have done."

"The wife's idea," Minogue rejoined quickly. "She knows what the score is. She had it herself years ago. I used to think that I should have gone to the sessions with her, you know. I think I was too mad though, and I didn't know it. I shouldn't say mad, I suppose. More like I was raging. Wouldn't listen to anyone. Not much help to Kathleen, I expect, no. But . . . that's done with."

"The first child?" Herlighy said.

"Yes," Minogue said softly.

Minogue and Herlighy were walking slowly around Merrion Square. They had stepped out from the psychiatrist's office at Minogue's request. They kept to the outer route where the paths were closest to the railings. The railings were quite buried by the shrubs and trees. Merrion Square held its Georgian grace to all four sides. As the two men walked slowly along the path, views of the eighteenth-century houses emerged between the trees. Here a row of windows, ivy cossetting railings which formed balconies on some, there a door at once simple and refined.

As usual, Minogue did the leading. He was walking slower today, Herlighy noticed. Minogue had not hesitated to ask for an 'out' day today. On his first visit to Herlighy's office, Minogue had gazed out the long windows onto the square. He had been surprised when Herlighy had simply asked him at the next session:

"Do you want to go out there? There's no need for us to be in here at all."

Minogue had been amused too, but not suspicious.

"You mean it's all right to be out there? I thought you had to be in a room, like going to confession." ·

"Interesting idea. No. I find it helps," Herlighy had replied.

Herlighy was still puzzled. On the one hand, Minogue seemed bound up, complete and self-assured all these months. Then he was speculative and yearning, even playful sometimes. Must play hell with him, having to work as a cop: 'unsuited' written all over him.

Minogue seemed to be thriving, despite the trauma after the explosion. Had he been faking it? Why did he seek out these sessions then? What did he want to tell? Herlighy still believed in Minogue's need to confess. Guilt was the motor for this, survivor guilt. There was some other story coming through, like a descant, but still faint however. Some old story in Minogue was starting to talk again.

Herlighy often felt nervous with Minogue. He felt that Minogue was ready to confront something soon. Oddly, he also found himself looking forward to their sessions. He had begun hypnosis with Minogue five sessions back. For a cop, Minogue was neither suspicious nor hostile.

"How's your list coming along?" Herlighy asked.

"Great, so it is. Once you get over the first ten or so, you can't stop. I think I could go on to a thousand," Minogue replied.

"Good," Herlighy said.

"I'm working on a few of them actually, bit by bit. Funny, I have the craving for a smoke again," Minogue added.

They walked on in silence.

"Some of them are hard, but I'm doing all right," Minogue murmured.

Herlighy's eyebrows went up, and he slowed the pace so Minogue would notice.

"With the children, like. I'm more . . . more: I shouldn't say 'physical.' More direct, like. I always wanted to be. You were definitely right about that, I can tell you," Minogue said.

Herlighy noted Minogue's embarrassment. They resumed their walk, under the trees.

Just after eleven o clock, Agnes McGuire arrived unannounced at the door of Minogue's office. She stood in the threshold.

"I'm Agnes McGuire. You were looking for me."

Minogue was taken aback. He stood quickly, his mind alive with details. Her accent carried up the ends of words and phrases and it added what southerners mistook for earnestness. A soft hiss on the *s*, a changing of vowels.

Agnes McGuire had dark red hair and a pale face. Her eyes had red edges to them. The centres were gentian. Thin hands joined in front of a handknit cardigan. In a sense which shocked

39

him, Minogue abruptly decided that Agnes McGuire was some-how used to grieving.

"Will you sit down please, Miss McGuire?"

"Agnes will do," she said.

"And you can call me Matt if you wish. Agnes, I'll be asking you questions which you may find very trying. I don't need to tell you that we want to get to the bottom of this thing as quickly as possible and although part will be painful to you, I trust you believe that it'll be worth something in the end. Every little thing counts."

"Well, do you think it was a madman who did this, Mr Min-ogue?" said Agnes.

"Because, to be quite frank, I don't think it was at all. That is what bothers me the most, you know," she continued.

Minogue decided to level with her.

"I can tell you that we don't have much to go on right now. It's not one of those things that results in an arrest within a matter of hours. Do you know how much of this kind of thing is done by another member of the family, a relative, a falling out among friends? This young man's background suggests none of that at all. Unfortunately Jarlath's parents are too distraught to recall a thing with any clarity, but, to be honest, I expect they will have little to offer to help find a resolution. If you follow my reasoning, or should I say, my speculation, I'm thinking of what happened as an event in this area, not just geographically, but in this part of Jarlath's life. College, his life here. Does that sound a bit cracked to you, Agnes?"

Agnes didn't reply immediately. She toyed with her long fingers and then looked to the window.

"I follow you. I didn't want to think like that. Jarlath was not what you might call an extremist." Was she smiling faintly?

"You're saying that Jarlath would not have been involved with radical student politics, whatever they might be?"

"Far from it. Jarlath was always talking about the Enlighten-ment. That sounds daft, doesn't it? Well, he thought that Irish people had to become more rational, more enterprising about politics."

Minogue said nothing. He waited.

"I suppose it was like a debating club with him really. But it's no sin to be naive. Or is it? Sure, he was laughed at by some of the students here. You know, the 'bourgeois apologist,' the 'light weight' tags here. I think they were jealous of him, do you know that? He had an optimism that they hadn't. I remember one of the sociology crowd telling him that he needed to visit the North once in a while to get to reality, that he needed to get out of his cosy middle class ghetto in Foxrock. It's like the Malone Road, I suppose. You know what was so silly about that? These radicals came from the same backgrounds. They felt they had to be full of thunder and opinions because they felt guilty about being well-to-do."

Minogue believed in wisdom at twenty for he had felt it stirring in himself at that age.

"Jarlath comes across as a gentle type of lad the way you talk," he said quietly.

Had to do it, damn and blast it, thought Minogue. Of course she began to cry and wasn't that the idea, you cruel bastard? When Agnes stopped crying, Minogue asked her:

"Agnes, can you tell me if Jarlath had any notion of drugs?"

"No He had nothing to do with them. You can be sure of that."

Although Minogue had read the preliminary statements taken from Agnes that Friday, he needed to go back and flesh out the details. Agnes made no protest. She spoke as if reciting. They had both studied in the library — the 1937 Reading Room — until a bit after eight. They skipped tea-time. Then they went to her rooms where she prepared a meal. *Linguini?* Strips of pasta. A bit of meat made into a sauce. They had a couple of glasses of wine. They talked a bit, then he left. About half past ten. *Did they arrange to meet? Anything out of the ordinary they talked about?* No, a plan for a cycling holiday in France. *Oh, Jarlath wanted to visit Belfast. Curious?* No, she smiled. He had never been there, said he wanted to. *Were they thinking of going steady,*

41

getting engaged? Pause. No. *Did he leave any belongings in her rooms?* No, he took everything in his bag. The bag was falling apart, she said. *Hmm.*

"His school-bag?" asked Minogue, with a slight stir in his stomach.

"No, that was gone. He had it stolen from him. He had to sneak in home with his shopping bag so no one'd see him. The one that was taken was a present from his mother so there'd be wigs on the green if they found out."

"Stolen in college?"

"Right out of his locker, locked and all."

"And did he have valuables in it?"

"Not really. He caught up on the lecture notes by borrowing. Notebooks and bits of things went. A fountain pen he won in debating competition in secondary school. A snap of me." She blushed lightly.

A minute's silence filled the room. It seemed to rest on the grey light which morning had brought to this part of the college. Minogue remembered that it was sunny on the other side of the square when he came in. He felt Agnes willing herself not to cry. He pretended to note things on his sheets. He was thinking of Iseult. Agnes' composure had returned.

"Agnes, if you don't think it's forward of me, may I invite you to come for coffee with me above in Bewley's? I'm allowed some freedom on this case and I intend to sustain myself well. A sticky bun. Maybe we'll risk a large white coffee too, upstairs. If I'm not presuming too much . . . "

Upstairs in Bewley's the sun roared in the windows, shocking the wood into showing different hues. The newspapers were luminous sheets in the rage of light. From halfway across the room, he could see where an old man hadn't shaved. Minogue didn't ask any more about Jarlath Walsh. Nor did he mention anything about the North. Emboldened by the coffee, Minogue found himself talking with a young woman his daughter's age about the National Gallery and the recitals he planned to go to.

He talked on and on. Agnes looked from him to the sunlit

42

windows and then back. Sometimes she laughed aloud. Minogue, for his part, kept on talking while the sunlight—in its slow and grudging move through Dublin—graced the next table.

Minogue's profligacy with time still allowed him to see Captain Loftus before dinner-time. He climbed the circular staircase slowly, trying to sort out the impressions. History, an alien history, came to him with the lavender smell of floor polish and the echoes of his own footsteps. As he mounted the staircase, his hand rested at times on a varnished banister. Below and to the left of him always, the flagged floor turned lazily with Minogue's ascent.

He knocked and pushed at a heavy door. Loftus turned from a cabinet.

"Ah, Sergeant . . . "

"Minogue."

"Indeed. Is it me you came to see?"

"To be sure. I was hoping to find out more about that boy's locker. It was broken open some time ago. Do ye keep any reports on such goings-on in the college?" Minogue asked.

"Let me see . . . "

Loftus opened a drawer and glanced at a document. Minogue worked hard to conceal his humour, or rather his ill humour. He smelled a cloying scent of aftershave off Loftus. Let me see, indeed. Let me see your Aunt Fanny's fat agricultural arse.

"Some three weeks ago, Sergeant. Four lockers were broken open. As a matter of policy we don't trouble the Gardai with these things. Little enough was lost. Notes, someone's rugby shirt, another lad's lunch." Loftus smiled.

"Jarlath Walsh's bag."

Loftus looked back at the sheet.

"Yes, that too. Yes"

"Do you by chance have a list of the items reported stolen, Captain Loftus? Might I see it?"

"No problem," said Loftus.

Must have learned the 'no problem' stuff off the Yanks. Jarlath

Walsh, 24 South Park, Foxrock, County Dublin: one leather briefcase, black, containing two notebooks and various lecture notes, mementoes/personal, no cash, pens, pencils, a tape recorder.

"A tape recorder?"

"Apparently so. Mr Walsh likely used it for lectures, I expect."

"What's the usual routine on this stuff, Captain?"

"Eventually compensation. We stress that the college is not liable for damage or theft, but we don't like to leave people hanging. Especially in this case. I had authorised payment to Mr Walsh the day I heard the news."

"Yes. I suspect that the thief used a crowbar or the end of a heavy screwdriver. Determined. You'll understand, Sergeant, that manpower needs preclude constant patrols."

"Dublin isn't what it used to be, is it, Captain?"

"Indeed, Sergeant. The needs must. We do what we can. A person desperate for anything to steal really. A drinking problem. Maybe just vandalism."

Yes, thought Minogue, plenty of that. Drive out by Tallaght in your BMW on the way home to your enclave. You'd probably spend your next few weekends adding glass to the top of your walls.

"Thank you, Captain."

Minogue phoned in a want card on a tape recorder and a black leather briefcase if any citizen should turn it in. Fat chance. He phoned Kilmartin's office.

"Matt, the hard man."

"Jimmy, how are you? Any give on the spot where this Walsh boy was killed?"

"Divil a bit, Matt. The two lads from Pearse Street scoured the college looking all day yesterday. Did you bump into them at all?"

"No."

"Well, the gist of it is that they found nothing. Tell you the truth, I think they're praying for rain so that they have the excuse to give it up. They are wall-eyed after a day of that. The fellas in Pearse Street found nothing on the weekend anyway."

"Hmm . . ."

"Do you want manpower?"

"No thanks, Jimmy. Slowly but surely. I'll put a few notes together and rocket them over to you."

"Incidentally. Connors is gone to the Walshes to go over things with them. Save you the trouble. He needs the practice in this kind of thing. A bit weak in the shell. Have a look at what he says tomorrow."

Minogue put down the phone. He was glad he didn't have to interview the parents. He thought about Loftus, about how he wanted to show he was running a tight ship. What was he hiding, though? Crossing Front Square toward the room he had been assigned at the college, Minogue passed Mick Roche.

"How'ya, Mick?"

"And yourself, Sergeant?"

"Will you direct me to Dr Allen's place?"

"The headbanger? The psychology fella. Oh yeah, you'll have no trouble finding him. Follow the crowds."

"How do you mean?"

"Just joking. He's a bit of a guru. He has a loyal following, especially in Agnes McGuire."

Minogue followed directions to Allen's office in New Square. Allen greeted him with a tight handshake. He seemed to have expected him.

"Professor Allen. Thank you for your time. I tried to make an appointment but your line was engaged."

Minogue examined Allen's face. He was drawn to the eyes. Unbotherable, confident. The eyes rested on an outdoor face which looked open. A full head of hair, though quite grey. An attractive man to women, Minogue concurred without thinking about it. Allen was dressed casually. He had stepped out of his shoes. His fortyish face smiled in an unsmile, a formal ease.

"I sometimes leave the phone off the hook. Things find me eventually and the more necessary ones will reach me first, I find."

"Sergeant Matt Minogue," and Minogue proffered a hand.

"Not Malone, then. That clears that up," Allen smiled.

They sat. Minogue glanced at the rubbings of figures taken, he guessed, from old stones lying around the ditches of Ireland or from monuments as they were called. These poster-size rubbings were all of whorl patterns.

"They're very nice, Professor Allen. The rubbings. They're hard to do though. I did them as a child."

"Minogue. That's a Clare name, is it not?"

"It is to be sure. And yourself?"

"I'm an Englishman actually. What you hear is an overlay of ten years of being in Ireland, with a heavy foundation of Lancashire."

"You'd never know it."

"More Irish than the Irish themselves you might say, Sergeant."

He had the charm and the small talk too, Minogue reflected.

"Actually, my mother was Irish. An emigrant. Regrettably, she died before she could return for her old age."

"A hard thing to leave go of, the mother country. How well you knew I was from Clare now."

"I do a lot of ethnography, more as a hobby. See this?" Allen pointed to one of the rubbings.

"I got it in West Clare. I went on a dig some years ago in Sardinia and I found a pattern almost identical to this one. A type of mandala. Some people get a bit upset about finding these kinds of similarities, isn't that odd?"

"It is, I suppose," Minogue allowed.

"People don't like to realise that others had the same inspirations or troubles or joys as countless others. Sort of offends against one's sense of uniqueness. Our treasured assumptions about how we control the world."

"You have me there," Minogue murmured.

"It's nothing really. Some of us think that causes and effects are out of our hands. Other people like to think they have more control over things. Illusion really, but it's the belief that counts."

"Superstition, like?"

46

"In a sense, yes. Look at Americans for instance. They seem to think they can do just about anything. They have a nice, cosy, irrational belief in Progress. Now, Irish people are a bit passive perhaps, but there's history too . . . Shouldn't generalise really."

"Well you've given me a lot to be thinking about now, Dr Allen," Minogue said thoughtfully.

"I wonder," Allen replied, "I wonder why I'm telling you this. It's not what you're here for, is it? Maybe you have some facility as a seer, drawing out things."

Minogue affected to be surprised. He laughed lightly.

"Ah, I'm a bit pedestrian at the best of times. But continuing on from what you were saying about people believing they can effect things, can I ask you where you'd place Jarlath Walsh there?"

Allen sat back and crossed his legs at the ankles. His forehead moved slightly and his hair moved with it.

"Hmm. Interesting you should ask. Yes. You know of course that what I say is not in the nature of a report. Mr Walsh attended one lecture a week with me. I hardly knew him. I'm not sure why he chose to do this course."

He paused as if to think deeply. "*Switched into his official style,*" Minogue memoed himself.

"I can't say that Mr Walsh was the brightest student in the class. He definitely had an interest in the subject as a whole, but from an essay he wrote me at Christmas I feel that he didn't have the background for attempting what he appeared to be attempting."

"What was that?"

"Well, he was trying to develop a psychology of a typical Irish person, I suppose you would say."

Allen's forehead went up again and he studied his toes. "Let me see if I can explain, Sergeant. Stuff like this might have worked in the last century. No, I should be more charitable about it . . . Psychology has come a long way from metaphysics in the last century. Mr Walsh wanted to plug in an easy theory into his understanding of Irish politics. He had taken an interest in the

47

violence in the North, of all things. Let's say more than others in the Republic anyway. I suppose he thought there was a simple psychological solution. He was quite emphatic about this. One can understand naive enthusiasm, but Mr Walsh had not moved from this position. There's quite an attraction for people in this stuff about national character. You hear a lot of it. The Russians are supposed to be dour and bearish people who favour despots, or the Irish are charming dodgers. Any good psychology has to account for individual differences as well as commonalities across cultures. Mr Walsh was tempted to reach for what we call Grand Theory." Allen paused. A trace of amusement passed over his face.

"Am I lecturing?" he asked softly, as if taken aback at a great new understanding of himself.

"Not a bit of it," replied Minogue with conviction.

"It may be that Irish people don't feel they can effect any solutions in the North. Pessimism and acceptance. However, one can't be too careful with those wild, huge hypotheses. With Jarlath Walsh, it was becoming a Pollyanna-ish thing really. Still, he had done a lot of work and he got better than a passing mark."

Minogue was thinking about Agnes McGuire. Maybe she was lying down in her room, thinking of the boy. Perhaps Walsh had been learning something but not something a university could teach. He had found Agnes anyway. Why wouldn't a callow young man believe that some psychology could fix the mess up north? It would have that attractive simplicity, a parallel to feelings which were newly arrived to him with Agnes perhaps, and he could have been swept away with inexperience and optimism.

"I think I see what you mean. Tell me, did you know that Jarlath had a relationship, can I say, with a student in your class? Agnes McGuire, she's in your class too, am I right?"

"Yes. You may have touched on the chief reason he was in the class in the first place."

Minogue could detect no trace of sarcasm in Allen's voice. As if in answer, Allen said:

48

"I'm not being flippant or dismissive. Have you spoken with her yet?"

"This very day," Minogue replied.

"Perhaps lecturers are not supposed to notice, but I think Mr Walsh was very taken with her."

"I had the same impression. Like we say though, she's young."

"Ah but Sergeant, years aren't everything. I imagine there was a wealth of difference between her and Mr Walsh. Sometimes the facts, big as they are, escape us."

"In . . . ?"

"Agnes McGuire has lived through a lot, Sergeant."

"Oh yes. Belfast."

"And more," Allen replied, leaning forward in his chair to ruin Minogue's day.

"Her father was a magistrate in Belfast. He was assassinated three years ago."

Minogue felt as if the afternoon had run in a window and fallen on top of him. It wasn't the faint touch of smugness in the delivery that suggested he hadn't done his homework. It was more the thought of Agnes' composure, the control she had. She had had the cruellest practice.

The silence in the room lasted for a full minute.

"Three years."

"I'm Agnes' tutor. We take on groups of students to help and advise them. She was assigned to me alphabetically. My specialty is in the psychology of aggression, of all things. I do public lectures all around Ireland, North and South. Everything's coloured by what happens in the North, of course. Here I was, sitting across the table from her. I'm trained in various therapy techniques, you see. I expected that she'd be a candidate for help. Given the right suggestions, learning is improved, relationships bloom. I cannot disclose anything of our chats, you'll understand, but let me tell you that Agnes McGuire gives credence to some unfashionable notions. Health, freedom . . ."

"Strange to think . . . " Minogue began.

"That she and Walsh could get along? She's Catholic. Her

father was killed by Protestant extremists. Isn't that something in itself?"

"I don't follow," Minogue said.

"You'd think they'd leave him alone, wouldn't you? I mean they talk about law and order and enforcing the rule of law when it suits them. The thing was that McGuire was the one who started the process of getting Loyalist paramilitaries behind bars, not just the IRA. I imagine the other side couldn't countenance a Catholic putting away one of theirs, no matter that he was part of the institutions they said they were fighting for."

Minogue said nothing. A whorl of pity eddied down his stomach. No, not pity: regret.

"So much for rationality and politics," Allen said.

"So much indeed," Minogue muttered.

It was beginning to dawn on Minogue that Jarlath Walsh had been naive all right. Still, there was a pedestrian heroism to his ideas. In the end though, what did this all have to do with his getting killed? Ireland entertained a lot of people with the most lunatic ideas. Some were even elected to promote those ideas.

Minogue made to go. Allen's eyes had gone out of focus. They returned to focussing on his feet. Then he looked up at Minogue.

"Sergeant, I last saw Mr Walsh after last Thursday's lecture. That I've told you. I'm not sure if what I'll tell you now has any bearing on your investigations. For some weeks now, Walsh has been asking me privately at the end of the lectures for books on the psychological effects of things like cigarettes, alcohol, narcotics and so on."

Minogue tried to look unconcerned, but apparently it didn't work.

"That shocks you a little, Sergeant?"

"I'm a bit taken aback to be sure. I'm sure that you can understand how one forms an image as one investigates someone's life." Minogue liked the sound of the way he had said that, very neutral and analytical.

"Narcotics. You mean hash and grass basically?"

50

"I suppose I do," Allen replied with the faintest of smiles. *Touché*, thought Minogue.

Minogue recalled the bland assurances he had had from college officials about this kind of thing not being on their turf, oh no.

Minogue's mind was tired. He was beginning to feel irritable. He felt uninformed. He hadn't really one promising lead, not a sausage. Intuitions meant nothing, less than nothing, because they deflected his attention. Look: he had spent ten minutes talking about Agnes McGuire. Romancing, he was. Go home to your wife.

CHAPTER FIVE

Instead of going home to his wife, a contrary Minogue knocked on Captain Loftus' door. He caught Loftus leaving. Loftus stood in the doorway, half-coated, reaching for the sleeve. The office had a strong smell of aftershave.

"A minute of your time, Captain. I'd like to see Walsh's locker."

"Ah, that'll be a job. I'm afraid those lockers were too badly damaged now. They've been replaced."

Minogue felt the beginnings of indignation.

"I had the understanding that the lock was jemmied. They'd be those little locks you get in Woolworth's. There'd hardly be damage to the locker itself though, would there?"

Loftus dodged, pretending to search for keys in his pocket.

"There was a lot of damage done, Sergeant. The hinges were torn out. You can't just weld on a door. They make you buy the whole unit. There was nothing for it but to be rid of them."

"Where are they now?"

"They'd be gone to the dump, I expect. Good for nothing."

"Actually, Captain, they'd be good for my investigation. When did you have them taken down?"

"Last week, sometime," Loftus replied.

"Friday, then?"

"It might have been that late, yes."

"Who gave the order?"

"The requisition . . . ? I did."

"So there'd be a record of the date."

Loftus stopped fiddling. He stood to his full height.

"Sergeant Minogue. I'm beginning to wonder if you're not overworking yourself here."

"Let me enlighten you then, Captain, because I think you're not enlightening me much. Now I didn't get out of bed on the wrong side this morning, but that doesn't mean that I'm interested in getting the run-around. I'm paid to look into all the bits and pieces."

"An empty, damaged locker, Sergeant?" Loftus said slowly to heighten the effect.

Minogue didn't reply. He didn't want to tell Loftus that he'd wanted to look for signs of what might have been in the locker. He wondered if Allen had misread the questions that Jarlath Walsh had put to him. Minogue was beginning to believe that this was the case. Minogue guessed that the boy wanted the information for something more prosaic, like a debate. He caught a little of this Jarlath Walsh and it wasn't encouraging. A boy, not a man, tipsy on book-learning, his trust in the power of reason, boyscout's honour. Knowledge is power for good: Walsh was a dupe for the university. No. He was a trier. Minogue was dried up with cynicism. Maybe. Walsh didn't have the edges smoothed out by experience yet. He noticed that Loftus was eying him. Why not give him a swipe?

"It may look odd to you, Captain. Let me be candid. This student wasn't killed by some random act. All the signs are against it. He had something, he did something or he knew something. He probably didn't know that he did any of these things. At least not powerful enough to warrant his murder. I'm no Aga-

53

tha Christie, and I don't have a computer to calculate odds. The thoughts I'm having are what they call hunches in the thrillers. The word 'drugs' keeps popping into my head. I hear it a lot. Dublin isn't what it used to be. Nor, might I add is Trinity College or its students. What do you think?"

Loftus' nostrils had been sucked in. Minogue recognised signs of breath held in. Loftus was staring intently at him, struggling with a decision. Then, abruptly, he turned away. He took off his coat with an air of resignation and he walked around to the other side of his desk. He fumbled with his keys and unlocked the desk. Without a search, Loftus drew out a large envelope. He handed it to Minogue. Minogue saw defiance in the place of the smugness he had read on the face before.

Minogue removed the note and read it. It had been typed, poorly.

JARLATH WALSH MAKES A MOCKERY OF THIS COL-LEGE. WHO WILL ACT? WALSH TRAFFICS IN DRUGS. DRUGS POISON PEOPLE. DON'T BE DECEIVED. ACT. WALSH'S FRUIT IMPORTS LOOKS AS INNOCENT AS WALSH.

Minogue read over the note again. Loftus sat down.

"Get many hoaxes, Captain? Your students here have a reputation for high jinks."

"My thoughts exactly, Sergeant." Was there a hint of vengeance in his voice?

"I made a decision quite a while ago. Forbidden fruit is a lot less tasty when there's no talk about it."

"I don't follow your analogy, Captain."

"My chief concern here is not whether this note was written in a serious vein or not. I'm sure there are people capable of trying to ruin someone's good name for spite. I'm sure there are self-appointed people whose paranoia leads them to make serious accusations without any reasonable evidence too."

"So . . . ?" Minogue probed.

"On balance, I think this is just a malicious slur," Loftus said slowly.

"Hmm," from Minogue.

"The way we see it here, Sergeant, the more talk of drugs the students hear, the more glamorous the stuff appears. You know how it is at that age. It's the same thing with the bank robberies and the shooting: glamour. We deal with so-called drug problems in the college in a very low-key way. We're not entirely naive in here about the ways of the world out there. We go through the Drug Squad when we need to. Check that out and you'll find how good our liaison is with the Gardai."

Minogue wasn't listening. He was thinking of the way Loftus was saying "we."

"A person of lesser sophistication might call this sweeping things under the table, Captain," Minogue offered.

"The college doesn't employ such persons, Sergeant," replied Loftus.

Minogue realised all of a sudden that a few years ago he might have gotten on his own high horse with this sparrowfart.

"Uh," Minogue said, trying to appear thoughtful.

"So whether I believe this rubbish or not has little to do with the matter at hand for me. Of course I cannot stop you believing what you will. We're all responsible for the good name of the college in here. It's not so much security as reputation. That is a commodity, once traded, impossible to buy back. This is the college of Edmund Burke and Oliver Goldsmith. Samuel Beckett too, if that's your fancy. Our graduates and our students as well as our staff are our stock of good will."

Minogue was tiring of this speech. He wondered if Loftus had practised this one or had used it before. Minogue also wondered if he should be standing here barefoot and illiterate as his ancestors had been, while this haven of scholarship buttered up the gentry whose daddies had sent the bailiff to batter down peasant houses. Careful, Minogue, your inferiority complexes are showing.

"We see this current fetish with drugs as part of history, you might say," Loftus was saying. "It's a small part of our first four hundred years and we'll ride it out."

55

A picture of Mary Brosnahan, the cleaning-woman who had tripped across the body, came into Minogue's mind. Her statement read like an apology for nearly having dirtied the college with her discovery. Why this loyalty, and she paid little enough, and her knees probably gone these years? And Walsh, trusting in reasonable propositions, boyscout's honour. Loyalty to those notions on this island?

"I take your point, Captain. I'll be dispensing with pleasantries as such while I effect economical answers to present concerns. Doubtless you'll see to the reputation of the place in your own good time. Now: why did you remove the locker in its entirety only on Friday? When did you get this note? Before answering, be assured that this is a very serious matter and I'm well able to step on toes."

Loftus' answer immediately gave Minogue the impression that Loftus had prepared for this eventuality.

"I take it you've not been in the army, Sergeant. I'd know it if you had been. You don't need to look beyond a man's bearing and general attitude to know one of our own. Finbar Walsh, the boy's father, and I had the privilege of serving together. It was for a short time only and it was quite a number of years ago. Mr Walsh was a senior officer to me and the army lost a valuable man when Mr Walsh left. I was happy for him that he managed to be so successful in business. I don't give a god's curse basically if there's one iota of truth in this note or not. If indeed there is some substance to it, you can be certain that my loyalties are to the college and this man's reputation. Particularly so because the boy is now deceased. Don't mistake me. I want to see the culprit caught too."

Great speech, thought Minogue. He nodded resignedly.

"And something else too. I hope you don't mistake my concerns for obstruction. I suspect that you haven't been adequately briefed by your superiors on this matter. As for myself, I'm not a desk jockey with no backing," Loftus said with a tight smile.

"There are things that matter more than incidents," he added with a tone of finality.

Minogue was sure now that he loathed this twit. Loftus had stopped little short of a criminal offence. The thing was that there was no point in throwing the book at the likes of Loftus. He'd probably been given the lead from someone else anyway.

Loftus wouldn't have said what he did without some umbrella, some nod from a handler. Probably your man with the tweed brain, Griffiths. All sweet eminent reason, of course. What was more, the note might well be rubbish, a bad joke, and nothing would come of tests on the bloody locker anyway. Notebooks and a bag. Far too like James Bond.

Minogue looked at the sliver of sunlight which the late afternoon had carried into the office. It held playing motes of dust and it showed up the grain on the edges of the desk. History rolls on like the afternoon. Time and tide. Jarlath Walsh would be buried tomorrow. The parents would be in no condition to talk tomorrow. Connors would draw a big duck egg there too. Well, Minogue decided, with a finality quite alien to the dreamy light around him, might as well leave this twit hanging.

"Be so kind as to give me that note and an envelope to hold it. It will be returned to you when we have gone over it. Good day to you, Captain Loftus. We'll be meeting again perhaps. You have a way to get in touch with me?"

Loftus nodded once.

Minogue smelled wax and confidence in this building as he walked down the stairs. Immovable, assured.

Minogue awoke to the sounds of rain. It had been raining for some time because the heavy, slow *pat-pat* of the drops oozing from under the gutter was a steady pattern of sound. Minogue swore silently. He could see the rain washing away the traces of a murder. He saw the water swirling toward a drain, a face grinning. It was Loftus' face.

The dawn light came into the bedroom like smoke. Minogue crept out of the bed and went downstairs. He made tea and turned on the radio low. Then he switched on a bar of the electric heater and leaned closer to the radio. He craved a smoke. Not even the stay in hospital had given him the urge as strongly as this.

It was too early for Radio Eireann. Minogue turned to the BBC just in time to catch the tail end of a sentence.

" . . . at his front door in Limavady about seven o'clock last night. A spokesman for the RUC confirmed that Mr Elgie had received death threats in the past. Mr Elgie was active in the Peace Now movement in Northern Ireland. He is the forty seventh civilian to die of violence in Northern Ireland this year. Security forces are reportedly stepping up searches and surveillance in the area in the wake of several shootings in this area within the last fortnight. A spokesman for the Army did not deny that all the shootings appear to be part of a pattern as similar weapons have been used in recent incidents. Concern was voiced during question period in the House of Commons that more weapons appear to be entering Northern Ireland. Rocket-propelled grenades and heavy calibre machine-guns have been used in ambushes in South Armagh. Police believe that Mr Elgie was killed with a Russian-made semi-automatic rifle. So far, no organisation has claimed responsibility for the murder. Conservative MP Mr Stanley Robinson accused the government of the Irish Republic of being lax in border security. Mr Robinson said that the IRA is indiscriminate in its use of weapons and sources of supply and this indicates how bankrupt their politics are. The Prime Minister today visited . . . "

Minogue felt awake enough to want to go back to bed. Words like 'terrorist' and 'security forces' rolled off the announcer's tongue just like that. Indiscriminate, lax. It was all loaded of course, we can expect no less, Minogue thought. His wakening mind rambled on to an image of Allen and the work he was doing. Seemed so calm, so rational, even confident. Did he really believe that his lectures could change people?

In many ways, Allen was a man to be admired. He didn't hide in the academic cloister. Instead, he went out and gave ideas their acid test, to see if they could make change happen. A composed man, a bit cautious, but with assurance. He didn't miss much.

Imagine an Englishman knowing so much about Ireland. Well it just went to prove that the Irish and the English were not inevitable enemies due to some chemistry or geography.

Agnes McGuire had composure and pride too. She seemed to be able to take it all in and to transcend it, but a sadness lingered. It actually shone out of her. Maybe Allen, as her tutor, had been able to help her make sense of things. But hadn't Allen said that she didn't need him to sort things out for herself? She had begun to soften and shape poor Walsh even, the son of parents and a country who didn't want to know about the North but wanted to be left alone with their lawns and their holidays.

Minogue abruptly realised that he hadn't touched on the relationship between her and Jarlath. Reserve, politeness? A cloud of doubt passed over the prospect of the day's work ahead. He could spin it out in the college for another day or two and that would be that, unless Connors had something from the parents or prints showed on the note.

Kathleen shouldered the door open gently.

"Matt. You're up."

"Good morning madam," Minogue replied, the advantage of tea resting him on the high ground of talk. "I awoke early. I may be entering my dotage."

"Is it the job?" Kathleen asked.

"No, lovey. The rain woke me, so it did."

Later, when Daithi and Iseult appeared at the table, Minogue couldn't keep his eyes off them. It occurred to him that he might indeed be going dotty to be scrutinising them like this. Daithi looked up from his cornflakes several times. Finally he raised his hands.

"Honest to God, I didn't do it," he said.

"What?" Minogue said.

"Whatever it is, I didn't do it. If you're looking at me bloodshot eyes, it's the library to blame."

As they left Minogue's car outside the university, Minogue managed to kiss both of his children. Iseult blushed and drew away a little, her eyelashes down. Daithi was more than bashful

59

and he tried to ease his father's caprice as well as his own irritation.

"We can't go on meeting like this, darling."

There might be something in that remark, Minogue thought as he drove off.

Kilmartin was sitting behind a copy of the *Irish Independent*. It crumpled down as he began his effusive greeting. Greeks bearing gifts, Minogue figured.

"Matt, me old ball and socket," Kilmartin said. "How is she cutting?"

"Fair to middling. Nothing to write home about."

Both sat. This is not like him, Minogue registered. For his part, Kilmartin felt a companion gas pain. Its occurrence marked awkward moments in his life, a constant sentinel these days. He hoped he wouldn't have to fart here in this office. Better hurry it up, Minogue knows there's something in the wind.

"I took the liberty of bringing along Connors' notes of the interview with the Walsh boy's parents. A very sad business to be sure, to be sure. The missus is under sedation. She might have to go into hospital. Do you know, her memory is gone almost completely. She remembers the boy as a youngster and little else.

"An interview? Yesterday?" Minogue said.

"Well, a few words to be exact. Connors just kept his ears open."

"The Da?" Minogue led.

"Oh he's a very busy man, you might say. Very busy, yes," Kilmartin said with reluctance.

"Not saying he wasn't a good father at all, don't get me wrong. Let's say he let the wife look after domestic things. And the family sort of fell under that heading. At the moment, Connors said he doesn't know whether he's coming or going really. That's the gist of it," Kilmartin concluded.

"Thanks. I'll go through it myself later."

"And the bloody rain has put the kybosh on searching for the murder-site. Isn't that the divil?" Kilmartin said.

"It is," Minogue allowed.

"And I have to sit in on these meetings to do with the latest stuff in the North. Would you credit it but we're all involved? There's to be some of that crowd from A division up in the North — you know, the joint RUC and Special Branch thing they have up there. They'll be sitting in too. They have the wind up, so they do. I don't mind telling you, Matt, that that particular crowd has hooligans in it, what with the way they treat people in Castlerea . . . "

And what about our own Heavy Gang here in the South, Minogue mused inwardly. Banana republic. Kilmartin lit a cigarette and inhaled. Minogue glanced over the transcriptions of Connors' notes.

"Not so hot, is it?" Kilmartin offered.

"Best he could do, I suppose," Minogue replied.

"You're managing O.K. though," Kilmartin said tentatively. "Overall, like?"

Minogue studied the desktop. So that was it. Kilmartin wanted to be reassured.

"Fine, thanks. I'm always quiet like this when I'm Sherlocking cases."

"Right you be, Matt, right you be. Sure didn't I know that when I had you put on the case?"

Kilmartin smiled, affecting contentment. His belly rumbled and the pain burned him again.

"The Commissioner was inquiring after you. Asked to be remembered to you. 'Glad to hear Matt is on this one,' says he. 'The man is out on his own, so he is,' he says. 'And don't I know that myself?' says I. Isn't that the trick, Matt, picking the right people and then getting a pat on the back for the results, hah?"

It was Minogue's turn to smile. Out on his own is right. Did he mean outstanding or remote?

"Oh and he says to tell you that Wexford will wallop Clare when their turn comes," Kilmartin said with some satisfaction.

Minogue had to hand it to Jimmy Kilmartin. He was making the best of it, trusting Minogue to fill in the lines. Letting Minogue know in a low-key way. A bit of chat about what the patricians were hatching, keep in touch. He liked Kilmartin. He didn't envy Kilmartin's go-betweens, his rank, his obligations. They had known each other for twenty years. Still, Minogue was growing frustrated at waiting for the rest of it.

"So Loftus put a flea in someone's ear?" Minogue asked.

Kilmartin didn't balk.

"Yep. He was on the blower. Nothing direct, you see. Polite enquiry and exchanging pleasantries."

"And . . . " Minogue waited.

"Wondering if maybe you were concentrating too much on something. You gave him a bit of heat about a locker the other day?"

"Lucky I didn't run him in for destroying evidence. There might be a drug angle to this so —"

"— and you're the man on the spot, Matt. Tell you the truth, I haven't the time of day for the likes of your man, Loftus. Just to let you know. Now if you need staff to work on this part with you, say the word. We're stretched but, you know."

"Thanks."

"Loftus was peeved. The Commissioner got the impression that you might have felt under pressure to produce results and that you were pushing a matter of little consequence."

"Sounds like Loftus talking," Minogue said. "Tell me, was the Commissioner ever in the army himself?"

Kilmartin hesitated.

"Matter of fact, now that you mention it, he was. In the early fifties. Did an unusual thing, changed career. Paid off."

"The contacts are always there," Minogue observed delicately.

"Look, Matt. That note—I know about it—is from a crank or some yo-yo who didn't like Walsh. As for his Da's importing fruit and the like, well you can't get much for bananas on the drug market here. Walsh wouldn't know one end of a reefer from the other. Neither would the young lad, God be good to him. It's just a student thing. You know how the papers would lap up any stuff like that though. That's Loftus' peeve, I'm sure."

"One of the boy's professors told me he had an interest in the effects of various drugs," Minogue said.

"Ah," Kilmartin sighed. "Well, that's how I tend to think about it meself. He probably wanted to have something ready to say to his pals if they were poking fun at him for not smoking up. A debate maybe. He was well able to talk, by all accounts."

Neither man spoke for several seconds.

"Be that as it may, though," Minogue said quietly, "Loftus won't be the one to determine whether police work should or shouldn't pursue something, no matter how far up the bog it might look."

"Absolutely," Kilmartin said. "But listen. Maybe you did rub Loftus the wrong way, maybe a personality thing. The Commissioner is wondering if maybe your own views on things aren't squeezing in on things a bit."

"You mean Loftus and where he works? The old school tie stuff and the gentry beyond in Trinity? No."

"It's been a rough year for you, Matt, more than a lot of people could take. Wouldn't you prefer to work on another angle? Look, I can get Connors to do the legwork for you. He's a smart lad. He has his wits about him."

"No thanks," Minogue said, in the quietness which seemed to fill the room after Kilmartin's remarks.

Kilmartin turned back to the pleasantries. He did not want to leave any friction in his wake. He suffered for his understanding, however, with the knifing pain in his bowel as well as with the knowledge that Minogue read his strategies.

63

CHAPTER SIX

With no plan in his head, Minogue went to Trinity College. Driving into the centre of the city, the buildings passed him in a grimy, purgatorial progression. The rain greyed everything. Women's stockings had splash marks on them. Motorists were drowning people at the streetcorners. The buses seemed to go even faster than usual. Tramps stood sodden in the streets downtown, their hair matted on their foreheads. The parking practices of Dubliners were bad enough on days you could philosophise about them, but today they were three deep in Leeson Street. Grafton Street was blocked.

Walking from his car finally, Minogue felt the gloom approach closer. No doubt it would meet him and swallow him whole in the room. Burying Walsh today. What a send-off in this downpour. Minogue shivered.

Closer to the door of the room he had been assigned, Minogue had a little change of heart. He headed off toward Agnes' rooms.

Breathless after three flights of stairs, he tapped at her door. He heard footsteps inside. She opened the door and smiled faintly.

"Well, Sergeant. Come in."

She was dressed in black and grey. The outfit was a size or two too big for her, probably borrowed. The dark colours made her face even paler.

Minogue stepped in. Sitting at the table was Allen, uncharacteristically dressed in a jacket and tie.

"I was just about to leave," Allen said, rising. He turned to Agnes.

"I'll be back at a quarter to. The car is parked up near Pearse Street Gate."

"Sit down, will you, Sergeant. Will it be tea?" she asked. Minogue was taken with the accent again: sot dine.

"I had hoped to carry on our conversation from yesterday, Agnes. But if I'm intruding . . . " he trailed off.

"Not a bit of it."

"Well," Minogue began, "Yes, tea would be grand."

He felt his heart pushing still after the climb. Agnes lit the gas, walked back into the room and sat across the table from Minogue. A picture of two people dressed up as clowns on their way out to a party hung on the wall behind her. It was at dusk and the two figures were dwarfed by the black branches of a winter coppice. Between the branches was a sky of light blue which fell imperceptibly to cream behind the trees. Miraculously, a moon held the stillness and peace without a trace of a message for the astonished Minogue. A Rousseau?

The place was very neat without being fussy. Minogue noticed that all the books were shelved alphabetically. Rain beaded the window. Drops broke away with the help of gusts and they gullied down the glass. A faint smell of gas came from the kitchenette. It was mixed with a light staleness of age, maybe a trace of bedwarmth. Nobody smoked here.

"You'll be off soon then, Agnes?"

"Dr Allen's giving me a lift out to the funeral. So . . . "

"I'm still trying to figure out details, so I am. Every little thing can have a bearing. I don't know if this is the day to be pursuing it though."

"I can try in the next twenty minutes or so. I'm in one piece now. I can't say about this afternoon though," Agnes said. Her voice had the questioning quality which Minogue was familiar with from listening to Northerners. Hers had none of the suspicion or dare-me he associated with the talk he heard in that accent. He was quite mesmerised by her voice. The silence finally jolted him back from staring at the poster.

"Em. Agnes, did Jarlath ever discuss things to do with drugs with you?"

"Drugs?" she asked. Drugs. She shook her head, not taking her eyes from Minogue's.

"He wasn't that type of person. I would have known," she added. "Jarlath talked about a lot of things. I'm not sure I was listening to him all the time. It wasn't what he said or anything, it was more that he liked ideas, liked a listener."

"He had notebooks that were stolen. Would you know anything about what he used the notebooks for?" Minogue asked.

"Well, he wrote down ideas. He was full of them. Anything really, I suppose. Quotations, references maybe . . . He said it made him look organised, like Woodward and Bernstein, documenting everything," Agnes said.

"Who?"

"The men who blew the whistle on Nixon. The Watergate thing. Jarlath was very interested in that stuff. He wanted to get a scoop, he said. He used to joke about it. He'd keep me in suspense, you know, pretending he had found out something big and I'd be dying to know. It'd turn out to be a yarn, having me on. He had a sense of humour. People didn't see it very often though. They didn't give him much of a chance. He'd have me on the edge of the chair with it, and it'd turn out to be something like the Provost's cat peed on his shoes. Silly, but he did it for laughs. He wasn't the way others here thought of him, you know."

66

"Yes, your president beyond in the Students' Union mentioned Jarlath's interest in the journalism," Minogue said.

"Mick Roche? Not too complimentary, I'd suspect," Agnes said wryly.

"Not really. Said Jarlath had potential," Minogue said.

In between talking, he could hear the kettle gathering strength. Soon it would whistle. It dawned on Minogue that he liked this room. He would like to try this other life out for a while. Going to lectures, chatting, making friends, reading. To be this age, to be going to libraries, to be in touch. Minogue wanted to do silly things, to make mistakes.

Agnes went to the kitchenette to make the tea. Minogue listened to the numerous domestic sounds. His mind reeled effortlessly back to his own youth. Had he had a youth? Maybe that's what it is, he speculated: he didn't have a youth and he spent his adult life trying to make up for it. He didn't mind being thought of as a bit eccentric. It served as well as any other dressing. Over the years he had watched some grey creep in, even into his beard. Kathleen had bought him an electric razor. With some fascination he observed the dust of hairs which he blew out the bathroom window. His hands had lost their strength. His shoulders weren't back. Stairs reminded him of his age. His few friends looked old sometimes, straitened, very usual.

Minogue had gone all the way through school to the Leaving Certificate. He and his brother, Mick, had run the farm. Their father could do little enough after the bouts of TB. The boys were a new generation in the Irish Free State. The war on the continent had brushed them in their early teens. Big things happening abroad, the names of battles and towns and generals coming across the wireless. The Local Defence Force hanging around in ditches trying to look fierce at the occasional roadblocks. Cars were scarce on the roads.

The Christian Brothers had done their anointed task and Minogue had endured. He could almost carry on a conversation in Latin. At least he could entertain a few Romans with recitations from Livy. He remembered the stupidest things even yet: which

67

forms took the subjunctive, expressions like *iter fecerunt*, Hannibal with the vinegar, breaking boulders in the Alps.

The odd teacher along the way indulged him. He read out parts of the *Aeneid* by gaslight at home in the kitchen. His parents listened with a reverence for the holiness that Latin brought to the house. His father would cough and say that Virgil borrowed his stuff from the Irish stories.

They heard about camps for Jews on the continent. A lay teacher risked George Orwell, God forbid, and even loaned Minogue books by Steinbeck and Sinclair Lewis. The wet fields waited for them in the spring. One of the fields might flood. A pig might get stuck in a dike. They bought a tractor, the talk of the townland.

In school, the civics classes taught you codes of conduct. May brought the altar to the Blessed Virgin into the classroom, lilacs inevitably. The Catechism showed him how to answer hypothetical questions which a Protestant might ask you if you were in a bus, say. No opportunity for converting was to be lost. Minogue's mother thought that one of her sons might have a vocation for the priesthood. She fastened her hopes on Mick and he turned toward her hope. Minogue watched his sisters grow up, do civil service exams, go to dances, get a job in the bank and more. Minogue stayed on the farm while Mick deliberated.

More cars appeared on the roads. There was a change in the music at the dances. Minogue began to favour pints of stout and he found that he was well able to drink them all evening in the pub. Coming home on the lane, the drink tidal in his belly, he'd stop for a piss in the ditch. He'd hear the rustlings in the hedges when the stream stopped. Swaying in the dark, he'd be pissing on his shoes as he looked up for stars. He was twenty and tired of waiting.

At night he'd hear the cattle lowing or the hens being disturbed. Up at six, the clang of the milking buckets, a cigarette in the mouth early, the rhythmical swish of the teats squirting into the bucket.

What decided it finally was not his father's deteriorating condition or his own frustration. Rather, it was the questioning of his brother by the Garda one evening. It was a casual thing, to look as if they were doing something about the IRA. Mick came home late. He was triumphant, Minogue realised. He had been questioned in the barracks in town about his connections with the IRA, a proscribed organisation. It didn't matter that it was moribund, maintained by diehards and barstool heroes. Mick had found his vocation, Minogue understood. Ireland was to be his religion.

Maybe, as Mick accused him, it was the books he read. Books full of pessimism and anti-religious feeling. Maybe it wasn't fashionable to be devoted to your country anymore, Mick would sneer. Youth? Mick didn't have it either. Curious though, Kathleen had remarked after they had all met at a neighbour's funeral years later, Mick didn't seem to age.

Minogue tried his hand at bartending in Dublin. His mother wanted him to do the Civil Service exams. He spent a lot of time in the libraries. He saved money for a trip to America. He met Kathleen O'Hare who was new to the Civil Service. She poked fun at his accent, knowing his irritation to be waxing love. He in turn complained about Dublin people. She teased out his plans. She said she had to be fair with him, not to lead him on, because if he was serious about America, she couldn't go. Her family needed her and America frightened her, she admitted.

"You're nobody there, Matt," she'd say.

Minogue was reading the Frenchman, Sartre, and he felt that he wouldn't mind being a nobody for a while. Maybe a holiday in America, Kathleen said.

She had been very fair to me, Minogue thought. He was determined to repay her honesty with a loyalty the intensity of which surprised him. Minogue didn't fancy himself as a man who went in for the lovey-dovey stuff, but not because he wanted people to think he was a hard man. He would be happy with loyalty and company. Within a year, he was through the Garda training in Templemore, surprising himself even more by doing well at it. They married. With the America money and Kathleen's economy, they saw themselves into a new house in Kilmacud. Minogue didn't mind it at all, not even the cliff-heights of a mortgage.

In that same year, Minogue's father had died, leaving Mick the man of the house. Their mother grieved for a long time. The doctor called it reactive depression. Minogue's sisters and their husbands called on weekends. One sister, Maura, gently asked him what he thought about her moving to Canada and how would their mother take it. Families grew. Something was stirring in the country, money.

Kathleen delivered a baby boy, Eamonn, a big hairy child. Eamonn died unaccountably some seven months later, forgetting to breathe, it seems. The death precipitated the worst years of Minogue's life. For all their cleverness, , the poems and the books meant nothing after that. Kathleen overcame her dread and went to see a psychiatrist. Minogue was helpless, encumbered. They promoted him to detective.

It wasn't until six years later that Kathleen conceived again. Minogue felt frightened being an expectant father again. None of their acquaintances joked with them. Minogue had been marked as different already.

Iseult was a different baby from the start. Kathleen took heart. The coldness leaked out of Minogue. As if to remind them that it wasn't chance, Daithi was born the following year. Minogue was always watching. He was careful not to live for his children but his determination was manic. They would have university, the loan of the car, good teeth, pocket money, clothes, French, parties, books. Fearing his own intensity, Minogue immersed himself in it all the more.

As they grew, Minogue wondered—but didn't much care about — his promotion. He became a detective sergeant. Others passed him on the ladder.

Optimism seeped into Ireland in the sixties. One evening he watched civil rights marchers being beaten up near Derry. Was that still going on? He knew vaguely that the civil rights people were Catholics and that the Unionists controlled the North. The police beat up the marchers. That Paisley lunatic and his huge

70

lips and mouth sneering on the television, a hysteric from another century. A new IRA appeared in the streets. Minogue was relieved. The people he worked with and the people he met were glad too. There were rumours of sending in troops to Derry to protect the Catholics. Hooded bodies turned up in ditches. Bombs demolished shops and factories. Men were shot to death at their doors. Troops went berserk. Petrol bombs arced lazily and burst in the night on the evening news. British Ministers recoiled at the hatred. Minogue's brother called in and had a glass of whisky.

"Majority my foot. How is it that a country that's held up to be the birthplace of parliamentary government can give in to a crowd of seventeenth-century bigots who represent about two percent of the population of Great Britain. How is that, can you tell me?"

New laws and courts, armed guards and the army at trials. The word 'terrorist' showed up in the news a lot. The old guard of the IRA, well clear of Belfast and Newry and Derry, lauded their northern heroes. Mick exhilarated in talk. He was well-to-do now. The country was to join the European Economic Community although Mick didn't agree with the move in principle. Still, Mick was not an activist, Minogue knew. Mick was for Ireland going it alone and his zeal couldn't countenance socialism. He couldn't approve of guns from Libya or Russia or from the madmen in Germany.

The brothers met intermittently at hurling matches. In Hayes' Hotel in Thurles, they'd be pressed together by the swell of men trying to get to the bar, eager for pints after the game. Both locked into the throng of countrymen in the streets and pubs of provincial towns. Minogue would catch sight of his brother through the struggling mass; the strong smells of his own youth — the porter, the cowshite, the hair oil — rising up around him. They never quarrelled.

Minogue knew that his brother knew more than he'd tell. The mannered ambiguity and the lifetime's practice with evasion meshed the two men. Ah, Minogue thought sometimes as the

71

stout hit his stomach, we have the same sisters and mother and father, isn't that the strangest thing? How's things Matt? Grand and how's yourself and yours? Can't complain, Matt, back to the wind. And how's Kathleen and the two children? Good, thanks be to God. *Not thanks be to God at all, to Kathleen probably.*

Minogue had felt a God in the singed grass at the side of the road, in the slowness of things winding down. The young fellow with the scattered blots and freckles of blood thick all over his face and everything silent and slow and slower as the smoke moved off. Minogue had spent a long time thinking about it in hospital. It was never fear really, more a surprise, especially so because there was something so familiar there at the time. It was like a face maybe. Maybe like those Zen fellas, a face he had before he was born. Not smiling or puzzled or anything at all really, more a feeling that something was there. A watchful presence, interested and disinterested at the same time. Great calm, silence. Maybe a trace of regret as it receded. Life marches on, each wave of people full of themselves, but less so as they get closer to the edge with the years. Then it's our turn.

Lying in the hospital bed, Minogue had imagined all the life, plants and animals, all the plankton in the sea, all the organisms in his body. This small hating island off the coast of Europe . . . There were people dying of hunger elsewhere, without the time or the energy to be on their mad summer marches, without any dirty little pubs to plot in. Ah, but that wasn't the half of it even. People are nice here a lot of the time. More inane phrases drifted by Minogue and he'd turn aside to sleep.

Then, driving back up to Dublin after the games, Minogue would sometimes dream what life would have been like had he left for the States those years ago. He might be a cop on the beat in New York City. He might be a farmer in Montana with a Ford pick-up truck and steers. His wife would be a blonde with big white teeth and a skin that'd tan. Maybe two cars. The kids would have American accents.

No end in sight to this business, is there, Matt? That is if the

English insist on being blackmailed by those Orangemen. No, Mick, it doesn't look like it.

Mick didn't shoot the guns, but Minogue was sure he cheered the count of soldiers or loyalists killed.

Maybe it'll spread, Matt. It may well, but we'll do what we can, Mick.

Minogue listened to the things his brother left unsaid. Minogue had by then given up any ambition of rescuing his brother or indeed any of his countrymen from whatever threw them effortlessly between savagery and kindness.

Agnes laid the vapouring cups on the table. Slowly the two of them sipped their tea. Occasionally, a gust sprayed rain on the window and rattled the frame. Finally, Agnes spoke:

"A great day for going to the library . . . or a funeral."

Minogue couldn't deny her. He had been sitting there as a visitor drinking tea. He was afraid to intrude upon her by asking her questions about her own family. That was none of his business. She had told him as much as she could about Jarlath Walsh. Agnes prepared to go. He couldn't stay here. He was supposed to be detecting, not sitting here with a girl, daydreaming.

He walked down the flights of stairs ahead of her and side by side to the carpark. Allen leaned over and pushed the passenger door open for her. When Allen fussed with attaching her seatbelt, Minogue believed that this was a different Allen, a solicitous man taking custody of a precious cargo. A fatherly concern? Easy in a man with no brood at home to be keeping him in the real world, a part of Minogue's mind jeered.

Minogue closed Agnes' door. It closed with a solid clap. Beads of rainwater quivered on the waxed paintwork. A nice, big, new Toyota without an excess of chrome, Minogue mused. He would have had to put his boot to his own door on the Fiat to get it to close first time. As if reading the thoughts of a poor but secretly favoured suitor, Agnes looked up briefly and smiled through the glass. Unreachable, going. As he walked aimlessly back into the college, Minogue worked at persuading himself that he was not somehow envious of Allen. A moment of juvenile insecurity, he chided within.

What Minogue could not put aside, however, was the belief that the case had left him beached with the ebbing tide no longer touching him. Funerals. The last funeral Minogue had attended was that of an old IRA man from 1916, one who had survived the Civil War and a spell interned in the Curragh, to write memoirs and die renowned as one of the last of the hard men. There couldn't be many left. Three old men, propped up by their relatives, had stood over the grave. Mick had been among the hundreds of mourners there. Minogue had caught his brother looking over at him several times. He thought it was a look of some satisfaction on Mick's face, as if to claim the damp countryside and its people as his inheritance, not Minogue's.

CHAPTER SEVEN

Back in his room, Minogue doodled. He wrote down names and events. Then he tried to join them with lines so he could work out cause and effect later. Nothing.

They'd be burying the boy now. There'd be beads of rain on the coffin. The wet would give the bouquets more colour. Minogue reached a disagreeable decision. He phoned the Drug Squad.

While Minogue doodled, thought and telephoned, a well-dressed man in his late thirties took up a padded barstool in the Bailey public house. He held a copy of the *Irish Times* under his arm. He had stepped from a taxi but feet from the door.

The barman prided himself on recognising customers' occupations by the way they dressed. He took the order for a small Paddy, and he registered some surprise at an American accent, soft but there all the same. The customer unfolding the paper had the ruddy tan of a robust Yank with any amount of rhino for holidays and grub. Took care of himself.

The barman put him as a legal eagle, but that was a long shot, he realised, as he poured the water into the jug. Irish-looking, all the same, probably in the early thirties. The barman recognized a forty quid shirt when he saw one. The plain grey suit had the looks of having cost three hundred quid. Although he hadn't seen the customer hang up his coat, the barman guessed an Aquascutum.

The customer opened the paper to the editorial, which concerned itself with a condemnation of the murders of policemen, culminating in another one yesterday. He sipped at the whisky. The barman returned to his preparations for the lunchtime crowd.

When the customer's pal showed, the barman pegged him for a journalist or a theatrical type. Maybe not though. He served him a pint and returned to setting up glasses. He felt the light grab at the small of his back, the twinge that would grow to an ache by lunchtime. The barman's name was Gerry, and he wasn't any more interested in politics than he was in soccer, but he talked about both endlessly every working day. He heard enough guff. The tanned and fit-looking barrister who was not a barrister was likewise disinterested in what passed for politics. He was so anti-pathetic toward the way politics ran on this island that he carried a large-calibre automatic pistol holstered under his armpit. The magazine was fully loaded and there was a bullet in the spout. The man wanted nothing to do with talking politics or any other conversation which policemen might wish to engage him in.

Before starting out on this project, he had weighed the things he felt were necessary and those which he could get around. Daily, and with no sense of excitement, he cleaned the gun in his hotel room. Carrying it was a non-negotiable item in his list and he felt quite at home with yet another hard and fast rule in his life.

Gerry the barman's guess about the other fellow, who was dressed half as a farmer and half as a priest, was partially correct in that the man was a playwright. The playwright had spent the best part of a half hour making sure he was not being tailed.

The tanned man disliked the playwright, not least for the maudlin viciousness of his nationalism. He regarded him as a fool whose brains were stewed by decades in fifth-rate theatricals. He did not trust the playwright, but he knew that having to work with him was a test which others were watching.

"You can see that results come quickly," he began.

"There's no gainsaying that," agreed the playwright. "So it went smoothly this time and the volunteers got away. Maximum effect, oh yes, I can see that."

"But . . . ? You have reservations?"

The playwright observed the bubbles rising to the ice in his glass before replying.

"I'll say this much. All this firepower and technology are fine and well. You are well able to do the fancy footwork. But I've been in this thing for most of my life. I know how the lads on the ground feel. I can tell you that they're not too excited about the Russians getting in on this like they've started to."

The tanned man saw the beginnings of a faint irony in the smile on the other's face. Patronising.

"What don't they like?"

"Don't get me wrong. The movement is all for arms supplies, even from the man in the moon. As long as there's no strings attached. What do I say when they ask what we're supposed to hand over in return? Some of the lads'll think maybe it's too much of an assembly line thing. They wonder what we had to give to get this kind of support."

The tanned man looked directly at the playwright.

"Does it really matter to the active service units where the stuff comes from? It's a command council decision. I haven't traded away the place to get this stuff. And that consideration has really nothing to do with either of us, has it? I'm here to monitor things. I have to report to them at some point otherwise they won't hand over any more," he added.

"Risk," the playwright said.

"Everything has risk. It was even a risk trying to persuade the council to go along with this scheme. The drop to the trawler

77

went off without a hitch, didn't it? The Soviet boat didn't pick up on anyone. And they're stuffed with monitoring gear. It went off perfectly. The guns were in use and even safely back across the border within a week."

"Could be the Yanks are stringing them along and waiting for a big haul so they can tip off the Brits. I read where those satellites can read the paper you have in your hand from up there," the playwright said.

Testing my patience, the tanned man thought, to see how far he can go with me, how much he can find out.

"Could be," he began. "But we're not talking of sheer numbers of weapons. The risk of detection is not as high as you might think. It's a matter of having the right weapon at the right time. Look at all the publicity about the grenade launcher. Let them think we have these things coming out our ears. They think we have any amount of nightsights. That's what works. Effectiveness, economy. There's more yet."

"Another toy?" the playwright asked.

"You don't need to know details. Just get your guys to set up a car to take something the size of a suitcase. The guidance and the sights fit into the suitcase too. It looks like a typewriter case. Light, portable; about twenty-five pounds."

"A suitcase?" The playwright had become very attentive.

"Have you heard of a Sagger?"

"I've heard of a shagger. I've met a lot of them . . . "

"They were big in the Egypt and Israel war in seventy-three."
"What is it?"

"It's a guided missile, an anti-tank missile. It'll go a mile and a half. If it hits dead-on, it'll go through 400 mil plate."

The tanned man watched the playwright lose his battle to keep his composure.

"Jesus, Mary and Holy Saint Joseph. Is it here?"

"It was in, as of eleven o'clock last night."

"Same stunt?" the playwright whispered.

"Same route, different boat. I told you they're serious about this. It's a whole new approach. You've missed out on the global picture here. They're peeved with the Americans sending in stuff to Afghanistan. There's Central America. We're all part of the big picture. It's not just a local squabble."

"So it could be released a mile and a half from target?" the playwright asked.

"It's proven accurate to that. It needs two men, one to sight and control as it's in flight, the other to set up behind. It's wire-guided. Not for space cadets. It's reliable. It works."

The playwright frowned. He wondered yet again what this Yank, or whatever he was, had as a stake in this. The rumour was that the Yank was actually Irish, even born here. Another part of the mythology which had gathered around his arrival was that he was a tycoon businessman. That was too much to hope for, that image of Ireland's emigrant sons renewing the struggle. In any event, the council had put their suspicions aside and allowed this newcomer some rope. So far, to their astonishment, he had delivered. Although they had no way of checking, few could doubt that indeed he had enough links to set up the deliveries right from the Soviet Union. Still, no one could fathom his motives enough to allay their suspicions. He hadn't approached any of the movement in the States. A search on him had turned up things that the leadership had kept to themselves, causing the rumours to fly around even more. Some suspected a plant, but again they were discredited when the guns went into use in the North.

As the playwright tried to digest this news, the tanned man observed with some scorn . Resentful, befuddled. This remnant of a green peasant Ireland was out of his depth.

The playwright and his like didn't want a rational solution to the mess, because they wouldn't be the kings of the pygmies any more afterwards. He had no commitment to unloading the mess, the national inferiority complex, the energy deflected into 'politics,' the bitterness. Like any neurotic, the playwright didn't see how he was clinging to the neurosis itself.

"And will you be wanting those couriers still . . . ?" the playwright asked.

"You sound like you want to tell me there's some hitch," the tanned man said.

"It's not a hitch."

"Well, what's the big deal then?"

"There's no big deal. I hope you've got a car lined up yourself for this. I don't have anything in the garage right now. Seeing as you don't like Mercedes and all that."

"Get your guys to boost something a lot less conspicuous next time, that's all I said. You ditched it like I said, right?"

"Almost."

"What does that mean?"

"Some of the boys are down from Belfast and I had to give them a car. The only one in the garage was the Merc, so I gave it to them for today and tomorrow. What's the point of torching a perfectly good car?" the playwright answered.

"Look. You know the cars are for this operation." The tanned man's voice began to rise.

"I know, I know. Don't be getting yourself—"

"Shut up for a minute. I say what goes here. Just because I say dump that car, that doesn't mean it's yours and you can loan the god-damn thing out. Get it back off those hoods straightaway. Tell them to boost their own transport if they have to. I want this operation watertight. Get it back and burn it, OK?"

The playwright held his palms up in mock surrender.

"Anyway. I have the guy I need for this one. Good cover and a car thrown in as well, all legal. I want you to use the gas—the petrol tank for the package."

The playwright finished his drink and got up to leave.

"Better get the car to me soon. Can't do much at the garage until they have the exact dimensions. It's a very precise thing. The cars are not as big over here," the playwright said.

The tanned man turned aside the veiled jibe and merely nodded his head. You must be kidding, he thought. Whip off the gas tank and secure the thing inside another one. No doubt this loser favoured putting it on his shoulder and running across the fields. Or taking chances on the roads even when they didn't know which roads the Brits were likely to crater from one day to the next. The British Army had infra-red and thermal surveillance as well as roving patrols out in the fields at night.

When the playwright left, the tanned man took up the newspaper again. Much to the chagrin of the barman, he ordered a coffee. Gerry was twenty years in the trade and still couldn't get used to serving up tea and cake in a public house.

As the lunchtime crowd began coming in, Gerry noticed the well-dressed fella get his coat and leave. The man crossed Duke Street and entered the shopping arcade. He went to a phone booth, deposited the money and dialled.

"I'm calling about the matter we discussed on the weekend. It's ready to go."

"Have you got a day on it yet?"

"No. But I'll know by tomorrow evening probably. It'll be your fellow doing it again."

The other person paused.

"Is there a problem with that?"

"Not really. We might need to let some things blow over."

"Like?"

"That business about the student. My fellow balked a bit. It scared him a lot."

"Is that it?"

"We have an irritation which prevents things from, shall we say, healing over. The dick who's looking into it. Not what you'd call a sleuth, but I have a bad feeling about him. Deceptive kind. Behind the scenes."

"Did you spin out the drug thing?"

"Yes. I think it's working."

"Well, we can't wait forever."

"No. I'm thinking that we should maybe nudge more things on him, set him going on the trail."

"That's your affair. Just make it work. We have to work this thing to show we can deliver. Then we can relax."

While the tanned man left the arcade, the person he had called sat wondering what to do about Minogue.

For his part, the playwright was not a happy man. He sat in a taxi which had been caught in a traffic jam in College Green. A bloody bomb scare, wasn't that funny? The playwright did not like the man he had met in the Bailey. He didn't like him one bit. He was a snotty, smart, pushy, well-to-do Yank. Telling him who he could give out one of the cars to. What was this well-connected Yank going to get out of this anyway? What would the Russians get out of it? Surely they knew that Irish people wouldn't accept their way even if they did help to win in the Six Counties. Although it was tougher and tougher to get in the stuff from the States, at least it didn't alienate the rank and file. What if the Yank was an undercover, a set-up?

It had come hard to the playwright to be told by the leadership to give this man all assistance. It might even be that this new thing could change everything. The taxi inched around College Green, under the portals of the Bank of Ireland and the haughty Trinity College. He smiled grimly at the sight: god-damn it to hell, he decided, if that institution can claim to have any say in the business of Irish liberation. He knew then what he would do. The preparations would go ahead, but the weapon would find a different route to the North. We'll test out this fancy scheme, he thought. Well and good if they make it through, then he'll have been wrong and he'll admit it. No one would blame him in the end for being so vigilant. He'd find a way to get the weapon in by his own route.

More and more as he thought about it, the playwright began to believe that this was the acid test. The Brits would have stepped up searches with the latest incidents. Any number of things could banjax this whiz kid's operation and all its glamour. A tip-off was the worst danger, of course. Tip-offs. At least such betrayals sent the command council scurrying around trying to find the traitors and made them rely again on the proven loyalty of men like himself. Tip-offs, yes. A constant worry, something that high-flying boyos with their shady deals overlooked.

The taxi-man swore long and loud.

"Everything'd be just dandy if people just knew the ropes in this city," he muttered. "The trouble is you have drivers who think they know bloody short-cuts and fancy moves. They're the ones that jam up the shagging place when a street is closed with a bomb-scare. Fuckin' iijits, pardon me language."

The driver switched off the engine. Exactly, the playwright thought. The war is being fought by Irishmen and women here in Ireland. For their own homes and families, their own country. Ordinary people like this taxi-driver, born and bred here. Living here, enduring, persevering. And the Yank, or whatever he was . . . ? The playwright didn't need to deliberate any longer. He caught sight of the tired face of the driver as he turned in the seat to share his exasperation. Right, he thought, certain now about the Yank: our Ireland, not his.

Minogue had that stupid feeling again. Anytime he was on the phone for more than a minute or so, he felt stupid. He became bored talking into it, no matter how important it was supposed to be or how well known to him the person on the other end. Minogue's attention wandered all the more because he knew he was getting a long and polite no with many hints and reasons.

He liked the man on the other end, Denny Byrne from the Drug Squad. For a Wicklowman he was a good old stick.

"The chances are very much against it, Matt. The crates and things do be open, you see, to air the goods. There does be a lot of loose stuff in them, compared to other things, you see. It used to be popular enough a number of years ago, I don't mind telling you, but we copped on. I shouldn't say it was us who copped on. It was others, like fellas unloading and finding burst bags of things. I remember even a fellow out in Fairview who ran a shop phoning up and telling me he had 'drugs' in a box of bananas. 'Go way outa that,' I says to him, thinking like bananas is the word for him. God, do you know he was right. So I says to him, 'How did you cop onto the fact that these were bags of heroin, then?' You know what he says? 'Why wouldn't I know they were drugs? Sure don't I see it on shows on the telly?'"

Minogue smiled.

83

"So, a slim chance."

"Yep. That's about it. I'm not saying we're sniffing around the port of Dublin every day. But I don't mind people thinking we are. We go through people, people we know about or hear about. We can't afford to go the random route alone, do you see."

That was that, Minogue thought. Walsh as an unwitting accomplice in a deal, then he stumbled on something? Wild guessology. Still, Minogue had had the direction from two people independently, and they were not the sort to be romancing. Loftus for all his prissy speechifying about law and order was not a fool, nor was Allen. Allen. What was it about Allen? Was it that he was so organised, so controlled?

Minogue decided that it was time to dose himself with a large white coffee in Bewley's. He stepped out onto the greasy cobblestones and felt the drops of rain pat against his coat. The air freshened him. He wondered if he was being played elaborately by somebody or somebodies. Even Mick Roche, the Students' Union president, had turned in a fine performance, one might think. As Minogue shouldered into Bewley's on Grafton Street he wondered: and Agnes?

After his second cup of coffee, Minogue had decided to return to Agnes McGuire. She wasn't popping up again and again in his mind for no good reason. There was something she hadn't said, he was sure of that. Maybe it'd turn out that what she'd say would not help him. Maybe she'd cry out her loss and break down, shed the stoicism and sadness and show her anger. It must be there, he thought, she's only human.

Minogue's timing worked. Agnes had returned from the funeral some minutes before he climbed the stairs and knocked. She didn't seem surprised to see him. She let him in.

"Agnes, I've held off asking you certain questions. God knows, I've never had much sense of timing so I'd like to try them now. It'll speed things up a lot. Or it will close off some distracting angles anyway."

"I think you want to ask me if there was a Someone Else. Isn't that the way it goes?"

"That's about the size of it, Agnes. Can you help me? You see, this thing has hallmarks of what might be called a crime of passion. It's an avenue I have to explore sometime."

Minogue saw reluctance in her. She examined her fingers before she spoke.

"It's a funny thing, I suppose," she began, "but when you least expect it you have something you never expected to have. Would it surprise you to know that I didn't have a boyfriend until I started college here? You'd think the opposite, wouldn't you, that the local thing would win out and that you'd go out with someone from your own background . . . ? Well, my father was assassinated when I was sixteen. You can imagine what that made of our lives."

Minogue watched her eyelashes as signs and when they stopped flickering, she continued.

"Well, I came here and, you know, I liked it. I didn't think I would. I felt that people in the South were not very sincere, if you know what I mean. This thing about violence. They didn't have to go through the results of their thinking. They just don't understand. It's not like 1916. I suppose you could say I was cynical." *Son-e-col,* Minogue heard.

"At first when Jarlath started following me around, I was annoyed. He was such a puppy. Embarrassing."

She smiled. Minogue was attentive at the same time as he was lost in thought. His mind raced on from her words, from her accent.

"Odd how things work out. Feeling sorry for him, I mean. The politicos used to tease him a lot here. You know how it is, the students who have a lot of ideas about society, have read a lot. Can you imagine how surprised I was when I heard myself defending and explaining Jarlath to Mick Roche? You know him?"

"The president of the Students' Union."

"Yes. Well, I was sort of going out with Mick. Or at least that's what he thought. I think he felt sorry for me, did Mick. Maybe even more than Jarlath. He knew my background. I felt I had to thank him somehow for feeling sorry for me. God. You know, I found out that people with any brains here in the South seem to be just hypnotized by the North. All Mick's talk is organised around it. There's a lot of fellas here in the South feel like that too, but all the most of them want is a bit of excitement or something like that. Mick is different. I think he felt guilty or something. Ashamed . . . How did I get to talking about this? Sounds like a soap opera."

Minogue smiled in return this time.

" . . . Anyway. I felt I was some kind of specimen. A ghost to haunt them here. But Jarlath didn't try to mine me for info like the others. Not head-over-heels or anything like that. He was very naive. Very. And, you know, I didn't mind that. He wasn't putting on like he knew or understood everything. Oh sure, he probably was opinionated, but he could feel things. That was the difference; he had a stomach. I felt bad for him when they laughed at him. His ideas used to get him into trouble."

"Dr Allen mentioned that Jarlath had a stake in something which wasn't in favour, academically at least," Minogue said.

Agnes' eyebrows arched.

"Something about a psychological model of Irish character that we could use to solve some of our, em, problems," Minogue offered.

Agnes turned to look at the window. Her hands were clasped together. Her head dipped as if to concentrate on her twining hands. Her hair fell to conceal her cheeks. Minogue waited. He saw a tear drop onto her arm. For no reason his sluggish mind could settle on in that room, he felt appalled. He shouldn't be doing this. This could be Iseult by chance of birth or geography. Without raising her head, Agnes picked a paper hanky from her sleeve and dabbed her eyes. Then she tossed her hair back. Minogue saw the film still on her eyes.

"It's all right," she said. "Just some things. Some people would say he was just thick or that he was a part of a class who helped cause the stuff up North so he'd never admit to the 'reality' of the situation. He hadn't been to the North once in his life. So there he was trying to build a big theory up for . . . for I don't know what. His family took care of him all his life. I mean what did he know about poverty or civil rights? Really?"

Agnes looked inquiringly at Minogue and then continued:

"The thing was—and I don't care what anyone else says—he was trying. I suppose it'd look sort of clumsy to an older person. When I think of it. Cooking Italian food and trying out wines. The Student Prince." Agnes' teeth showed in her smile this time. Then she frowned and looked straight at Minogue.

"Maybe I was the only one who noticed he was changing. I'll bet his parents didn't notice. I met them today for the first time. And the last time probably. I shouldn't say it maybe . . . but I felt I had seen them before. They didn't seem like strangers."

Minogue was thinking about Mick Roche. Could hardly call him jilted though. He had been circumspect, not the opinionated termagant Minogue had expected in a student leader. Perhaps give him credit for being able to conceal his feelings. Still, Roche had recognised the changes in Jarlath.

"Agnes, did Jarlath experiment with drugs at all?"

Minogue looked closely at her to try and gauge the risk. He had said it out of context, watching. Would she switch to anger? Minogue waited, seeing the frown on her face, not knowing if he had asked at the right time.

"Are you joking?"

Minogue didn't reply.

"Like I said this morning: *No*."

After a pause of returning his gaze, Agnes spoke slowly.

"Maybe I had better save you some embarrassment, Sergeant. You talk about drugs. Well Jarlath didn't so much as experiment with sex. He was all for cuddles and going to the pictures and walking me home. As for trying to stay the night . . . and it isn't even that I wanted things that way at all. But you know fellas, trying to prove things to themselves. Jarlath got pissed out of his brain after three pints. I mean, nothing doing. Can you believe that?"

"Yes," Minogue said simply. He turned away from the intensity

87

of her gaze. She had decided in his favour by the slightest of margins. She still retained the challenging candour in her voice as if daring him to push his luck into rudeness. "Yes." Minogue needed to believe as much about Iseult and Daithi, that they weren't part of the touted libertine rubbish which the magazines fed to the middle-aged on their stale weekends.

Minogue heard a little *ping* in the back of his head. It came from remembering Allen's reluctance in telling him about Jarlath's interests. Had Jarlath kept it to himself, this business about the effects of drugs? Wouldn't Agnes know? It just wasn't likely that he'd keep it to himself. Minogue found that Agnes was still looking directly at him, awaiting the signs of another challenge. No, he decided, he couldn't ask her now.

CHAPTER EIGHT

The south side of Dublin being snotty, plenty of the cars which passed Gardai Kehoe and Cummins cost more than twice their annual salaries, before tax. The two were sitting in a Garda squad car near the Bray Road, the main thoroughfare south from Dublin. There was an agreement between them that their priorities would be given to Jags, BMWs, Mercedes and anything made in Italy that wasn't a Fiat. Speed traps were rare on Irish roads, but such a potential source of revenue as the billiard table expanse of the new Bray Road couldn't be ignored.

Kehoe and Cummins had been sitting in the car before morning rush hour some weeks previously, and they had observed a reddish projectile rocketing under the bridge in Belfield. Kehoe burned his fingers as he tried to get the cigarette out of his mouth, looking for the ignition. The UFO had obliged them by mounting a curb near Stillorgan, ripping off the front of the car and grinding to a stop after it had rubbed itself like a drugged, frantic cat along a wall for over two hundred feet. All this at ten to seven in the morning. Later, the authorities were to report that the showband star inside, one Malachi O'Brien of O'Brien's Country Treasures, a band enjoying a large following in all parts of the republic except Dublin, was too drunk to get out of the car. O'Brien expressed his gratitude at being rescued by the officers and added that it was only because the new Bray Road was so well constructed that his life had been extended. The car had been travelling at speeds close to a hundred miles an hour.

"It's the bloody telly. Smokey and the Outlaw, or whatever you call it. Did you hear him? 'Arra boys, the blessin's of God and his Holy Mother on you. Amn't I only delighted to see ye. Sure the bloody car took off by itself and I couldn't stop it,'" Kehoe mimicked to his colleague.

"Blind drunk, I suppose, was he?"

"Man dear, he was nearly speechless with the drink. He didn't know what century he was in. I wouldn't mind but he's a favourite of the wife's. She was surprised, I can tell you."

"Pop stars? A pack of iijits. That's a nice how do you do."

Both Gardai guessed that the motorists had been flashing lights up ahead. In ten minutes, they hadn't heard the alert from the speed gun.

"We'll head off so," Kehoe muttered.

Kehoe clipped on his belt and started off on the slip road which joined the dual carriageway a hundred yards ahead. Cummins radioed in and sat back. Kehoe noticed a large car which had been coming up fast behind them. It had braked when the driver had realised he was passing a police car, itself doing the legal limit. Kehoe saw the bonnet of the car, a Mercedes, dip in his mirror. That'll learn you, he thought. For divilment, he slowed the police car. The car, a yellow Mercedes, was obliged to pass. Kehoe nudged his partner. Both looked over to the right at the slowly passing car. The car was no more than a year old.

The Gardai knew that the occupants would pretend not to notice them. There were three men in the car. It was a kind of play: the driver knew he had been speeding, the Gardai knew it, they all knew that each knew it, but the radar wasn't on. The driver and passenger stared ahead. As the rear passenger drifted by the police car, he darted a glance at the two policemen. Both Cummins and Kehoe noticed this. Kehoe, closest to the passing car, was the first to say it.

"Well, Lar. Will we give it a look?"

Cummins didn't answer immediately. Cummins was a Dublinman, an exception on the Garda police force. He came from Crumlin, a working class district. He had had to take a lot of stick for joining the police. Crumlin didn't harbour many Mercedes. Cummins didn't mind that many of the policemen he worked with were bogmen, even though he knew they acted the heavy sometimes because they wanted to get a dig at Dublin hooligans.

Cummins had a new house in Templeogue and his wife, Breda, had a job in the bank. He had bought a new car. Cummins and the wife had been to Greece on their honeymoon. He didn't think he had any reason to resent rich people. Cummins could not ignore the internal radar, that intuition which he and Kehoe, who was a Kilkenny bogman, along with other police had. Three men in a car starts you thinking.

"Keep an eye on him anyway, I suppose."

Cummins reached for the microphone and called in the registration, a Dublin one. A 280 SEL. He wondered if that was a six-cylinder model. Waiting for the reply, the Gardai could hear the chatter of the other units. Kehoe had sat in, two cars behind the Merc. They'd have to decide soon because the turnoff to Booterstown was coming up soon.

"Blackrock, Unit Fourteen . . . a yellow Mercedes, number is . . . Meath. Hold on a second until I get the number . . . reported stolen yesterday in Dunboyne. Model 280 SEL, year . . . "

"Blackrock, Unit Fourteen. Meath, is it?"

"Yes, Fourteen. Hold on a sec now . . . "

Cummins looked over at Kehoe. Kehoe nodded. Cummins wrote down the number anyway. Cummins radioed in their location and that they wanted to look over the car.

Kehoe pulled out and drew alongside the Mercedes. Faces

91

turned to the two Gardai. Cummins had put on his hat and he had opened the window. He signalled the driver to pull over. One of the passengers leaned forward and spoke to the driver. The driver looked over to the policemen and nodded briefly. The Merc slowed. Kehoe pulled in ahead of the car.

He unbuckled his seat-belt as he watched Cummins walk back toward the Mercedes. There were about two car lengths between them. In the mirror, Kehoe noticed that the three men were sitting quite still, watching Cummins approach. Just before it happened, Kehoe had a sudden understanding of something, like when he had fallen on the ground during a game of football as a child.

Cummins heard the engine race and he chose the right direction to run. He leaped over the kerb as the Mercedes shot forward into the traffic lane. It surged into second gear and Cummins heard the deep burr of the six cylinders pick up the load again, rocketing the car into the light traffic. By the time Cummins had run to the car, Kehoe had it moving.

The Vauxhall squealed out from the kerb. Kehoe switched on the siren and threw his hat into the back seat. Cummins worked the radio. He felt calm even when Kehoe threw the car around in traffic. He glimpsed the tail of the Mercedes already racing by Booterstown Avenue. The traffic light there was turning orange.

"Ah shag it," Kehoe said. He skidded to a stop and leaned on the horn. Then he started off again.

"Be better off on me bike," he added, disgusted.

Cummins knew enough about cars to put his faith in the two-way radio. Blackrock and Donnybrook stations were the closest, unless there were cars out on the road ahead. Maybe a Garda on a motorbike. Cummins began figuring the chances as he listened to the radio, waiting. A Merc could easily do the ton and it could peel the door handles off this car on its way too. The Vauxhall could wind up to a hundred or maybe a hundred and ten if it was going down the side of the wall with a strong tail wind. Main thing was to keep it in sight and get the job done by radio.

Cummins saw the Merc veer sideways across a lane ahead. The chances might be even better, he thought. Suddenly the Mercedes darted across three traffic lanes and took off over the kerb down Merrion Avenue. Over the siren, Cummins could hear tires squealing still. Someone blew on a horn. Kehoe, with his tongue caressing his lower lip, dodged the cars, their brake lights popping on, their drivers up over the steering wheels. With a sense of timing and dexterity which surprised and pleased him, Kehoe crossed over the three traffic lanes in the wake of the Mercedes, now but a couple of hundred yards ahead.

Kehoe shot a glance at Cummins. Might actually be able to stay with it, Cummins thought.

Merrion Avenue is a broad, straight avenue which runs toward Blackrock and the sea. Off Merrion Avenue run various avenues and roads which draw out the most florid prose in auctioneers' sale ads. A tidy amount of money is to be made installing and updating burglar alarms along the Avenue.

In theory, one can drive down the Avenue at a wicked speed. The risks involved in doing this include an uneven road surface, the entry of other roads onto the Avenue and the presence of several schools at the bottom of the Avenue, just before it joins onto the coast road.

Cummins and Kehoe knew the Avenue. Each separately wondered if the driver of the Merc did. There was a good chance that there were some kids knocking about at the bottom of the Avenue.

Kehoe was travelling at eighty and the Merc was still pulling away. The Vauxhall bottomed out on a dip in the road surface. Kehoe had put the odds at about even: the Mercedes had the power and the handling, but it had to open a path in the traffic too. Dispatch, a girl with a Cork accent, told them there was a unit turning up Merrion Avenue to meet them. She cut off and the other car radioed that it was passing Sion Hill School. The driver of the Merc didn't use the brakes at all now. He swung it across the road or even passed on the inside. The distance between the cars was widening. Then Kehoe spotted the flicker of blue light atop the other police car in the distance. At the same time, the brake lights on the Merc glowed. In an instant, the

Mercedes had turned off to the right. The driver had almost lost it. The yellow car had skidded to face almost completely up the Avenue. The tires left greying smoke in the wake of the car. Time yet, Kehoe thought.

The Vauxhall roared into the street behind the Mercedes. Cummins shouted that there was a cul-de-sac up on the left. Kehoe looked in the mirror to see the other police car come swaying into the street at speed. Ahead of the Merc, a County Council dustbin lorry was backing out onto the road. The Mercedes swung wildly to the left and careened into the cul-de-sac. Kehoe laughed aloud. Cummins groaned inwardly because it looked like another episode of leaping over walls and through bushes. They might be lucky. Maybe the Merc would crash and give them the chance to put the heavy hand on these fellas. The other police car was closing in behind them. Four against three. Shag it, Cummins thought, and he hoped to God that there was some fit lad in the car behind to do the leaping and jumping. Lucky there was no one on the street. The Merc sped up.

"How far ahead?" Kehoe shouted.

"Around the bend there's a crescent and that's it," Cummins replied.

The Vauxhall rocked and squealed over the concrete roadway. As it swayed around the bend, Kehoe saw a housewife look up from the plants near her front door, her hand full of weeds and a trowel in the other hand. Then a yellow shape appeared across the roadway ahead of them. Two men were jumping out the doors on the far side of the car. The driver was shouldering his door on this side. Kehoe stood on the brakes and with screaming tires, the Vauxhall dredged into the road.

Cummins was thinking: watch out, the lads are coming up fast behind. Kehoe was looking at the heads which appeared over the roof of the Mercedes. They're not running, Kehoe thought. They're not running; isn't that a queer turn of events?

The Vauxhall was slowing, skidding sideways. Cummins felt and heard a pat somewhere in the body of the car. Pebbles? More. Then something like one of those sticker things against the window, those joke bulletholes. One of the men ran out from behind the Mercedes. He was carrying some kind of torch, flashing it at them. The windscreen whitened and a chunk of it fell out onto the bonnet. The Vauxhall was almost stopped now, grinding down on the suspension on Kehoe's side. Kehoe grunted and sighed. Something went through the car, then another and another, in and out the windows.

Isn't that odd? Cummins thought. *It's me who should be leaning up against Kehoe the way the bloody car is going, not the other way around. Anyone would think he was trying to give me a feel. His hands are all over the place.* Something hit Cummins in the side of the face. *A warm snowball, like a sod you'd clip from the field when you missed with your kick at the ball. Sore thing, that . . .*

The siren had stopped. Someone was breaking glass. Before the car had stopped—at the very instant that Cummins looked at his partner—their car was hit by the patrol car which had come into the cul-de-sac behind them. Cummins' belt bit into his neck and his head shot out in reaction to the shock. The door was coming in at him. Everything became suddenly glarybright and the world turned sideways, then over. Cummins' car rolled but once before it hit the Mercedes. It came to rest on its side. Without turning his head, Cummins could see Kehoe half hung in his belt above him. His head and shoulders had slipped out and lay partly on Cummins. Bright red splashes covered the roof of the car and Cummins could feel the absurd drip soaking further into his navy blue uniform. Cummins felt uncomfortably hot as the darkness which welled in through the windows from the sideways world outside gathered him.

Minogue stood in the doorway of the building which housed Allen's office. He stroked his upper lip between thumb and finger. A group of passing students looked at Minogue and awoke him. Loftus he discounted. He was engaged in the administration of his fiefdom and his loyalties to the university and an old army buddy of his. Chivalry my royal Irish arse. Allen? Minogue gave it a chance.

He walked up the staircase slowly. On the way he stepped around a woman on her knees, washing the steps. That could be that Brosnahan woman doing that, Minogue thought. Maybe her knees'd give out soon or she'd have arthritis for her pains. He knocked, expecting and hoping that Allen wouldn't be there. Bugger: Allen's face appeared in the doorway.

"Sergeant," he said.

"Good day to yourself, Doctor. I hope you can spare me some of your time."

"Just a few loose ends, Sergeant?" Allen asked.

"I beg your pardon," Minogue said.

A smile crosed Allen's face briefly. Minogue thought he saw irritation replace it. Maybe something else.

"Nothing really. It's just that I expected you to say something like that. Like the films or the television. Yes, I can spare you about ten minutes. Will that be enough?"

Minogue marvelled at the mixture of sentiments which Allen's remark could conceal. There were touches of sarcasm undoubtedly, and even a little arrogance too. There were also traces of relief and apprehension. In a strange sense he seemed relieved to see Minogue, almost resigned in some way, but he was guarded.

Minogue stepped into the room. The place was cluttered with books. Some order informed it all though, Minogue's glance affirmed. Allen sat next to his desk. Minogue noticed Allen's eyes. They seemed bigger than normal, whiter. Perhaps they were more opened. He looked as though he had just run up the stairs or he had been walking for some time.

Behind Allen, a view of the greenery and trees of New Square was framed in the tall window.

"Oh, I think I get it all right. I really should polish up my lines. You're quite right about the loose ends, I don't mind telling you. I'll be calling them straws soon enough. Where there's life . . . "

Allen, his arms folded, was displaying a patience which was

not easy for him, Minogue realised. He was privately pleased that Allen should be uncomfortable.

"To follow up on every little thing," Minogue continued. "I need to convince my superiors and myself that this is not some lunatic random thing."

Allen frowned.

"Yes. I suppose that I've hidden my light under a bushel, Doctor. Do you know that I hadn't even admitted to myself out loud in the middle of the day that this simply couldn't be a random thing? Well, there you have the gist of it. We can't escape it. I feel badly that I don't have some class of solid stuff for my superiors to digest, you know. It's like I can trace out elements, but I can't put things together in a way that appears rational. I'm waiting for a part of my brain to catch up with me," Minogue allowed himself a grin before continuing.

"Yes. What do you call it, free association. Like we allow ourselves to believe certain things without even stopping to think. We don't know the half of it, do we? A hint here, a suggestion there. It's my experience that people are easily led, if you know what I mean."

Allen eased himself in his chair a little.

"I think I follow you. Your technique for thinking out loud is a very good exercise. What I'm asking myself though is why you do it here."

"Ah, there's a good one indeed, Doctor. I confess I was drawn to your office by the need of your insight. I mean that I think I'm up the garden path at the moment. For instance, the drug thing you mentioned to me. I'm stymied by it. Agnes McGuire knew nothing of his interests in that line. He wasn't the kind of lad to hold back, was he? I mean, that was almost a failing in him, the way he had so much to say, to offer. He was naive, like."

"Well, he'd hardly advertise it to someone he wanted to impress, Sergeant," Allen observed.

"So you put some store in the whole thing then?" Minogue asked quickly.

"Actually I'm almost sorry I mentioned it at all. You seem to be saying that it is a red herring."

"Were you aware that an anonymous note had come to the college security officer, Captain Loftus, suggesting that Jarlath Walsh might be involved in drugs?"

"Matter of fact I was. I'll grant it may have coloured my interpretation of the questions he was asking me. Like I said, I'm almost regretting having told you about this in the first place . . . "

Allen sat back in the chair and folded his arms again. Then, like a cloud passing over his face, Minogue watched the idea come to Allen. Allen leaned forward slowly.

"I have the distinct feeling that you're not asking what you really want to ask me, Sergeant, but you're trying to provoke me in a way."

Full marks, Minogue thought. Go to the top of the class. Did it really look that obvious?

Minogue said nothing. He watched what looked like indignation loosen Allen's manner. Finally he said:

"Doctor, I'm sorry if I left you with that impression. I wonder if I might ask you to sleep on the matter. Any small details or memories that come to you. A remark in class, a fellow student, anything."

"You think I'm concealing something, don't you?" Allen said.

"Not at all. I haven't been able to firm up anything on this effort about the drugs, you see, and it's distracting me. I must be a very suggestible person."

Not fooled for a minute, Minogue thought. Allen's gaze suggested a knowingness but an amused ambivalence too. Maybe he was working hard at not being rude, Minogue considered. Hard to blame him, with a detective who is flying by the seat of his drawers.

Minogue returned to the room he had been lent in Front Square. He determined to make an early day of it. At least it had stopped raining. Walking to the carpark, he found himself searching the faces of passing students for any signs of a son or a daughter. Were they all the same, students?

Climbing into the car, he assigned the day a four out of ten. Little remained of the rain except a saturated city and oily roads. Could it be that they might get a bit of sun?

Minogue wanted to sneeze but the sensation passed. A police car with sirens and lights going full blast went by him as he rounded into College Green. Damn and blast it, he thought. It would be better if he at least phoned Kilmartin's office and checked in. Go by the book. Minogue stopped at two phone-boxes in succession. Both had been vandalized. Reluctantly, he drove up Dame Street toward the Castle. Another police car passed him at the lights at George's Street, screaming away. Maybe it was a bank robbery, another one.

Outside Kilmartin's office there was no work being done. Several uniformed Gardai sat on the edges of tables, smoking. Minogue could hear the monitored voices of men out in the streets, patrolling. The voices and clicks drifted down from the dispatch room. Nobody in Kilmartin's office. Minogue strolled toward the dispatch room, nodding at several Gardai as he passed them.

"Inspector Kilmartin, lads?"

"He's above in dispatch, sir," a Garda replied.

Kilmartin was sitting in a chair next to one of the girls. She was studiously concentrating on her earphones, nervous at his presence. He was smoking a cigarette. He stood up when he noticed Minogue and he walked over to the doorway.

"Did you hear about it?"

"What now?" Minogue asked.

"They shot our lads out in Blackrock. It's still going on. They got the driver, but the two fellas with the shooters are on the loose still."

Minogue felt an approaching swell. He waited. Kilmartin was mooching about for someplace to kill the butt of his cigarette. His arm was wavering. Minogue felt light, cold. The day was transformed. Somehow the room looked lurid. It pressed in on him.

"The IRA or the INLA or whatever crowd, I'll wager. One of

99

our lads was killed outright. The other one's alive," Kilmartin murmured, still wandering around the room. Minogue was taken up with watching the girl's nervousness as Kilmartin paced.

"Only a pack of animals would react to a uniform like that. They have automatic rifles. The place is upside down so it is. They have a cordon up. The army and the whole shebang is there."

"Where?" Minogue heard himself asking.

Kilmartin stopped walking.

"Out near the bottom of Merrion Avenue, near enough to Blackrock."

As hard as he tried, Minogue couldn't get the taste out of his mouth. The fear was like cheese on his breath. It sticks in your throat, it actually chokes you, he thought. Smell it on your breath.

CHAPTER NINE

The tanned man replaced the phone and walked over to the window. His room at the Shelbourne overlooked St. Stephen's Green. He watched couples and children and old people enter the Green. They haven't a clue, he thought, about what goes on less than a hundred miles from here.

Parked cars glutted the streets around the hotel. No one feared that one might contain a bomb. No searches, no midnight raids by troops. The shops were full, the pubs were open. A soft city in a soft country. It even made visitors soft. People became so flaccid that they feared slight changes to their self-satisfied equilibrium. A decision had to be made within the hour. The danger was in over-reacting, of pouncing too soon.

The Green was swollen with trees and shrubs, all dense with the day's rain. The tanned man was thinking of Minogue. The photo showed a tall man in a cheap suit walking in the Front Square of Trinity College. Totally out of place. A redneck. There was something cautious and reluctant about the face. Soft, maybe. He didn't put his hands in his pockets walking. Certainly not stupid. Was it possible that this Minogue had a hidden sense of an adversary out there, that this boy's death was linked to another world of events? It didn't matter now, be pragmatic. Kill Minogue or not?

Why kill? To be sure. Take such a risk, just get this one crucial delivery across the border to prove he was right. The place would be crawling with cops if that happened. That moron playwright would leak eventually. Get him too. No, needed him for this.

The tanned man decided that Minogue would live. He would stick with the story about drugs and build one more block onto it. It had to be something fairly dramatic, a bit of Mafia or something to it. Like being done in with a stone. The papers would say, 'Assault the work of drug related-criminal element' or 'Suspected drug link in assault of Garda.' It would have to do, even though the tanned man didn't like it. As he waited for the playwright to answer the phone, he wondered if Minogue knew that his probing was forcing somebody's hand.

"Are you getting the car ready for that trip?" he asked.

"Yep. He'll bolt on the goods tomorrow," the playwright replied airily.

"Another thing. Minogue, remember? Like we discussed. Get a car, that way. Leave something behind."

"Yep."

"You know how important this is. We're buying time until we can deal with the other thing that's come up. I'll be dealing with that other asshole before his knees give out completely."

The playwright laughed. He hadn't heard the Yank using bad language until now. It didn't fit with the suit. Could it be that Mr Whiz Kid might be human after all?

"Yes. I'll do the other thing myself. Kilmacud, is it?"

"Yes. No Roy Rogers stuff now. Think of it as a part. Imagine yourself as a gangster."

The tanned man hung up. He suppressed the little ice of anxiety which was rising in his stomach.

He returned to gazing out the window. The waiting was the

102

worst of it. He acknowledged the burrowing truth that ultimately, no one was completely reliable. No one should be trusted in extremity. As the stakes rose with the latest dangers, he had felt his own control slipping, his sense of agency diminish. Like a bank of clouds, chance and circumstance were drifting in to conceal the elements. He had no choice but to wait and see what came in from the fog. He thought about Minogue again. Would his nerve go after a bit of pushing or would he dig in his heels?

He was drawn out of his speculations by the rising *wawa* and the car horns which came in over the trees in the Green. Two police cars, an unmarked van and an army Land Rover sped by the hotel. Reflexively, he pushed his elbow into his side to feel the belt at his shoulder better and to feel the butt of the gun meet the inside of his jacket. Not for me, he thought. Only in the movies. He felt slightly claustrophobic with the noise filling the air.

He took his gabardine and went to the hotel foyer. He stepped out into the street. On the footpath outside the Shelbourne, a newspaper seller squatted on an orange box. The radio beside her chattered on and then broke into a monotonous disco beat. He walked over to the woman. The doorman from the hotel was watching the Mercedes and the Jags strewn along the double yellow line. The doorman rubbed his hands. The woman looked up at him.

"Looks like a nice how-do-ye-do, now. Shoot first and ask questions later, I say. Thugs down from the North is what they are. Disturbing the peace."

"Right enough. Thugs isn't the word for them. And them driving around in a Mercedes like they owned the bloody country. Unarmed pleecemen, I ask you. Where's the fairness in that. Shoot the buggers I say," said the doorman.

"I have a nephew out in Monkstown. I wonder if he's caught in the cross-fire," the newspaper woman said.

The doorman tried to ease the full weight of his sarcasm.

"Jases sure Monkstown is miles away. Cross-fire is it? What

103

fillum was that in. Your cousin is under the bed if he's not inside in the shaggin' bed itself."

The tanned man stood quite still. He felt the ripple pass right to the top of his head. He turned to the doorman.

"What's going on with all these police cars?"

"Ah sir. There's some class of gunfight going on in Blackrock. There's a Garda after being killed and there's two of them on the loose—"

"—with tommy-guns," the woman interrupted.

"—and they think that they have the two of them boxed in. Turn over to Radio Eireann on that box of yours and you'll get it on the news . . . Hanging is too good for them. You see we're doing fine down here as you can see for yourself, sir. It's that crowd giving us a bad name abroad . . . "

"Indeed," the tanned man replied.

"Well, they have one of them captured so they have. I'd like to get a dig at him myself. In cold blood. What's the world coming to?"

The tanned man turned to walk toward Kildare Street. He was almost dizzy with the anger. The doorman had said there was a Mercedes involved . . . It couldn't be a coincidence. Some incompetents in a useless shoot-out. No discipline, probably free-lancing on a bank job. That proved exactly what he had been busting a gut trying to convince them, that personnel like the damned playwright couldn't run things. After getting them to set up a proper garage and a mechanic to do the cars for the couriers, the playwright had blithely turned over one of the cars to some amateur thugs down from Belfast. All the work and preparations and the moron had given them a car, a toy to amuse them. A car gone to waste, weapons probably captured or abandoned. Cops on edge all over the city. He'd have to close the place down right away. If one of the losers knew about the garage and he talked, the cops could be kicking the door in fast.

The tanned man tried to rescue some benefit from this episode. At least it might divert some attention away from his operation for a few days anyway. When he finished with this part, he'd have the playwright's head on a plate for this.

Minogue felt light-headed and pukey after the cigarette. It was like learning to smoke all over again. It left him feeling bloated and nervous after even the first few pulls. Kilmartin sat with his elbows on his knees listening to the odd parts of the drama that were interspersed with the other messages.

The two gunmen hadn't been sighted since the shooting. They had taken off across the gardens. The danger was in cornering them where they might use hostages. Two units from the army had set up in the area. The Special Branch and the Gardai were running down streets and behind houses. There still wasn't enough manpower to get to all the houses and evacuate people. Just over thirty-five minutes, Kilmartin reflected, and the damage was done. There was a maze of streets just south of the cul-de-sac, just a few gardens over. It was likely that they had split up and ditched the guns. Aside from a thick lip and a bang on the head, the driver was in one piece and in custody.

Minogue decided to phone Kathleen. She'd have heard something on the radio anyway, he guessed. Fair play to her, Minogue pondered as he heard her talking, she's determined not to show anything now.

"Tis a bad state of affairs to be sure. Lookit, I'm not much help here so I'll be off home soon. Do you want me to stop off at the shopping centre for anything?" Minogue asked her. The phone was greasy in his hand. He smelled his own fetid breath curling out of the mouthpiece.

"A bit of black pudding and some sausages," she said.

Kilmartin looked to him as he re-entered the dispatch room.

"Do you want a few smokes for the way home, Matt?"

"No thanks. Sure it'll be another while before I take them up again, I'm thinking. They're a great comfort though . . . I'd forgotten that. I'm off home now. You should go home yourself. The Special Branch lads will have the matter well in hand," Minogue murmured.

Kathleen Minogue answered the phone for the second time in five minutes. This time she didn't predict right because it was neither Matt nor the children.

"Em, no. He's due home though. A school reunion? Well, isn't that rich," she laughed. "But sure that's years ago."

Kathleen thought that the caller must have moved well away from County Clare himself. His voice had a polish to it, deliberate like Richard Burton, with a trace of country accent. "Indeed and you should, Mr . . . ? Mr Murphy. Oh I'm sure he'd be tickled. We have the tea about six. In actual fact I'm waiting for Matt to stop off at the shopping centre to bring home sausages and the like. I wasn't out on account of the rain. Yes, do. About half six and you'll be sure to get him."

The playwright left the booth and got into the Granada. The car was no more than a year old and it had been in his possession for approximately twenty-seven minutes. It would remain in his care for about another three quarters of an hour, then to be ditched. With luck, he wouldn't leave a mark on it.

He drove off out the Bray Road, in the direction of Stillorgan Shopping Centre. He was pleased with his performance. It would look like he was giving every assistance to Mr Whiz Kid. The car insulated him from the road and the sights which slowly swept by him as he stop-started in the traffic. He observed the frustration on the faces of people standing at bus-stops. Cars inched by him, then fell back again to pass him again. He made studies of the faces in the cars. Bank managers and accountants on their way home to the vacuum of suburbia. This was the Ireland which we had fought the British for?

A woman laughed behind glass in a Jaguar. She looked like a carnival mask with that sinister leer. Made up to the hilt and wearing those stupid glasses, copying anything and everything American.

No one would have the nerve to even think that he'd tip off the Brits. After they'd taken the car apart, the council would know that he'd been wise not to entrust such a valuable weapon to the Yank's scheme. Him and his cars and his couriers. We haven't come through the lean years just to hand over the reins to some jumped-up Houdini opportunist who was trickacting with the Soviets.

In a room on the second floor of Blackrock Garda Station sat two hefty middle-aged men. One, Galvin, remained on his feet, pacing the room in a measured pattern. Formerly dark-haired, he was now balding. He had found suits disagreeable these thirty years and more and it showed. A shelf of shirt stuck out from his belt and gathered the end of his tie, itself at half mast. Galvin had the face you'd see squinting on the steps of a Sunday church in Tipperary as he'd edge out into the daylight before the end of Mass. When he moved, however, no fat jellied around him. Removed from the company of farm animals these thirty years, nature had compensated him with the attributes of a suspicious bull.

His companion, Moroney, remained seated. He contented himself with picking imaginary pieces of lint from the knee of his pants. Moroney lacked the physical presence of his colleague Galvin; his body was beginning to sugarloaf at the belt. His face, mounted on thin lips, was completely out of place. Where one could reasonably expect swarthiness and a ruddy, heart attack complexion, a marbled model of cerebration rested atop the collar. To the side of Moroney was a pitted wooden table salvaged from a civil service department. The sole window in the room had been painted over with a heavy cream on the inside. A grid of wire mesh had been screwed to the window frame some years ago. The room smelled of damp and waiting. Under the window, a radiator which looked like a failed bellows tried to heat the air. The floor was made up of cracked and worn lino tiles which were flecked with cigarette burns.

On the table lay a portable tape recorder with a microphone attached. The seated man sat with his arms folded now. Occasionally he'd uncross his legs and then cross them again. He didn't speak to Galvin who was circling the room like a wrestler before the bout. They had been waiting for ten minutes. Every now and

107

then they could hear the sounds of the building, the ticking of the radiator, steps outside. Five minutes ago, a young Garda had stuck his head in the doorway.

"Momentarily now, sir. He's on the way."

Galvin and Moroney had travelled from Dublin Castle. They had made their arrangements for the proceedings in the car. Galvin stopped pacing as he heard footsteps outside. The door opened. Two uniformed Gardai walked in, followed by a young man in handcuffs. Another two Gardai followed in his wake and after an interval a plain clothes Garda, whom neither Galvin nor Moroney recognised, followed.

Moroney stood up slowly, watching the young man's face intently.

"Right, thanks," he said to no one. The uniformed Gardai left. The plain clothes stood leaning against the wall and ensured that the door closed fully.

Moroney looked at the elastoplast over the man's left eye.

"Sit there," he pointed to the chair he had vacated.

Galvin stood behind the chair. The young man turned slightly to look at him. Then he sat on the edge of the chair. His hair looked wet. His skin reminded Moroney of a jail-bird. Which is probably what he was. Moroney put him at about twenty-four.

The prisoner held his handcuffed wrists up from his knees. Moroney ignored the gesture. Instead, he switched on the tape recorder.

"Your name in full."

"Volunteer James Duffy," the man replied with assurance. Moroney glanced over the prisoner's shoulder at Galvin.

"And where are you from, Duffy?"

"The Six Counties," he answered.

Without warning, Galvin grabbed him by the hair and lifted him out of the chair. As Duffy reached to his head with his arms, Galvin punched him under the ribs. Duffy wheezed and tottered sideways as Galvin released his grip on his hair. He squirmed on the floor, his face knotted. His sharp intakes of breath stopped abruptly as he was lifted into the chair. He sat crazily leaning with his eyes watering through the slits of his eyelids.

"I insist on medical treatment, to be examined by a doctor, that's my right," he wheezed. He was beginning to open his eyes more to let the tears escape. He didn't open them in time to avoid a knee in the side of the face. The blow filled the room with a *thock* sound just before the screech of the upturned chair. He fell uncontrolled to the floor.

Galvin raised his eyebrows slightly. He nodded to Moroney who was now standing over the prisoner. Duffy was breathing through his nose in bursts.

"Up," Galvin said.

Again he was lifted up by the hair. He was determined to keep his eyes open. Duffy sat shakily, fearfully checking the man standing to his side in the edge of his vision. His body was like a spring, arching away from the threat.

"We'll try again now. Your rights as you call them don't mean anything here. The policeman who was killed had rights too. Common sense should tell you to say all you know. There's no one else, just the three of us," Galvin said quietly.

Duffy edged onto one buttock and darted his eyes from Galvin to Moroney standing beside him. He could feel his cheek thickening already, pressing up to his eye. He probed with his tongue and found two loose teeth. A glaucous liquid was leaking into his mouth from somewhere.

"Don't delude yourself. Your outfit talks about a state of war, so stop playing public house solicitor and bellyaching about your rights. You answer the questions put to you and I'll see what I can do about you leaving here in one piece," Galvin added.

"Now. Where are you from?" Moroney asked.

"Newry," Duffy said thickly.

"What were you at this afternoon?" Galvin asked.

"Well—"

The chair was kicked from under him and he fell heavily to the floor. Before he had time to cover it, Galvin kicked him in the side of the head. A flare of light exploded in his brain and he

109

heard a sound like a waterfall. Dimly he tried to roll onto his knees and get away. Halfway up he felt steadying hands on his back. Then a tremendous kick in the stomach almost lifted him off the floor. As though from a long way off, he heard someone telling him to get up. He decided that he wouldn't. A blinding pain in the small of his back made his legs tingle. He heard a yelp. He found himself back on the edge of the seat. Something was in his way as he looked to the side where he expected the cop to be.

"What were you at?"

"As true as God, nothing," a voice said. His own voice, like out of a pipe.

"Continue." No kick.

"We're down for a while to get a rest. Fun, a bit of a holiday," he whispered. He looked up into the impassive face of the policeman.

"Are you part of an active service unit in your area?"

The prisoner hesitated. Then he recoiled at the slight movement of that shadow to his side which could only be that other cop.

"I'm a driver," he blurted out. He swallowed more of the liquid in his mouth. "I don't do the other stuff at all."

The policeman by the door lit up a cigarette.

"Just a driver," murmured Moroney. He looked at the prisoner's feet as if he were studying them. Then he returned his gaze to Duffy's bruised face.

"There's no just-a-driver here. Killing a policeman is a capital offence. You did just as much as your friends. That's the way the law looks at it too. Your two pals are singing like canaries. According to them you do a lot more than driving."

Duffy tried hard not to show some relief. He knew this cop was lying. He kept his head down. Maybe he'd get out of this one.

"Where'd you get the car?"

"In Dublin."

"Where'd you get the car?"

110

"Like I—"

The chair leg shrieked as Duffy rolled toward the wall. The plain clothes at the door kicked him in the shin. As he tried to roll away, Galvin kicked him in the small of the back. His legs went numb. The light in the room began to pulse and run up to him. He remembered the name they gave these cops in the South, The Heavy Gang. He felt himself pulled up and he was left trying to stay standing. He couldn't. He fainted.

When he came to he was in the chair again. A smell of baby came to him, strong. He had puked down his shirt, he realised. He looked up. Nothing had changed. He tried to turn slightly and check where the other cop was. How much time had passed?

"Where'd you get the car?"

"I swear to God," Duffy began. The voice, his voice, resonated through his skull. He was sure it was someone else's voice. He knew what he wanted to say, but his hearing wasn't picking up what he thought the voice was saying.

" . . . I came down on the train is all. That's all. I was told to meet the others at a hotel."

"What hotel?"

"The Bur . . . the Burg. The Burlington."

"When?"

"The day before yesterday, yes."

"Who told you?"

"I just got a phone call. A fella phoned."

"Where did you meet these two before?"

"As true as God, I never did. They're from Belfast."

Vaguely, Duffy wondered if he could control what he was saying. It was like being stoned — you didn't know if you said it or just thought it. He understood he had to keep the shared illusion about the other two being caught. He doubted they'd be taken. They were hard men and they were wanted, so they had little enough to lose. They had made him nervous the way they hardly said a word all day.

"All I know," the voice continued," is that they told me to lose that patrol car. I remember we ran into a dead end and they

111

jumped out of the car. I remember them shooting. And me trying to get out the door on my side. I was half-way out. I was lucky not to get me leg sliced off so I was."

"What were you at this afternoon?"

Duffy hesitated. Like a magnetic force, he could feel the closeness of the cop behind him. His skin tickled alarms.

"I think it was a bank job. The boys was bored."

"Where?"

"Cruising is all. They never told me anything, as true as . . . "

"Where have you been staying?"

"At that hotel. Same as them," Duffy added.

A light knock at the door. Plain clothes opened it. Galvin left the room. He closed the door gently behind him.

In the hallway, the Special Branch man whispered,

"No sign of them or the guns. We think they got out of the area right away."

"This yo-yo says they're Belfast and that's all he knows. They'll be headed back into the city now. They were staying at the Burlington so set the place up overnight anyway, though I doubt it. Get in first and have a look around. Remember who you're dealing with. They might have handguns."

"What about your man inside?"

Galvin stroked his chin.

"Ah, he's only a dummy. He's not trained at all. He has the willies with Moroney in there."

"We have the check-points up on the Bray Road and Merrion Road. Nothing yet. We're starting the house-to-house about now," the Special Branch man said.

And there'll be nothing from the check-points either if that little shitebird is telling the truth, Galvin added silently. Hard men.

"Set up something for this fella in the Bridewell, would you. They can't keep him here. We'll be done with him in a few minutes. For the moment anyway. Make sure the door-to-door thing is kept up. And I want every house on our lists visited by a policeman tonight, especially on the south side of the city. Sympathis-

112

ers, politicos, hangers-on, I don't give a shite. Show the flag. They'll know that they can't hide out there."

"Yes, sir."

"And get a bit of first aid for this fecker in here. Maybe a concussion or eardrums. Don't take any guff out of him. He fell down a few times and hurt himself."

"Yes, sir."

When Galvin re-entered the room, Duffy looked over to him. Duffy was hunched over in the chair. The room smelled bad. It was hot now.

"Duffy. In between now and the time we see you again, you have some thinking to do. You should opt for self-preservation if you have any savvy at all. Your mates are in the same boat. And here's something else to dwell on while you still have fond memories of my colleagues here. Your outfit will be told that you're singing away here, so you'll have to square it with them in the clink when you get there. Who knows, we mightn't have you alive enough after that to hang you anyway. Doesn't matter what you say. We have the finger on plenty of your lads here and all we have to do is lift a few of them and drop your name, Volunteer Duffy. You don't know the half of it. Start remembering quick. You're up to your oxters now so all you can do is buy your way into some kind of protective custody. And even that won't mean much unless we see our way to some allowances later on. Remember: you killed a Garda officer. We can have you looking like a Hallowe'en mask at the end of a rope."

Moroney saw the wariness in the prisoner's eyes. The side of his head was swollen already and there was a drying film of blood at the corners of his mouth. Galvin felt a final rush of contempt for this pathetic fool. He thinks he has one up on us because we're codding him about his cronies being in custody, Moroney reflected. No training. Maybe it'd never dawn on him how suggestion worked. We know that he thinks he knows, that's the control. Moroney believed Duffy would get his story in soon enough. He also believed that it wouldn't amount to much.

"Get this worm out of here," Moroney said.

113

CHAPTER TEN

Minogue felt it was taking him forever to reach the shopping centre. His mind was cluttered with dark forms whose details escaped him as he tried to concentrate. He felt cold and he felt old. Maybe this is how it is when you lose your nerve, or when you let yourself admit you've lost your nerve, he thought.

Minogue parked his Fiat two rows away from the supermarket. He checked his pocket for money. He stopped walking and stood between parked cars, fingering coins to the side of his palm. The air was thick and moist around him. He pocketed his find and resumed walking. An expanse of glass confronted him beyond the rows of parked cars. He could see himself, head and shoulders above the car roofs as he stepped out onto the roadway. He felt damp and creaky out of the car. The sky was low, greyed and browned. He smelled a faint diesel scent hanging in the air. In the gutter ahead of him lay a discarded umbrella, like a broken bird. He stepped across rainbowed splashes of petrol now quite prominent after the rain.

Ahead of him, his figure became larger. This is how I must look to other people, he realised. People were moving behind the reflections in the glass. He heard the baskety metal clash of the shopping carts shoved away. Minogue thought of Debussy. Music under water, shimmering. Everything slow. Iseult had taken Kathleen and himself to a recital in the Art Gallery some weeks after he had come out of the hospital. Minogue had been astounded at what he had heard. He was sure the doctor had been wrong about the hearing loss. There in the hall, with the musicians warming up, the sounds had been like a dream. They walked toward the great hall, Minogue hardly feeling his feet move under him, quite lost to the gathering sounds which washed over and enveloped him. Was that what it was like when you kicked up your heels and your soul took off? Like a big underwater cave and everything changed and shining.

Silly to be thinking of Agnes McGuire and that at the same time. And then that young Guard in the car, dead now, just like that, like he never lived, another gravestone being made, an editorial on the outrage. What was the use of it all?

To Minogue's left, a movement between cars caught his eye. Ahead of him, the glass was now a darkening mirror. Rows of cars to his left and right in the mirror. Minogue wondered if he should go to a record shop later. A flicker of movement registered in Minogue's unconcern. He stepped over a worn yellow line. Debussy was like breathing under water, so it was. Minogue was vaguely aware of a soft hiss of tires on the tarmac. As if you could swim next to the dolphins and go into coral caves. Minogue realised that he was not surrounded by cars anymore. In a ridiculous second, he was standing on the strand in Lahinch, again a child, with the ebbing tide pulling the grains away from under him. He'd feel the tug and he'd turn and realise how far away the others were. All the way to Boston, Mam said as she pointed out over the waves.

Minogue heard the squeal as the tires bit in. He stopped. He looked to his left to see the car bearing down on him. A silhouette and beads of old rain on the glass. The engine roared and gulped as the automatic grabbed onto second gear. A pulse ran up to Minogue's scalp. Where? Minogue's body was all wrong for heading for the kerb ahead.

Still he moved a foot awkwardly in that direction. He dropped onto his flexed knees with his arms spread in a move from a deadly Chubby Checker dance. This can't work, he was thinking, as his body ran ahead of him, shifting from foot to foot awaiting a decision. *I can't stay here I'll be run over and killed.* Where? Don't think. Minogue's take-off foot wrenched him back toward the parked cars. His brain followed. He could feel rather than see the speeding car change direction. His legs seemed so long and so slow. They weren't really propelling him, he was tottering. The car was a breath away, bigger, final. The space between the Fiesta and the Mini parked ahead of him seemed huge but unattainable. The colours of the cars were now almost luminescent. The rush of the approaching car filled up all the space under the clouds.

Then Minogue was on his knees, pitching forward. His palms grazed along the wet tarmac. His shoulder bounced off a panel. His legs took him over on his side and he catapulted over the downed shoulder, heels drumming a door on a car and the tar grinding and pulling his hair as his head came over. The cars trembled and wavered as the white car shot by the gap. Tiny drops of water sprayed up from its wake fell lightly over Minogue's face as he lay there. A dull burning came from his forehead. He tried to get up, his hands splayed on the tar. *They might come back, I don't know.*

His leather soles slipped and he fell down again. It felt dangerous to be so near the underside of cars, so close to the wheels. As he elbowed up again, he felt wetness at his knees and in his socks. He crouched between the cars. Then he darted to the back of the car and looked up through the back window. A white car was speeding out onto the Kilmacud Road. It bounced on a kerb and moved abruptly around cars. As it passed out of his sight, Minogue heard horns blowing. He was trembling, ready for doing something but there was nothing now. His body was twitching. He began to breathe deeply as he leaned on the Fiesta. He looked up to find a middle-aged woman, head and shoulders, two car roofs over from him.

"Are you a'right now?" she called out.

Minogue's body was beginning to tighten and ache.

"Did you see that, Missus? Did you see that car?"

"What car, now?" she said, softer.

"A white car. This minute."

"No, I didn't."

Minogue swore.

"And your head. Is your head all right?" she asked.

Minogue reached up to the burning. His fingers showed orangey blood.

"Here, I have an elastoplast in the car. Come here. What happened to you at all?"

Minogue leaned on the bonnet of the car. His neck was beginning to hurt.

"Well, Missus, unless I'm mad entirely, someone tried to run me over."

The woman stood away from Minogue and raised a hand to her mouth. Her eyes widened.

"On purpose? Go away, you're codding me," she whispered.

"Indeed and I'm not, ma'am," Minogue said resignedly.

"But that sort of thing only goes on in . . . " she hesitated.

"In America? In the movies is it? I wish you were right," Minogue replied.

"Shouldn't we call the Garda then?" she whispered.

Minogue had found enough control over his trembling to flick at the particles of wet dirt which had been ground into his coat. He looked quizzically at the woman who was suspended, tongue over lip, in that ageless motion of trying to get the sticky parts of the elastoplast away from the wrap without dropping the whole thing or sticking her thumb into it. He bowed to let her apply it to his forehead.

"Thanks very much now. Sure I am the police, there's the rub," Minogue murmured.

The tanned man hissed as he spoke into the phone.

"I don't give a shit. Take anything that'll lead them further out of there and get to hell out of the place as fast as you can."

The tone of the man on the other end turned more petulant.

"After all the trouble we went to? There's a lot of me own tools in there as well. That'll take time. I mean to say, I can't just walk out the door. Look—"

"Shut up for a minute and listen. There's been a royal screw-up with that Mercedes you had in the place. Sooner or later the cops will trace that car to your place, and you won't be whining about your tools then. Just get them and get out. Go take a holiday or something."

"Here, it wasn't me who handed over the car. And those tools cost me a fortune, mister. Lookit, whoever you are I don't care. I just did the plates and built hidey holes for a few cars. I don't ask any questions."

"Exactly. You don't ask any questions. No one will know you worked out of that place. We looked after everything else. If you did what you're supposed to do, there'll be nothing to tie you to that place. It's all a dead-end, the cheques and the rental thing. Christ, you couldn't have been in the place more than half a dozen times."

"But who'll pay for me tools?"

"Look. You've never been fingerprinted so no one can trace you unless you damn well hang around! Don't you know they have one of those guys in custody?"

"Here now, hold on a minute," the mechanic said. "I don't want to know who I'm doing this for. A job is a job. I do the work and I gets me pay. Ask me no questions and I'll tell you no lies. I'm like the three monkeys, you know what I mean? And I don't like being let in on this stuff either. It's none of my shagging business."

The tanned man spoke quietly into the telephone now.

"Listen here now. It'll become your business if you don't get out of there inside of five minutes. If by any little remote chance, I get the slightest irritation because you screwed up somewhere

. . . you'll be getting a new face knitted for yourself. You'll be playing with fucking Lego for the rest of your life, do you hear me?"

"I'm not deaf."

"Where did you leave that Merc off for those guys anyway?"

"Ah sure I didn't have to leave it off anywhere. Just outside in the back lane here. I left the key under the wheel like that other fella told me. Your pal, whatever his name is."

The tanned man almost threw the phone across the room. His hand tightened around it. Outside the bloody garage, of all the places on this island. Outside the garage. That was the bitter end.

The mechanic listened but heard only breathing on the line.

"Are you still there . . . ?"

"When did that other car go out, the one with the new tank?"

"Yesterday. Picked up, no bother."

At least the main part of the operation was intact, the tanned man thought. He eased his grip on the phone.

"No hitches?"

"No. Your pal must have come over some evening and packed in whatever it is. All I know is I came in and there was a note saying bolt the thing back on, the thing is packed in and sealed. That's what I did. Dirtied it up good like I was told and left it parked on what-you-me-call-it Street, er . . . Nassau Street."

The tanned man felt his body ease into the chair more. So that part had gone fine.

"Look. We'll pay you for your tools or whatever you can't get out of there in five minutes."

"Five minutes?"

"The cops will look around the lane first probably, damn it! Just make sure there's nothing with your initials or that sort of thing. Go to the post office in Rathmines tomorrow. There'll be an envelope in your name."

The mechanic's voice lightened.

"Right you be, chief."

"And remember what I said. If I get so much as a ripple because

119

of anything you do, the organisation will take care of that too. There's nowhere to hide."

The tanned man hung up. He surveyed the hotel room. The problems amounted to little more than a few stones falling away. There would be no avalanche. Maybe in the future he might have the leisure to rethink this. By then he might even see that this series of mishaps was very functional. It plucked out the gangsters in the movement, the inept. If anything, the old guard in the movement would be discredited even more for not being able to control the mobsters they brought south for R&R.

He didn't feel any sympathy for any of those men. In fact, it would have been better if the two were shot out of hand. As for the third one, he'd probably spill but he was just a gofer. He might even distract the Branch with a few yarns.

He rose and walked to the bathroom. He felt sweaty. While the bath was filling, he hung his jacket. He took out the gun and laid it next to the telephone. He unhooked the harness, cursing inwardly at the sweat dribbling through the Velcro. The phone was still warm as he spoke into it again:

"A beer. Any kind. Has to be cold."

Such habits, he mused, as he put down the phone. Bathing at the first signs of sweat; a cold beer. He returned to the bathroom and laid the gun next to the handbasin. In the mirror he saw a strong and youthful man. His mother had said it well, 'If you don't look after yourself, no one else will.'

The bellboy wore an outfit that made him look like a New York leprechaun. He tipped him a pound at the door out of spite.

"Thanks very much, sir. Anything you want now, just give a little tinkle." A little bow, the door closed.

He swallowed a cold draught from the neck of the bottle. Roll on the future, he thought, that we may never have servile Irishmen like him born here again.

Minogue stood aching in the telephone booth.

"Uh-huh, yes. A white Granada, newish. Yep. The new model. No, I didn't get it. Call me at home, so. Anytime."

Agnes McGuire had heard police sirens at intervals while she studied in her room. It took little to distract her. By times, she awoke from a trance, exasperated that she had not turned a page in the book for ten minutes. She was thinking of her family and Italy. The two scenes alternated. She imagined herself walking with a packsack through dusty roads in Tuscany. It'd be dusk, an infinite orange world, glowing and washing into pinks. She'd stop at a farmhouse and be welcomed. She'd chat with the family for hours, listening to their stories. Agnes would be a pilgrim of sorts and people there would understand that.

Then Agnes was walking through streets in Belfast. It was raining. She had messages to get. Her arms ached from carrying groceries. Her fingers were numbed by the handles of the plastic bags which bit into them. Her mother was waiting at home. She was afraid to go out herself.

In the mornings, Agnes would bid goodbye and shoulder her bag now laden with home-made wine, bread and cheese. It would be no weight at all. She might even sit at the side of the road for a half hour and watch the mist dissipate, revealing an ancient land.

Agnes looked out over the sodden garden three floors below. Enclosed by enormous railings, Trinity resisted the bustle outside. Traffic was clogging Nassau Street. Agnes could see forms behind the steamed windows of the double-decked buses as they crawled by. A hand would work to clear part of a window, a face look out.

In Tuscany there'd likely be animals drawing wagons of some description.

Leaving the Belfast supermarket, an armoured carrier they called 'pigs' drove by like a sightless dinosaur and, gone by, the hard and challenging faces of soldiers appeared, looking to the wake of the vehicle's passage. Itching to play with their guns. Maybe somewhere nearby men were watching from a window too, deciding if they would shoot.

Piazzas at dusk, candlelight on the faces of the working men as they sat at tables, gathering in the cool of the evening.

Agnes was aware that Jarlath had no presence in these journeys. She could see him clearly, besuited, walking the streets of his own city here in a few years. He might wind up doing law or concentrating on economics. He'd work in an office. He'd be kind though. He mightn't get far on the ladder so his Da might pull him into the fruit business quickly to get him set up. Maybe Jarlath would take the year off like he said he would. Still, Agnes could not see him so changed as to be out on those roads and streets in Italy, or leaning on the railing of a ferry leaving Brindisi . . .

Lights were now gathering strength out in the streets. Traffic was easing. Behind her, the room was obscured. Agnes switched on the light. It was time to eat. She returned to the table and sorted the photocopied pages. Agnes, who could not now summon up the golden landscapes of Tuscany, began to shiver. Her eyes salted as she worked. She made no attempt to stop the steady roll of the first tear.

What straightened Minogue out was the unforeseen arrival of Iseult for tea. Kathleen's mock chiding, now that she had to include Iseult in the pan, helped him to land.

"What happened to you?" Iseult said breezily. "Ma, did he make improper advances, is it?"

Iseult turned to him and play-punched him in the shoulder. "You're a bit of a divil I'm thinking, Da. At your age. Ma you did the right thing. Feminism is coming of age. Down with patriarchy. What's in the pan?"

"Hafner's sausages. Do you want an egg, lovey?" Kathleen asked.

"I think Da has the duck egg. Give me a look. Did she hit you with the pan or what?"

"Very smart, I'm sure," Minogue said. He reached to touch the elastoplast and the lump which swelled it out from his forehead.

"Have a bit of sympathy now. Your daddy fell down in the carpark. A terrible day all around," Kathleen murmured.

"Did you spill any out of the bottle, Da?"

"Any what?"

"Whatever it was. Powers or Jameson."

Kathleen looked over from the cooker at her daughter.

"How well you know the names of all the whiskies. Is that the sum total of third level education these days?" Kathleen asked.

Minogue poured the tea. He was careful to keep his finger on the lid so it didn't fall off. This heartened him, this familiar precaution bedded into the rituals of the household. All the little idiosyncrasies of the house were shared knowledge. How to get the lawnmower started. How to tighten the shears and keep them sharp. How to get the garage door to close properly. Which ring on the cooker didn't heat up well. How to make sure you didn't bugger up the washing machine because the switch was contrary.

"Did you hear about the Garda being killed out in Blackrock?" Kathleen asked.

"I saw the headlines. Was it a fella you knew, Da?"

"No, actually."

Kathleen scooped sausages, black pudding and a fried egg onto Minogue's plate. Iseult leaned her chin on the heels of her hands, and elbowed into the plate exactly the way her parents had tried to train her out of doing for years. She watched her father attack the sausages. He looked up at her.

"Isn't it awful entirely?" he said quietly.

Kathleen sat down. She watched Minogue pour her tea.

His shirt-cuffs were dirty. He had missed a bit shaving under his ear. Hair was bushing out of his nose. She looked over to Iseult and saw her looking back. Her vision changed with the salty film which came between them. When she blinked, a drop popped on the table-cloth. Kathleen kept her head down then. The odd time, when she looked up, Iseult was looking at her, a big open face like the moon on her, as if she knew.

"Tell us now," Minogue said at last. "Any chance you'd set us up for one of those music recitals again?"

As was his habit when working to a deadline, Allen skipped his tea. He felt that his public lectures needed to be revised now. The

123

danger, he felt, was in routinising the delivery. He had noticed his own inner voice telling him that he was drifting into clichés. His metaphors strained him. He was actually tiring himself out by trying to suppress the inner critic. He tried to persuade himself that every audience was a new one, but that didn't satisfy him.

This time it wasn't just a matter of setting up some new idiom or sprinkling in new anecdotes and metaphors. He had come up with a good one during the week: '*We cannot live in the subjunctive or pluperfect anymore than we can live in the future. Mental illness is also a case of people largely living out false histories. Living out life in the wrong tense. Wrongs done us in childhood, wrongs done in history must not put blinkers on the future . . .*' That'd certainly strike a chord in any audience.

Allen sat back. He wondered if this sounded a bit academic. Where would he deliver this one? Newry? Allen remembered that Newry was largely a Catholic town. He determined to blot this understanding out so that he would not skew the lecture because of the fact. He would not pander to partisan learnings. He had spoken in Newry before and he had been heckled a lot, but he had also been applauded. There was an informal committee there to welcome him and to put him up.

Allen switched on the radio for the half-six news. Two armed men were still at large in the Blackrock area after a shooting incident today. A Garda was dead and one of the group was in custody. Police believed that they had intercepted the group *en route* to a bank robbery. All roads in the vicinity had road-blocks manned by armed Gardai and members of the armed forces.

He stiffened in his chair. The small of his back began to ache. He began his habitual inner talk to relieve the stress. He tried to loosen his muscles but couldn't. Abruptly he switched off the radio. He noticed that his hand trembled slightly.

Allen tried to return to his notes. He could easily take six months off. Greece, say, or Sardinia; someplace warm, distant. Maybe the break could be complete: he might never come back.

At this notion, Allen's thoughts of the lecture all but fled from his mind. He could not afford to think of this possibility. It threatened to burst completely through the dike he had built to staunch such thoughts. Again he tried to rescue his former life by concentrating on his notes. It wouldn't work. Allen threw his pencil across the room. He let his arms hang loose over the arms of the chair. The silence after the radio seemed to indict him as he looked at the refined clichés in his notes. He saw the hopeful, expectant faces of his audiences, those thoughtful, law abiding citizens—exactly the ones who were not involved in the violence. Those others were out in the night somewhere, planning, watching, waiting. They had waited for Allen. Now they had drawn him into their cycle of malignant atavism.

Daily he had checked to see if he was drifting into that helplessness and passivity which his training led him to expect. He had noticed a distance growing between his waking thoughts and his work. Some sleeplessness too, but he had preserved a spark by dint of his own powers. He could not always staunch the fear which came to him when he was reminded of where he now stood.

Allen willed himself up from the chair. He stood for a count of twenty, barely quelling this bout of panic. He knew that it would get worse too. How many more crises could he withstand, keeping up the manic façade of a normal life? How long before he broke . . . or before he would make his break? Maybe now, this evening, this miserable evening, the reckoning had come. He hadn't risen to being a professor of psychology in Trinity College from a poor emigrant family in Birmingham just to go under meekly, another victim.

Allen felt the fear and hatred ebb and a determination setting in in their place. He looked about his office, at the remnants of what was his old life. He could phone travel agents for a start.

Allen reconnected the phone. It rang almost as soon as he took his hand off it. "Allen?"

"Yes?"

"I've been trying to reach you for some time now. You should stop this childish business of unplugging your phone. We must meet. As soon as possible, actually."

125

"Your office?"

"No. It's better if we meet outside Trinity."

Loftus paused as if trying to sense the atmosphere for cues.

"O.K., then. I'll be dining alone in the Granary. I'm leaving now. I'll expect you there presently."

Allen put down the phone without answering. The image of Agnes McGuire came to him. He had watched her from a distance in the church at Walsh's funeral. Her face radiated a calm, even when she paused to whisper to Walsh's parents. There was an irreducible truth to her which Allen had recognised in a handful of people he had met over his lifetime. She was an enigma to him but overwhelmingly of this world at the same time. Not the longing for a matriarchal comfort in him, no, more a feeling he remembered as a child, on a visit to Liverpool. He had seen a great tanker anchored offshore, mysterious and inaccessible to him. Promise.

Outside, puddles at the edges of the pathways held sections of Trinity buildings, moving them as Allen walked by. Parts of the cobblestones had dried. The grass seemed to breathe. The air was close. Students were calling to each other across the echoing stone square. A gowned lecturer helloed him in the gathering gloom, pipe smoke smell trailing him. Lights swelled soft yellow out onto the stones. Allen felt that he had let down a load, a load that had clung to him for most of his life. He did have a choice, one choice at least, and he was determined to use it.

CHAPTER ELEVEN

Moroney and Galvin, the two Special Branch detectives, stepped from their car in Baggot Street. They had been preceded by plain-clothes officers from a surveillance unit some hours before.

Neither of the detectives was happy with what they had heard. The driver of the Mercedes had picked up the stolen car with its plates doctored in a lane behind Baggot Street. On the way in from Blackrock, they had been radioed that the garage had been located. They had had to decide whether to keep a lookout on the premises or whether to go in right then and there. Curiously, it was Galvin, the detective who had done the heavy with the prisoner, who was in favour of keeping watch.

"You never know. They mightn't have heard . . ." he had said.

"It's been on the radio and the telly," Moroney replied.

"But they mightn't reckon on our pal telling us anything. They might be kind of slow on the details. Might come in a hurry to tidy up or something."

Moroney wondered if perhaps they hadn't an embarrassment

of riches. Perhaps they had done their job too well, getting the driver to tell them what he had.

"Ah, give them credit now. They'll have been mobile and ready to get the hell out at a moment's notice. I have an idea that there might be something useful in this place for us. My guess is that it's part of a network. I think we have to move fast. We have to get some results, that's the politics of the thing right now. The shootings and bombings are on the up and up. Can't wait."

Galvin said nothing.

"We'll go in, what?"

"All right," Galvin said.

The two men walked by the entrance to the lane. The light was poor. They recognised the old coachhouses, garages and sheds which had formerly been servants' quarters, stables and the like. Now they were used as storage buildings or for parking. Often they were gutted and turned into pricey mews houses. They wondered if they hadn't gone to the wrong lane. There was nobody about, no cars. A man in a light raincoat stepped out from the shadows.

"Sergeant?" he said.

"Hello. Special Branch. Yes. We're just in from Blackrock. What's the story?"

"Very discreet. We met a fellow up the lane who has an electrical shop there. He knew the place."

"Are you sure?"

"I am. He even remembers walking by and the door was half-open. Said he saw the Mercedes in there."

"See anyone?"

"He didn't. We haven't seen anyone either. There's men over beyond and a few in the garden there with night glasses. We're ready to go."

The way he said it irked Moroney. These fellows were more like paramilitaries. They didn't let you know they were in the area half the time. Strolling about the place with submachine guns, like they were out walking the dog.

"Hold on there now. What's the chain of command here?"

128

"We were called in sir. Told to wait for your instructions."

"Who?"

"Superintendant Reynolds."

Moroney almost smiled. They had been given a surprising amount of leeway. That'd be one in the eye for those yobbos.

"And you're . . . ?"

"McAuliffe, sir."

"Right McAuliffe, give them the billy."

McAuliffe fingered his earphone more securely into his ear. He turned back a lapel and bent his head toward the mike.

"We are going when I say. Have you got a clear field up there? O.K. Back up 1 and 3. Clear? Any lights in there? Right 9 and 10, back door to yard opens inward all right? Ready units 2,4 and 6. What? Yes, jemmy it."

He paused and looked down the silent lane. Only the centre of the lane was in light.

"Stand to the side, gentlemen," he whispered to the two detectives.

Leaning to the mike, he said "Go, now."

He reached under his coat and drew the sling tight to his shoulder as he poked a Uzi out. He ran on his toes down the lane.

The detectives saw a half dozen men sit upright on the roofs of sheds to the front and sides of the garage. Three more men in what looked like jogging suits ran to the door. One produced a crowbar and levered a crack between doors until a loud splintering sound echoed down the lane. The man swore and quickly inserted the crowbar again. This time the doors gave way and the crowbar fell to the ground. Another figure yanked open the door and leaped in, shouting. The men on the roofs jerked their heads slightly from side to side, listening intently to their earphones, all the while training their weapons on the doors. A can was kicked over inside. The shouting died down. A light went on. Still no one appeared in the lane. No one had noticed, the Special Branch men realised. They recognized McAuliffe's silhouette in the light which spilled from the door. He beckoned to them.

Inside, the men who had stormed the place stood around looking both disappointed and relieved. One of them was speaking into his radio and staring off into space as his head inclined to listen to the reply.

The garage was not really a garage. It was a dusty shed. Some planks lay haphazardly on the floor. They could see right up to the rafters. There was a faint smell of paint. Some rusted garden tools lay piled in a corner. A homemade stool made of rough plank scraps lay on its side. A car pulled up outside. In it were two uniformed Gardai. A small old man sat in the back.

"He's the one up the lane. The electrical shop," McAuliffe said.

The detectives walked over to the car.

"Hello. We're police officers," Moroney said, leaning in the window.

"You're the man who spotted that the place was being used as a garage . . . ?"

"I am that."

"Anything unusual at all lately?"

"Not to speak of. No. But didn't I see a fella working on that Mercedes Benz the other day."

"Yesterday, like?"

"The day before."

"And did you know him? Did you know his face, like?"

"You know, I never even seen him. I saw his legs I think. He was doing something at the front of the car, down near the bumper. 'Hello I says to him.' And he says 'Hello' back. That was it. The only time I seen him and I didn't see him at all."

"Never saw his face at all?"

"Not a bit of it," the old man said with a look of satisfaction.

Moroney looked away to his colleague. The two Gardai remained in the front seats listening to the dispatcher on the radio. Galvin's eyes went toward a heaven he privately doubted.

"Tell you what," the old man said suddenly. "I saw him, or actually didn't see him fiddling with another car."

"And . . . ?"

"And nothing. I don't know what class of car it was at all."

"No idea? When was this?"

"Early in the week. He had it up on one of those jacks. He had the back up, I know that. He had the car backed in that time. I heard him wriggling around under the back. 'Hello' I says—"

"— and he says 'Hello back,'" Galvin interrupted.

"How did you know?" the old man asked.

"Was there a colour?"

"Let's see. You know when something is crimson and purple at the same time . . . ?"

"Magenta?"

"Ma what?"

"Was it new?"

The old man's face took on an indignant look.

"And how would I know? Do you think I'm an encyclopaedia of cars or something?"

"How well you know the Mercedes, though."

"Sure that's a quality car, mister. There was a singer in Dublin by that name back in the thirties. Would you credit that? Mercedes McNamara. A bit of an actress too. Before your time, I'm thinking."

Moroney looked down the lane. He was aware of McAuliffe standing next to him.

"Will you be wanting the fingerprint brigade in, sir?"

Moroney wondered if McAuliffe was being bloody-minded. 'And should I try picking my nose, sir? Or maybe will I let a fart, sir?'

"Where are they?"

"The van's out on Baggot Street, sir. I think you passed it on your way in," McAuliffe replied.

Moroney scrutinised McAuliffe's face for any visible trace of insolence. He could find none and this irritated him all the more. These lads had been trained in leaping about like the Chinese, living off the bog, killing people with paper cups and that sort of effort. Very modern men entirely. Toughs who'd probably never have to start on the beat and get promoted into plain clothes.

131

"I'll be needing you to bring this man here to the station and go through the car book with him," Moroney said.

"I took the liberty of assigning that work to the two Gardai here from Harcourt Street station. It's my understanding that we've done our part," McAuliffe said.

"What?" said the old man in the back of the car.

"Here, leave me off at the bus, the number 10. I have to get home. The missus'll be wondering if I've run off with a young wan. Hee hee. Are we right?" the old man continued.

The Garda behind the wheel looked wearily at McAuliffe, then at Moroney.

"We need you to look through a few pictures of cars for us," McAuliffe said to the old man.

"Are you joking? Sure I've done what I can. I have to get home. Jases."

"You can call the wife from the station. We'll drive you home. You'll get your tea too," said the Garda in the passenger seat.

"Feck it, lads. God forgive me for cursing. Magnum P.I. is on the telly. I never miss it."

McAuliffe waved the van into the laneway. His men were putting on jackets and dispersing. A couple who had walked into the laneway stood staring as the van disgorged wires and lights and boxes. McAuliffe made himself scarce in the hubbub. When Moroney went off to look for him, he was gone. Moroney was still angry.

He found Galvin, gawking like an adolescent looking at donkeys at it in a ditch, a far cry from the heavy who had thrown the Duffy fella around that afternoon.

"Here. Leave these fellas alone. Do you know what I'm going to do? I'm going to buy a pint of stout apiece for yourself and myself and a big fuckin' sandwich below in O'Neill's. What do you think of that?"

Galvin frowned. It wasn't like Moroney to be so coarse.

As the two detectives walked out under the arch to Baggot Street, they passed several people looking down the alley at what must have looked like people making a film. There were three squad cars parked beside theirs now. As they passed one Garda, Moroney said,

"The hard man, is it yourself. How's things out in Blackrock?"

"Divil a bit," the middle-aged Garda replied and shook his head.

They walked on. As he opened the door of the car, Moroney's pessimism rolled up relentlessly behind him and broke over him. The birds had flown, he realised. It was dark now.

The following day being Friday, Kilmartin did not feel too aggrieved at having slept poorly. He had had a feeling which persisted into his dreams that something was unravelling nearby, but that it couldn't be detected. Were there a forced choice, Kilmartin would have preferred 'prosaic' to 'man of fantasy' on his gravestone. Nonetheless he felt as a child felt upon awakening, knowing it had snowed in the night, even before opening the curtain. This morning, Kilmartin's snow was quite invisible. He felt gruff. He smoked four cigarettes in the car on his way to work. Eight hours ago, the two gunmen in Blackrock had not been found. He had gone home after midnight, despondent and furious by turns.

Of the two men who waited outside his office, he would have preferred not to see Minogue. Connors he could send on some errand. Minogue's odd face gave Kilmartin a tiny pop in his stomach. He groaned inside at the thought of a morning's gas.

"Good morrow, Matt. Tea, then?"

"Good morning yourself," Minogue replied, fingering the folders under his arm.

"Step in, step in. Connors, would you kindly root out some tea?"

Minogue sat lightly in the chair. Kilmartin sat on the edge of his desk, wondering if the *clackety clack* of the typewriters would now add a headache to his woes.

"Any big moves, Matt?" inquired Kilmartin gently.

"Well now. This thing will be eclipsed by other concerns, I'm sure, so I'll make a long story short. Someone tried to run me

133

over yesterday. They could have tried a bit harder too, I've been thinking."

Kilmartin started. He stared at Minogue.

"Odd, isn't it? In a carpark. Of course I didn't tell Kathleen, but someone phoned the house masquerading as an old school friend, if you please. Some yarn about a reunion. All rubbish of course, but he knew where to find me and what I looked like."

This was it, Kilmartin was thinking. Minogue has gone batty. The signs were there and it's only now they're coming together.

"Yes. All part of an elaborate play. I'm thinking someone is trying to push this drug thing on me."

"I don't get it, Matt . . . "

"I'm being led. That's what I'm saying. I believe that boy's girlfriend or whatever you'd call her. I'm not sure why."

"Her account of the boy . . . ?"

"Yes. I'm not happy with the two yobbos in Trinity pushing those hints about drugs."

Kilmartin thought for a minute. Minogue seemed relaxed and somehow resolute about this. Had he changed a bit somehow? "What makes you feel that you're being led down the garden path, Matt?"

"There's the rub now. I haven't an inkling. Well, actually now I shouldn't say that at all. I have the feeling that something is happening and that time is a factor. Like while the show is on, someone is picking pockets in the cloakroom."

Kilmartin stood up and walked to the window. He risked a small burning fart for relief. Minogue's thing was contagious, damn it all. Hints and inklings, suspicions. What Kilmartin really wanted was to be called to help in this business last night, not to be left eavesdropping in the radio room for great events which made careers for other men. Something you could leap into and work at and get credit for.

"Anyway. I'm hoping the car was stolen and that it'll turn up. There's no reason for people trying to bump me off, you know. The old grey matter is nagging at me to believe there's something in this to do with that boy Walsh."

Indeed, thought Kilmartin. *Well now, Matt Minogue, I'm not going to come straight out and tell you what I think, but I'll give you a hint.*

"Tell you what, Matt. Give it until this evening or over the weekend. Then we can get someone else to start from scratch and rehash it."

Kilmartin caught wind of his newborn fart. It had emerged and lain in waiting only to burst when he had congratulated himself for his discretion. Holy God, it was a killer. The window was stuck. So was Kilmartin. A sulphurous aroma rose around him. Minogue uncrossed his legs and brushed lightly across his nose with his fingers.

"Right so. I'll look over the parents' statements again and rethink it," said Minogue, rising from the chair.

"Good, Matt. Look, do you want me to follow up on this thing yesterday? Where that car came at you?"

Minogue recognised the challenge. *Minogue is gone loony, right?*

"No. I'll go through the thing myself."

"Sergeant Minogue? Doherty here. You asked about a car."

Doherty? Right, the one from the Vehicle Bureau.

"Yes. Are you Pat Doherty's brother?"

"I am."

"Tell him they haven't a ghost on Sunday in Nenagh. The Wexford crowd will take the day. Ye'll have to play the wings and pass the ball more."

"Go on out of that," Doherty said. "If the rain comes again, we'll scalp that crowd. The Wexford crowd hate the rain."

"My eye," said Minogue.

"I'll put money on it," Doherty replied.

"I don't want to be robbing you."

"Well. A white Ford Granada was stolen on Churchtown Road in the afternoon. Are you with me?"

"I am."

"Reported at 10:53 three last night. Some old bollocks had

135

been in a pub all that time. And then he wanted to drive home, but he couldn't find his bloody car."

"Comical."

"The country is gone to pot," Doherty said. His Galwegian indignation came softly to Minogue, who thought of the long, open bogroads by Clifden with the clouds rolling in over the horizon, sea on the air.

"Well, it turned up today in Dundrum. Next to a bus-stop. The cheek of it, I ask you. Do you know, it caused a bit of havoc in the traffic this morning."

As if he intended we find it, Minogue realised.

"Where is it now?"

"Store Street Station."

"Good luck."

Minogue's years on the Drug Squad afforded him the chance to track down a pal, Jack Currelly.

"And how's the family, Matt?"

"Oh, pulling the divil by the tail, Jack."

"Where, now?"

"Store Street. Don't bother with the kit. Let's keep it informal for the moment. You'd know what I'm looking for straight away."

Minogue stood in the yard leaning on a freshly crushed Capri. Currelly rested on one knee on the driver's seat as he checked the interior. To Minogue, the white Granada looked threatening.

A uniformed Garda stood by, clasping a clipboard.

"Rain do you think?" a garrulous Minogue said.

"God knows now, sir. It's as like as not."

A fresh-faced lad up from the farm, big sky-blue eyes on him and a razor cut next to his chin. Trying too hard to be perfect.

Currelly kneed his way out of the car. He showed Minogue the remains of a joint nestling in the palm of his hand.

"One roach. In the ashtray, if you don't mind. Well, Sherlock. What do you think? Will we call in Dr Watson or what? Joy-ride, I'd say. Still though you'd expect the car would be done in a bit. Want me to give it the once-over in earnest?"

"No thanks." Minogue turned to the Garda.

"Do ye dust these yokes for prints or that class of thing?" Minogue asked.

"If requested, sir. If the items are part of a body of evidence. Commission of a crime, like."

"How about this one?"

"No, sir." The Garda pointed to the Comments on the sheet as he held out the clipboard for Minogue. Minogue read '*Joy-ride?*' and, below, '*No apparent damage.*'

"So?"

"Well, it's a question of volume really, Sergeant. Your man should be glad he got it back in one piece. There's a lot go missing in Dublin."

"And if we find a narcotic substance in it?" Minogue pressed.

"Oh in that case I'm sure that'd warrant full treatment, sir."

Whatever the hell 'full treatment' meant these days.

"To tell you the truth, sir, the car was just given the once- over very quick, like, when it came in. The real examination would be done later in the day, I'm thinking."

Good lad, Minogue thought, at least you're covering for your pals and that's no bad thing. Not the end of the world.

"Could you arrange to have it done, if you please? And have that Garda Doherty call me as soon as he has anything?"

"Yes, sir."

Currelly and Minogue strolled over to their own car.

"Is this a big deal, Matt?" Currelly asked.

"Ah you know, I'm just pulling on bits of things really."

"Terrible bloody mess that thing yesterday. Out in Blackrock."

Both men got into Minogue's car.

"And tell me, Matt, how have you been since that other business?"

"Could be worse, Jack, could be worse," Minogue heard himself reply.

The traffic on Friday in Dublin had staggered an already shaky system. Soon they became enmeshed. The sun came out and Currelly rolled down his window. On the path beside him, a well-dressed couple walked by speaking French loudly over the noise of the cars. Minogue knew there wouldn't be any prints worth a damn in the car and he was still being bobbed around on a string. He'd call Trinity to see if anything had shown up in lost and found.

The *Irish Times* headlines lay across Allen's desk, barely held in by the width of the newspaper itself. The picture of a Garda in uniform stood next to a picture of a car on its side, leaning against a Mercedes. He was sure of his decision now. Surprisingly, Allen had slept well. He had not dreamed. He felt light now. The sun threw light in the window, over his notes and against the bookcases. It was as good a time as any.

Allen was certain that he could persuade her. He returned to his notes and began trying to memorise the outline. Allen gathered his notes. He couldn't concentrate. He removed mementoes from a drawer—a pen won in grammar school, a medal of his father's. He looked around the room. There was little or nothing personal in it. A few plants—they could stay—a radio alarm clock, a poster of an old phrenology diagram. The books had been expensive but they could be allowed no weight now.

Allen fingered through the files in his desk. Anyone could take his place, marking tests, going to conferences, meeting with colleagues. Committees, proposals, luncheons. Student counselling, research, administration. Evaluation, theses, recommendations. Evisceration. Yes, that too. His friends? Allen's reserve and self sufficiency had allowed him distance. He sat at his desk and began writing a list of what he had to do: '*Bank, letter, solicitor.*' He'd go whether she agreed or not. He went through his office again, selecting and discarding.

The committee met in a carpeted room in Dublin Castle. Army intelligence arrived in civvies. The only uniforms present were those of two district superintendents from Dublin. Almost half of the eleven men present were from Special Branch. A civil servant who looked more like a priest, and knew it and cultivated it, sat at the table also.

"The basics are these," a Special Branch detective was explaining.

"We have a man in custody, one James Duffy, native of Newry. He has no record of criminal activities with the RUC. The most he has done in his life is thrown stones during riots, live on the dole and, the RUC suspect, drive other people's cars without their permission. He is on a list of theirs as under suspicion for involvement in IRA activities. Admits to driving the car yesterday. Claims not to have known the other two. Not even their names. You know the routine. Admits to being a 'volunteer.' He says he was here on a kind of holiday. We think he's small fry and that he will be no loss to them. That's probably why he was sent down here. Expendable."

"What does he know, Sergeant?" army intelligence asked bluntly.

"Yes, he picked up the car—incidentally the plates were fakes—in the vicinity of a lane behind Lower Baggot Street. We found the garage that probably hid the car and fixed the plates. So, to answer your question, he knows bugger-all. He's more or less a stooge. He says the two were bored so they wanted to crack a bank in south county Dublin."

"How did he get his instructions?" the army man persisted.

"Over the phone. As for the garage. We got in yesterday evening. It was decided by the boys on the spot. As it turns out, nothing would have been gained by setting up a surveillance. They had flown the coop."

"They?" said the civil servant.

"Whoever. The owner rented it out, paid in advance. He says the man who rented it was, what was his word, 'civilised.' Well-to-do. Youngish and fit-looking." The detective flicked to a page: ". . . 'well groomed' . . . 'obviously a businessman' . . . The man told him it was for preparing antique cars for restorations. The name doesn't mean anything and the address is rubbish. The man was 'refined.'"

"In other words, nobody."

"Has the owner been through the books?" one of the super-intendents asked, more to get a word in than to advance the understanding of the meeting.

"Yes, sir. Nothing." The detective sat down. The man next to him stood and put his hands in his pockets. He had no notes to brief him.

"A man who used one of the sheds up the lane identified the Mercedes straight away. He couldn't be sure about another car he saw there earlier in the week though. He settled on a Japanese car and that's as good as we'll get. The thing which may be of concern is that one of them was getting some substantial atten-tion. Some alteration or repair job."

"What's the significance, Inspector?" queried the super-intendent.

"Well, we believe the car or cars are being prepared for some operation. If this old man is right, a car has been modified most likely. We're working on the worst interpretation here."

"With respect, Inspector, I have to explain to the Minister why you are considering this. Seems tenuous to me," the civil servant said. The inspector, who had twenty years on the bureaucrat he was silently eying all the while, continued.

"Fair enough. We discount legitimate purposes. We don't think that this outfit went to the trouble of getting a place just to switch plates on a stolen car. A babe in arms could do that blind drunk on a wet night. We think there's some kind of a shift on but to be quite honest," he paused and looked directly over to the man from army intelligence, "we don't really know more than the next man."

He didn't have to spell it out. Sources in the British Special Branch and anti-terrorist squads had been unusually communi-cative lately. This was the case with the Brits only when they were grumbling. They grumbled because there was little they could do about it from their side, and they grumbled because the RUC's grumbles weren't listened to as keenly in the South. Ergo there was something going on in the South they wanted to stop but couldn't do it themselves. The increase in shootings and the sophistication of the weapons and techniques involved had them stymied. Their usual sources knew nothing about how the weapons were getting in. They had stepped up the border patrols and they had undertaken aerial surveillance with helicopters. The inspector let the silence sink in with its eloquence. Then he reminded them.

"There are signs that there's a new twist to the arms supply. You all know that our department feels the political pressure very quickly. We're pulling out all the stops. This business yesterday has turned up the heat even more."

"Will you outline the courses we can follow, gentlemen?" the civil servant asked.

"We're at a disadvantage. Our sources have either dried up or they don't know anything. There seem to be new men in the game. Whoever this 'refined businessman' is, we don't know. We should acknowledge that. We think that there's a connection between yesterday and our current problems. A slip. The human factor, if you like. No organisation is completely watertight. I'm suggesting that every available man be on a surveillance roster for each and every so-called republican on our books. The two murderers have to go to ground somewhere. I want taps on phones . . . I have a list here and it's as short as I can make it."

He pre-empted the civil servant whose face was already taking on a set of disapproval.

"And I don't like it either. There's no point in picking them up and interrogating the whole lot of them."

He slid the list across the table toward the civil servant and he sat down. Nobody spoke for a half minute. The civil servant looked up from the list and said,

"Inspector, can I see you after the meeting?"

A rustle of papers moved the committee on. The army intelligence had reports of sightings of Russian trawlers just outside the boundary last week, the week before and again this week. They had left the area before fishery protection vessels could get there and confirm the sightings. Nothing special, he said, time of year perhaps. A report from British Intelligence that it was almost certain one of their men had been killed by a sniper who used a Startron nightsight. Nothing else could explain him being shot in the head at nearly three hundred feet in the dead of night. Queried to the States because it was restricted on the Munitions List from their State Department.

Toward the end of the meeting, the inspector looked up from his fingerplay to find the civil servant's limpid gaze fixed on him. The civil servant was absent-mindedly drawing a thumb to and fro over the edge of the sheet which listed the names for the telephone taps. He looked away as the inspector met his stare, affecting attention to the speaker.

Scared, the inspector reflected. He feels things are slipping, but he doesn't want to tell his Minister that, because the Minister would rather believe otherwise. The inspector gave him a lingering look, knowing the civil servant would be aware of his mild scrutiny. Not as scared as some of my men, he's not, the inspector guessed. Probably not as scared as me.

CHAPTER TWELVE

The playwright listened to what he knew were Americanisms. He looked around the pub for some relief from the tight-lipped anger of the Yank.

"I had to close the god-damn place down rightaway after I heard about your goons," the tanned man hissed. "So much for you loaning out a hot car to those assholes."

"Who gave you the job of deciding what I do?" the playwright retorted. "I gave them the car because I didn't want them trying to lift one for themselves and getting caught. We need those men up there—"

"Right. We don't need them screwing up the works down here, I tell you—"

"—They're coming from a battle zone, mister. Maybe you don't realise that. Your crowd can have your Vietnams and your Chiles a thousand miles away. Our men on the ground are under pressure all the time. They need a break. We do what we can for them—"

"—Like tell them to take on a bank? Shoot cops?"

"That's out of bounds and they know that. They'll answer for it. To the appropriate authorities."

The tanned man heard the changed inflexion in the playwright's words now. So that was it, his trump card, the appropriate authorities. At least it was more out in the open now. He felt a grim satisfaction take the place of his anger. He'd have the playwright's head on a plate after he got through with this.

"Look, let's drop it for now," said the tanned man. "We'll be bringing the present for Aunt Maggie tomorrow. Everything is settled isn't it?"

"That car? Yes," the playwright replied.

"No screw-ups, O.K.?"

The playwright returned the Yank's glare but said nothing. The only other detail really is that you are out of the running, my fine flowery mid-Atlantic fancy man. You're washed up as of tomorrow. He smiled up at the Yank.

"By the way, your home phone is being tapped again, so go through your list consecutively if it's on business," the tanned man said. Show-off, thought the playwright, as he smiled more broadly at the departing pest.

Minogue had sought refuge in Bewley's. Needed something to keep him going. He had been on his way out to Walsh's despite the reception he had gotten on the phone from Mr Walsh. A mixture of tentativeness and arrogance which mystified Minogue had been his reward for phoning. Mrs Walsh was under sedation and the doctor was ready to send her to hospital at the drop of a hat. Did Minogue really need to see her today? She couldn't stand to be around the house with memories. Mr W. hadn't been to work in the last week. What good would it seem to talk now? Hadn't they told the police everything they could?

A large white coffee and a gooey bun brought some solace to Minogue. He ensconced himself near the window in the non-smoker's section on the first floor. Sun streamed in over the rooftops opposite. Between Minogue and the office windows across

Grafton Street lay the paralysed traffic below, a snake of exhaust and metal.

Minogue began to observe the waitresses. They were perked up by the arrival of Friday. Some of them appeared exceedingly gorgeous to Minogue. He attributed his rush of feeling to the coffee. Then he began to go further and understand that he had been gladdened and emboldened somehow. The near miss with the car had brought him another taste of the calm perspicacity which had cradled him for those weeks in hospital. Minogue saw the cashier throw her head back and laugh at something a customer had said. A tramp snored lightly at the far end of the room. Each woman seemed stubbornly real to him. They'd be tired after the day, their backs, their feet. But look at the one still laughing. Maybe some of them were married to slobs, ah-good- ould- Dublin characters who came home late from the pub. Dublin. It dawned on Minogue that he was almost free. There was an ungetaroundableness to things now. Sequestered truths awaited him here in Dublin, which was neither Clare nor Montana . . .

Truths? Did we always have to believe that things turned out well, that there were answers and happinesses ahead? Maybe they were badly paid here. Maybe someone was being shot in the North. Maybe Daithi might fail his exams. Maybe his brother Mick was unforgivable.

Minogue opted for a second cup of coffee. Confidence welled in him, barely overshadowed by his sense of the puzzle of the murder waiting for him beyond this happy afternoon, the body of one Jarlath Walsh waiting for answers.

Leaving Bewley's, Minogue reinserted himself in the traffic jam. As he finally made some headway beyond Merrion Square, his precarious caffeine optimism dulled and then died. Pulling into the manicured driveway of Walsh's house, he saw a curtain drawn back slightly to show a man's face, more disapproving than curious.

Portly, Minogue thought, like out of a book. He expected to see Walsh dressed in a three-piece with a pocket-watch in his fob.

145

Hair in place, thinning, no suggestions of sideburns. Walsh preceded Minogue into another carpeted area.

"Step into the living room, Detective Sergeant."

Minogue tried to trace the accent but failed to get beyond a vague understanding that it was from some part of Munster.

The curtains were half drawn. Minogue was looking at a face which was used to being resolute but was now wavering. The man looked almost curious. Still, he was keeping together. Minogue noticed no decanters around. The room was large and tidy. The diffused light made pastels of most of the colours, themselves mainly beige or blue anyway. Minogue wondered if they lived in this living room. His eye was caught by a stand-up thing for holding magazines. *Time* and *Newsweek* looked out of it.

"Mr Walsh. Please accept my condolences."

There was a few moment's silence between the men. Minogue felt himself sinking into the upholstered chair.

"I'd offer you a drink, Sergeant . . . "

"Thanks, but no. It's semi-official."

"Semi?"

"Well, I'm looking for something or someone to fill the holes in my investigation. I'm less inclined to believe that your son was a random victim of violence."

Walsh seemed to sit up more in his seat.

"Random?" he said.

"I don't believe in a master plan or that class of thing. I'm guessing that Jarlath was in the wrong place at the wrong time, that he may unwittingly have been involved in something."

"Sergeant. I know my own son. He was not involved in gangs or whatever it is you're describing."

Minogue heard himself speaking and he was taken aback by his own tone. This man, whom he had met but minutes before, rankled him somehow.

"Allow me to say, Mr Walsh, that I have built up a fair picture of your son over the last week too. What I need now are some little details which might not have seemed important enough to mention before. A hint."

Walsh's face had changed. He licked a lip. Minogue wondered if he had been a farmer's son, big as he was, a big neck on a body going fat inside a few more years. A face you'd see under a cap herding cattle down a lane. The striped shirt and the marble fireplace belied that.

"Now, Sergeant, I had an inkling you—not you exactly now—but one of ye would come to that. I think that you crowd have run out of steam and now ye're worried about looking bad with no one behind bars for this."

"So what do you do?" Walsh continued, sitting forward in his chair and clasping meaty knuckles together. "Ye try to insinuate that there's something amiss with my son. Almost like he had it coming."

"Now Mr Walsh, that's not the way it is. What I'm saying is that many investigations are successful due to the remembering of details which initially seemed of no consequence."

"Oh that's a nice thing to say and a nice way to say it, Sergeant, but let me tell you. I think the place is out of control. That's what I think. I think you lads don't know whether you're coming or going here in this city. Ye're afraid to deal firmly with the likes of criminals walking the streets. Do you know, I don't care whether it was a lunatic or some gang. I want the fella or fellas caught. Punished. That's the size of it."

Minogue stared idly at the television in the corner while Walsh talked on. He realised that Walsh had to be allowed to vent his frustration on someone. At times Minogue nodded in a show of sympathy to hurry him up. It wasn't working.

"Sergeant Minogue. I came to Dublin over twenty-five year ago and I had nothing at all. Now those were not the best of times. But the first thing I learned was that Dublin people are not the same as us. They don't like us doing well for ourselves. They want to sit around over pints and complain. So you know what I think is the pity of it though?"

Minogue was tempted to say he did.

"That every year the Gardai on the beat are learning the same thing. Young lads up from the farm like myself. A bit too trusting,

147

I'm thinking. Didn't know how to deal with hooligans and vandals. Afraid of the firm hand. Oh don't get me wrong, I don't blame the Gardai entirely. I'm well aware of the way this country is going. I'll tell you that a spell of army service would do the youth of this bloody city a lot of good. What galls me is that these vandals here can hang around the pubs on the dole and never get told to shape up or ship out. They're getting so brazen they're robbing people on the streets. Drugs and everything. Look, I don't mind telling you that, same as yourself, I had some high jinks when I was a lad. A few glasses of porter, a bit of divilment. But I never in my life thought that the rest of my life could be like that. There was always hard work the next day. 'Work hard, play hard.' That's my motto."

Walsh seemed to have spent himself. He was probably on the edge and confused for the first time in his life, Minogue guessed. How could a woman live with a man like that? He'd scarify her for any signs of weakness.

"Did Jarlath discuss any of his hobbies or interests, Mr Walsh? His girlfriend?"

Walsh's eyes widened, then narrowed and he shook his head gently. Damn, Minogue thought, set him off again.

"Girlfriend, is it? You mean that red-haired young one at the funeral? With the Northern accent?"

"Agnes McGuire," Minogue said pointedly.

"Look, no one minds young people having a fling. These are different times than when we grew up. I always say play the field as long as your conduct is good, no one can fault you."

Minogue was struck by the word 'conduct.' He hadn't heard it in years. He associated it with sentences or warnings, school or courtrooms.

"I said that to him. I said 'Jarlath, you are a free man. You don't owe anything to anybody so you're beholden to no one. You pick your own studies now and you make friends. Male and female alike. Your mother and I are a bit old-fashioned but you'll know later on what we mean. There's time enough for responsibilities later.'" Walsh paused.

Minogue felt a breeze of despair.

The words turned over in his mind. He thought of Daithi, foolish man-boy half astride a fence in these years. A mistake to call him a man. Kathleen had been at him to take Daithi aside. What did that mean, to 'take Daithi aside?' To prepare him for life with a little chat? Like those stupid American shows on the telly, 'Well, my boy, it's time we had a little . . . ' A little what? A little man-to-man chat? About what? Passing on the secrets of males, the pathetic bullying ways of half the world who threw children into wars and sat around pubs uttering platitudes.

"Freedom. They used to talk about it a lot more. The hippies and the rest of it. Freedom doesn't mean that same some gutty has the choice to kill my son out of turn. That's not freedom. Jarlath picked his courses. He had his own politics and I never said boo to that. I worked in this bloody city so he can have those choices. I can tell you that it took a while for me to learn it, but Jarlath had as much right to go socialist as I did not to—"

"Socialist?" Minogue interrupted.

"Well, left or whatever they call it. You have to understand that Jarlath had no experience of the world. He didn't know what socialism was in practice. 'We're all socialists at heart,' I told him. 'Even Jesus Christ was a socialist,' I told him. I pay the lads well at work. Not that I have much choice with the unions . . . "

Experience being the name we give our mistakes, Minogue's inner voice copied Wilde's mordant truth.

"Anything about Irish politics? The North?" Minogue said.

"You're back to that girl again, aren't you? He told me once that we didn't know anything because we hadn't lived through it. I mean that's all fine and well to say. The enthusiasm of youth is a thing that can be easily turned to bad ends."

So that was another gem, Minogue thought. He imagined father and son shouting at the foot of the stairs, Mrs Walsh trying to intercede. Mother Ireland.

"Anyway. I'd not describe her as a girlfriend. To answer your question," Walsh said and sat back defiantly in his chair.

"Why not?"

149

"Well, we never met her. She was never introduced to us. In a formal way."

Minogue's pessimism deepened. The boy had learned enough to be ashamed of them probably.

"I was just thinking, Sergeant Minogue. Doesn't the Bible say 'an eye for an eye?' Don't you think there's something in it all the same? Where's the justice even if the fellow is caught? Jarlath had a great future ahead of him with the business. Sure the university was just a general training. Did I insist he do accountancy or the like? No, I did not. 'Every lecture has something for everybody,' I told him. A liberal education as they say. Strange as it may seem, I believed in that."

Minogue realised that he was probably the first and perhaps the last visitor to the house since the funeral. The man looked like a bachelor somehow. The place was spic and span, unused. Walsh's face held an intensity which was still disbelief as to how the world had fallen apart. Soon it would turn to anger. Walsh would want answers and no one would be able to provide them.

Walsh was fingering his lip now. His voice had dropped and he was staring at a print on the wall.

"The North. Well, that's part of it, I'm sure. Not directly of course but it sets the thermostat, you could say."

He looked intently at Minogue and continued.

"They're not the same as us, Sergeant. Not one bit. They're a different race entirely . . . My suppliers sometimes ask things but I explain that it's like another world up there. It could be another continent. Still they ask. What about the vast majority though, I ask myself. They're trying to make a living and keep their businesses going, like the rest of us. They're the same as us in that respect. Unsung heroes I might say, the ones who put the food on the table and keep the economy afloat. Where's the justice in that though? Bitter people. Too much politics. We don't need that here."

Minogue's mind echoed with 'vast majority.' He heard it often, usually to do with bad news. He felt weak in the company of this man, surrounded by his achievements. Walsh stood up and pocketed his hands. Minogue, no psychologist, recognised his chance.

"Mr Walsh. I'm wondering about your son's brief-case. It was stolen in the college. Did he mention it at all?"

"Matter of fact he did. I haven't told his mother at all on account of it being a present she gave him. I suppose no place is safe now, not even Trinity College Dublin."

"Any strange phone calls or visitors looking for your son this last while?" Minogue tried.

Walsh looked carefully at Minogue, considering his answer.

"No, Sergeant. And your insinuations can stop at that point. You're trying to suggest that our son was a stranger to us. We made it our business to know what he did. We were interested in how he did and not just with the books. We knew our son. We talked and discussed things with him. If you leave here with nothing else aside from that fact, well that'll be fine with me."

Minogue stood. Too far, he thought. Yes, this Walsh was a country man and no stranger to Minogue. Minogue had been meeting these men less and less over the years. He remembered a line of a poem but couldn't remember the poet.

'Will it be the bourgeois coma or the bully's push?'

Walsh had enough of the bully in him not to be comatose in the suburbs here. Yes, Walsh had the age-old dislike for the peelers and the law. Walsh led him to the door. Brass fittings caught Minogue's soupspoon head in passing. *You're wrong, Walsh. Your son was a stranger to you because he was learning to know you too well. Familiarity . . .*

"Thank you, Mr Walsh. I regret the inconvenience."

"We all do our job, Sergeant. Good day now."

Another bloody clumsy hint, Minogue realised as he heard the door clunk behind him. A cement statue in the middle of shrubs reminded him of a cemetery. Who had educated Jarlath Walsh really? Agnes McGuire, that's who.

Within a mile of the Walsh house, Minogue was faced with a choice. The Friday traffic was flowing south. Minogue's home was but three miles in toward the city. Couldn't he justify staying out here rather than returning to the city?

At this same time, the playwright had executed his choice. He replaced the phone. Maybe, on reflection, he should have phoned the Brits instead of the Gardai. A car of a given make and colour would be worth inspecting. It would be going through Dundalk tomorrow. It wouldn't be exactly full of petrol.

Minogue pulled in beside a shop, aching for a cigarette. He sat in the car for a minute, listening to the engine. Then he drove off onto the Bray Road toward his work. On his way to the city centre, there were times when he couldn't remember how he had driven this far, paying no heed to what he was supposed to be doing. By the time he reached Trinity, his mind had caught up with him. He was surprised to find himself parking there. He gathered his notes and checked the drawers. He locked the door behind him. He wrote a thanks, slipped the key into an envelope and sealed it. He walked under cooing pigeons at Front Gate and handed the envelope to a porter.

"And thank Captain Loftus for me. We'll be in touch," Minogue said.

Instead of returning directly to his car, Minogue turned toward Allen's office. The heavy varnished door took his knuckles and offered nothing. Minogue put his ear to the door but he heard no sound. He felt relieved and disappointed at the same time.

In truth, Minogue felt washed up. Almost unknown to himself he was lying in wait on the bank for some moving thing to pass, something he couldn't predict or control. Like waiting for a bus after you've had a few jars, idly detached from things. The implacable closed door and the bird song coming in from the square made him feel silly and lost. Walsh was right, he'd run out of steam.

He gathered his papers better under his arm and turned to leave. Turning, he caught sight of a faint sliver of brightness under the door. He bent to look and noticed that a folded sheet of paper had been slipped under the door. Minogue fished it out with the end tooth of his comb. The note was from a secretary apparently, reminding Allen to phone Captain Loftus when he got back. "*When you get back Sun/Mon.*" Minogue slipped the note back under the door.

Minogue explored his way to the back of the building. Turning a corner, he heard a typewriter. He knocked and entered. No, Dr Allen would not be in for the remainder of the day. Who was looking for him. Mr Who? Minogue. Had he an appointment? No. Well Dr Allen is very fussy about that. No less fussy than yourself, Minogue thought. Where could he reach him? He had rooms in college but he wouldn't be there either. How come . . . ?

His lectures took him away at least twice every month. And where would he be delivering his next one? That's a private initiative on his part. Sorry for asking.

"Well, more power to his elbow, I'll be seeing you," Minogue said to annoy her. A face on her like a plateful of mortal sins, Minogue thought.

CHAPTER THIRTEEN

Detective Garda Connors was trying to unbunch the large muscle group which comprised his arse. Connors welcomed the break from Kilmartin's company. Kilmartin had become morose and then angry by turns. Connors could feel Kilmartin's imploding anger and helplessness. The two killers were still at large. It looked like every single Garda in Dublin would be on the job following suspects around. Suspects indeed. Connors had drawn surveillance on an old-timer, a playwright, who had been active nearly thirty years ago. He had faded into the background more and more as the war in the North became a city war. The playwright hadn't been under regular surveillance for over three years. The file read like a story about a film star in decline.

Connors tried to remember some of the plays this fella had written. All with a nationalist bent or some bloody propaganda. Well, at least it was only play-acting. Maybe he'd be flattered to think he was being followed. He could boast about it to his cronies, be a fecking hero.

Connors' backside began to ease. He ordered another glass of Harp and looked around at the Friday afternoon crowd in the Bailey. Oh very poosh. More like a crowd of gobshites. And the women dressed up, laughing like actors on the telly. Mutton dressed up as lamb. Vixens, they'd take a lump out of any honest man in their path. Hardly ideal company for the patriotic playwright. Who was the fella with him though?

Connors took a slug out of the glass and watched the playwright talking. The other one looked like a Yank. The playwright might be softening him for a few jars or maybe a bit in the theatre line. That was one of his plays, *At the Wall*. Connors was pleased with his memory. A play about what might have happened if the leaders in the Rising hadn't been shot in 1916. Maybe it'd go down well in the States. Hardly though. That fella had a good tan, typical Yank. Looked after himself with the hair and the clothes. How did the Yanks make good suits like that?

The way he sat on the chair suggested to Connors that he was fit and stronger than the suit might indicate. There was something about the consistency in his posture. They had been in the pub for fifteen minutes, but the tanned man didn't slouch. He still looked none too happy about something, but the vexed look he had when he came in was gone now. He now looked merely annoyed at a nuisance of some kind. Hard to put an exact age on the Yank.

Connors wished he had heard the few sharp words the two exchanged when the Yank had come in first. All he could make out was the Yank—or whoever he was—saying something about screw-ups. The playwright had snapped back at him once or twice. After that they seemed to settle down a bit, with the playwright giving him a few big salesman smiles. Wouldn't trust him as far as . . . Aha, maybe the playwright had fixed him up with a colleen, but she hadn't obliged when push came to shove. No, there was more to it. The Yank looked like he was working at staying polite. Like Paul Newman after missing a honey shot in *The Hustler*. Cool dude. Under control . . .

155

The tanned man made his call from a phone in the hallway leading to the pub. He spoke slowly.

"Your job is on for tomorrow. Confirmed. Follow your normal route. Your car will withstand even a minute search so don't sweat it. It's right inside part of the vehicle's structure."

"Why are you telling me that?" The voice was less anguished than bitter.

"So you'll have confidence. So you'll look confident. Is that too simple a proposition for you?"

"When I get there . . . ?"

"You leave the key, just the car key, under the right front tire. The car'll be back in the same spot within the hour."

The tanned man heard breathing over the line.

"Why did you tell me this? Why not just get me to do it without knowing about it?"

The tanned man recognised the bitterness clearly now, but he didn't resist the sarcasm in return.

"'The unexamined life isn't worth living' and all that."

He hung up.

Connors watched as the Yank stood up abruptly. He gave a parting glance to the playwright. Another big crooked smile from your man. Must have one up on the Yank: probably stuck him for the price of the drinks. Connors was out the door before him. He put on his raincoat and a cap to alter his appearance outside. He stood looking into a window full of crafts, waiting for either or both of the men to come out. Almost three minutes passed before the Yank came out. Must have gone to the jacks. No sign of the playwright though, damn and blast him. So what about this Yank, Connors thought. So what? He had hoped that the playwright would be with him, but that'd be too tidy by far. He saw the Yank squint in the daylight as he paused by the door to the pub.

Connors decided to follow the Yank. He could always say that this Yank had acted suspiciously. The playwright might still be in the pub for hours. Connors watched the Yank cross Dawson

Street and then step into a lane which was a short-cut to Moles-worth Street. He thought that for a Yank, the tanned man stepped out nicely and seemed to know his way better than the rest of them who stood around Dawson Street with their snake-skin wives blocking the path, lost just a few hundred yards from the hotel. Connors bet on the Shelbourne Hotel.

The tanned man had already taken in the skulking presence of the man pretending to be interested in the shop opposite. He had been in the pub too. He became aware of a little congestion in his sinuses. He felt the shoulder strap bite as he shrugged. He was certain this was the first time he had been followed since he arrived. The guy was either a cop or a heavy that the playwright had called in. Not drinking enough to be serious about his stay and not meeting anyone, which is why he'd have been nursing his drink so long. Didn't look like a cop.

More pieces fell into place in parallel lines of thought as the tanned man took up a brisk pace. He began a flush out. There was no way that the Brits would have a man tailing him here in Dublin. He stepped into the arched passageway with a piece of Molesworth Street framed in light at the end. He felt he should decide by the end of this tunnel. The playwright had been almost ingratiating by the time he left the pub. Was that a prelude to being set up? And he had been all too obliging about putting the fear on that cop with the stolen car and the dope.

He approached the end of the tunnel and, without turning to look behind, headed for Kildare Street. He thought of his time frames for what he must do. By tomorrow, Saturday, at about two o'clock in the afternoon he would know whether he could report success or failure. He'd be on the plane to Amsterdam, armed with this success, to lever agreement out of his liaison. A unit in Armagh had guaranteed to target a patrol for Sunday as conclusive proof. They'd hear of it before the evening was out from Hilversum or the BBC and the liaison would set up the meeting with the cover from the embassy.

Ahead of him was Leinster House, the Parliament. Laughable

that the National Museum was next to it. Could they be distinguished really? He knew that there were armed guards and army units in the Parliament and he allowed for that. His mind cleared with the arrival of his chance.

As he walked into the foyer of the museum, the thought struck the tanned man that his follower might well be looking for a chance to kill him. The image of the playwright's face with its barely hidden condescension went through his mind. Was he capable of sending in an assassin? The museum was surprisingly bright. Light fell in from the large expanse of skylight. It made the tanned man think of a church. He could see but four other visitors in this large hall. On the balconies which faced out onto the main exhibition hall, he heard the talk of other unseen visitors. An elderly museum guard nodded at him and resumed his measured, meditational walk. He stepped into the floor proper and strolled by the cases with early Christian artefacts in them. He passed spearheads and pots from the Iron Age. He tried to remember the run of the museum from when he had visited it as a child. It was probably all changed.

He mounted steps leading to a balcony overlooking the hall. There he was, this rather tired-looking follower, now in shirtsleeves gazing too intently at golden necklaces, of all things. Why would he follow him around the museum and not wait near the front door? Must be expecting some cloak and dagger meeting. He looked at his watch. The museum closed in another twenty minutes. He turned the corner to meet with a museum guard who looked restive, whistling faintly between tongue and teeth. He had come circuitously back to the stairs. With luck, the guy following him would be a few rooms behind him now. Across to the entry hall. His shadower would be checking rooms.

Connors' feet were bothering him. The Yank looked as if he had just got out of bed and could run a few miles. In all honesty, well, to himself at least, Connors admitted that the Yank hadn't acted in any suspicious way. There was still time to go back and check on the twit he was supposed to be following. Likely if he checked out a few of the pubs like O'Neill's or Davy Byrne's, he'd soon find what's-his-face again. The Yank hadn't so much as looked around. This struck Connors as a bit odd, that he should know where he was going. But he ended up going to the museum, so that was that. Why go to the museum when it was ready to close? He should have phoned in. He should have stuck with the other fellow. He should have watched outside the bloody museum. What class of meeting could a body have in a museum anyway? He should have spent the extra tenner and bought real shoes.

Connors had seen the Yank go up the stairs and into a room before he himself crossed the floor of the hall. He stood behind a display case near to the toilets and watched for the Yank. Follow-around be damned.

What Connors saw in five minutes sparked a faint lightness in his chest. The Yank had come back down the stairs and looked around once before leaving. Either the Yank knew he was being followed or he was looking for someone he expected to meet. Connors counted to thirty. Then he crossed the hall and retrieved his coat and jacket. He wondered if his guess about the Shelbourne Hotel would prove true. He could check this fella out from there.

Connors left the museum, elbowing into his coat. It was nearly five o'clock. There was no sign of the man. Connors strode to the railings which girdled the museum as it ran along Kildare Street. He looked up and down the street and across at Molesworth Street. The Yank was gone. The dying leper's vomit, the curse of the seven snotty . . . Had he stepped into a taxi or a doorway? Connors was about to let go a volley of curses aloud when a movement in a shop window opposite caught his eye. An assistant was taking an antique plate from a display in the window, all the while talking to a customer. Though Connors could not see the face well, he recognised the suit. The Yank: if I can see him, by Jases he can see me.

Connors' brain raced. He could not appear to be faltering. There was no phone nearby to get another detective to switch the surveillance. Connors walked up Kildare Street with a purposive swing to his gait, raging inwardly. His best hope was to get to St. Stephen's Green and wait for however long it took for the Yank to return to the Shelbourne. Connors felt the presence of the Yank behind the glass opposite as he passed up the street and wondered if they both shared some new knowledge now.

Connors reached the top of Kildare Street excited and angry. He dodged traffic and stepped into St. Stephen's Green. He found a seat just inside the railings which afforded him a view of the front of the hotel and, to his left and almost directly ahead of him, the tops of Dawson Street and Kildare Street as they led up to the park.

As the assistant reached into the window, the tanned man saw his follower looking up and down the street. He had looked up and pretended not to notice the antique shop. He had been seen and he knew it.

He listened to the assistant but watched the man recovering and heading up Kildare Street.

"It's from a set. It's Belleek china. Do many people in America know about Belleek?" the assistant inquired.

"Well, I'm from the west coast, ma'am, so I can't speak for collectors on the Atlantic side," he replied.

"Ah, I detect an Irish influence though," she said conspiratorially.

"How discerning of you, I'm sure. Yes, my mother is Irish."

"Isn't that rich now," the assistant said.

The irony was not lost upon him. He'd as soon throw the goddamned plate through the window.

"I'll take your card if I may, ma'am."

"Oh, I see. Well, all right," she said, visibly taken aback.

He retraced his steps back along Molesworth Street. He was surprised to find that his armpits were sweating. The tail might have an out somewhere. He decided to go up Dawson Street to St. Stephen's Green. As he walked by late shoppers and cars, he tried to control his unease.

160

Minogue's week was over. He'd not be called in on the weekend even with the sweep for the murderers of the Garda. Kilmartin would have him nixed off the list, because Minogue had some vague status as an invalid. It has its advantages, Minogue reflected. Someone had tried to run him over; he had found out that there were powerful old boy networks in the army and in Trinity. They wanted their reputations left glowing even if it meant sullying others. That Loftus was a bad egg, an organisation man. Minogue realised that Agnes McGuire entered his mind as an image, a face, unclouded by things she had said.

This was quite contrary to how Loftus and Walsh's father came to mind. Where she came across as singular, Minogue's distaste for the others made his recollections of them amorphous, webby.

Kilmartin probably didn't believe him about the attempt. There was nothing he could do about it really. No clues came from the car. Maybe it was some headbanger who was on the lookout for anyone to frighten. Minogue found that his resistance to certain thoughts had weakened. Dublin was a different place. There was a lot of heavy drug addiction that no one wanted to talk about, a lot of lunatics on the loose. It was the times. Maybe some deranged addict had finally unhinged when he had seen this Walsh boy, a well-fed student with his future ahead of him, a boy who didn't know that the likes of Coolock or Finglas existed. On balance, however, people with drug dependencies were usually more passive than violent. General rules didn't explain every incident. Could a boy like Walsh inspire such violence otherwise? Maybe whoever did him in panicked before they got to the boy's wallet. Maybe the realisation of what they had done broke through their frenzy and hatred.

Minogue had felt the violent impulse himself in recent years, the rush of contempt that came over him at times. The most he had done was jump out of his seat and switch off the television when the inanity overwhelmed him. A narcissistic rock star comparing himself to Bach, someone whining about their oppressors, oppressors they needed to nourish their own weakness. On "The Late Late Show," the accents did it. He had exploded once, una-

161

ble to even laugh it off, when some ex-airhostess who had been appointed to promote tourism in the States started talking in her *hoi polloi* southside fakery.

"And now joining us on the show is Mrs Blah, wife of the auctioneer Michael Blah, all the way from New York, USA. My, Deirdre, what a gorgeous tan you've got . . . "

How could it be that people who were so insipid and grasping could inspire such disgust? His own anger, so vital and huge a hammer, stood looming over these fleas of contemporary Ireland.

The slats of the seat bit into Connors' thigh. He sat forward, his elbows on his knees. He watched scattered groups of pedestrians waiting for the lights at the top of Dawson Street. He looked over to Kildare Street and checked his watch. His gamble should pay off within fifteen minutes or not at all. He had three minutes left in his limit. He stood up and strolled toward one of the entrances to the Green.

Again he scanned the footpath. The traffic was moving fast, swirling around the Green. Connors wondered what would happen if one of the cars stopped suddenly. Everything would be haywire all over the city. The place wasn't built for cars. Connors turned at the sound of a horn. Someone had tried to run through the traffic to get to the Green. Probably a tourist, taking their lives in their hands. Connors saw it almost daily in the summers. Some poor old divil from Minnesota or someplace after a near miss, with that expression you'd see on a donkey chewing barbed wire and just beginning to realise it, trying to laugh it off. 'Oh Elmer nearly got run over in Dublin. Charming city.'

A near miss by the sound of it too, down the far side of Dawson Street. The pedestrian skipped through parked cars to the safety of the Green. Connors could not see the person very clearly. In the instant that the pedestrian ducked into the Green, Connors' brain eclipsed his eyesight and he began running down the path toward where the person had entered. He had made out that it was a man, a man in a hurry too, a man in a suit.

Connors ran across the grass, scattering seagulls. Coming

162

around a hedge he almost collided with a woman pushing a pram. He stopped and looked around him. He could find no trace of the man who had entered the Green. Connors' rational sense began to catch up with him and nag him. The woman had stopped. She looked him up and down disparagingly. If he's in a suit, then it's no bother to speak your mind to him, she thought. Still, he was harmless-looking, not like the gurriers, the thugs who'd do the same and dare you to complain.

"You don't have to jog all over me and the child, mister. Watch where you're going, would you."

"Sorry, missus. I'm looking for a friend of mine. I saw him come in, but I don't know what way he went. I have an important message for him."

The young mother had Connors taped as a bogman who had nearly trampled on her child. Still, a nice look about him.

"Your pal seems to do his jogging here too then," she said and indicated with her head.

Connors ran. He rounded the pond and headed up a hill to where he knew there was a statue of Yeats. Connors stopped near the statue. The statue, in the abstract style, made Connors feel he was on the moon. Various granite blocks had been laid down to provide steps and benches around the statue. He felt his legs twitching. He looked around at the trees which enclosed this area. There was nobody here.

Connors stepped slowly off the granite blocks and began walking under the trees. The grass had been worn away here, what little could grow in the shade. For a moment, Connors lost his bearings and imagined himself far from the city. Only the constant hush of the traffic as it filtered into the Green reminded him. He had been diddled, but what excited Connors now was that this man must have had a reason for running. Connors could now justify his trailing the man. His next step was to report in and have that playwright fella picked up and questioned about the Yank he had met, then to go looking for him in earnest.

This is indeed what was to happen, but Connors' intentions did not effect these steps. Connors was surprised to find a man

163

in a well-cut suit standing with his back to him next to a tree. The man turned and stared at Connors. The face was indeed tanned. A mixture of pity and irritation animated it. Connors thought it was odd to see a man so well dressed standing there in the trees. Maybe he'd stopped for a piss, not knowing where there was a proper jacks. The man's hand came up abruptly from his side.

"Hey!" Connors said.

The man's hand jerked and Connors was falling back before he heard the *phutt*. As the back of Connors' head hit the clay, the sky's light became intolerable. He wondered how he could have been pushed from so far away. He remembered the lightness in his chest when he'd leap down into the hay. "Up and awaaay" his brother would shout, "Up and away."

Kilmartin listened to Minogue's voice over the phone.

"Yes, I'm just leaving Trinity. The idea is to throw the bits up in the air again and look at it all from a different angle."

"Yes, Matt. I follow."

"What about that lad you have, what's his name."

"Connors?"

"Yes. He's on the up and up, isn't he?"

"He's very quick, there's no doubt, Matt. Are you saying you want to give him a crack at this?"

"Yes. A fresh approach."

"Sorry now, but you'll have to take your turn. He's out on surveillance now if you don't mind. It's this murder out in Blackrock," Kilmartin said.

Minogue looked around. The foyer to the library was empty. Students kept office hours too, apparently. He felt chastened at having all but forgotten that other events took precedence over his concerns. Was this a sign of old age, retreating into one's own preoccupations?

"Well, do—"

Minogue heard clicks on the line as an operator interrupted.

"Inspector Kilmartin, line two. Hello?"

"Hello?" Kilmartin said.

"A priority call on line two, Inspector."

"Hold, Matt, you hear," Kilmartin said.

For thirty seconds Minogue listened to his own breath bristling through his nose into the mouthpiece. There was a faint smell of peppermint off the phone.

When Kilmartin spoke again, his voice was very different.

"Matt. Be over here directly now. Something has come up. Drop what you're doing immediately. We'll need all the manpower we can get."

CHAPTER FOURTEEN

Allen watched her balancing the coffee as she took the change from the cashier. She sat down across the table from him.

"You know best, I mean," she said.

"By half past, it should be O.K. It's just that I'm allergic to traffic jams," he said.

Agnes smiled.

"It'd surely spoil the impulse if we ended up in a traffic jam so it would," she agreed.

"Does your family know you're coming?" Allen asked.

"No. It'll be a surprise, I can tell you," Agnes sipped her coffee and sat back. Allen had watched her sling a packsack into the boot and had felt a strange thrill.

"Well," Allen said, "I decided to go tonight and not wait. They're expecting me tomorrow but . . . too much routine. How are the books, Agnes?"

"What a question," she smiled. "I shouldn't tell you. I forget you're one of them."

He laughed.

"Well, aren't you?" she teased.

"Oh come on now. This isn't school. You don't have to pretend," he said.

"Ach, I wonder. I could do with a break from the books."

"Sounds normal to me. You'll pick up again."

Agnes sipped at the brim of the cup speculatively.

"Yes. I know that. It's just that sometimes I think of the future, you know. Jobs and all that. It's better than thinking about the past," she said.

Allen smiled.

"I really like the placement though. That's real social work. When I started out I couldn't understand it, you know. People here—the South I mean—are so different from back home. I used to think they were worse off here sometimes."

"How do you mean?"

"They couldn't blame it on the troubles is what I mean. There's no reason for people to starve in Dublin, but they do."

Allen understood. Life had been whittled cleaner for people in the North. Their uncertainty was kept at bay by this constant involvement.

"You know, like you talk about rationalisation in your lectures? It's the national pastime really, isn't it?"

Allen laughed and nodded his head. She got straight to the point, he thought. Would he though? Later, after they crossed the border. Maybe her reserve was a defence to hide her feelings for him.

By the time Minogue reached Kilmartin's office, he had dropped his files once. He caught Kilmartin just as he was about to step out the door, followed by a uniformed sergeant. Kilmartin's face was tight.

"Put 'em away in my office," Kilmartin nodded at the papers under Minogue's arm. Minogue looked at the sergeant. He appeared to be angry. He was flicking car keys on his fingers. Minogue tripped out in their wake.

"As true as God, Matt, this is the limit. I'll do it myself if I have to."

"What?"

Kilmartin stopped abruptly and shouted.

"They've shot Connors. He's dead. They shot him."

Minogue could smell Kilmartin's breath. Later, Minogue would remember striding behind Kilmartin and his driver and sinking into the seat. The sergeant drove at speed with the siren on. He mounted footpaths and swore. His sweat smell permeated the car. Nobody spoke. The city looked hostile to Minogue as it sped by. Kilmartin sat looking out the opposite window. As they reached St. Stephen's Green, Minogue heard other sirens behind. Ahead of them, Gardai on motorcycles were shouting at motorists. Groups of pedestrians stood staring over at the growing numbers of police cars and vans.

There were fifty or more uniformed Gardai keeping an area free of gawkers. Minogue caught sight of a few faces he knew, plain clothes police. His tension increased. Those men were surely armed. The whole place was falling apart. The Green should have a few people strolling around, some youngsters necking, not this.

Detectives were unrolling red plastic, twining it around trees and shrubs to mark off the area. The body was gone.

"I'm Kilmartin."

A detective stood aside from a group and helloed Kilmartin. Minogue stood behind Kilmartin.

"Inspector—" the detective began.

"What I need to know is this," Kilmartin cut him off. "I need to know who did this. I don't care who or how many."

The detective looked over Kilmartin's shoulder at Minogue. Minogue began to understand why he had been brought along. He felt a tenderness for Kilmartin. Kilmartin could never say it, but he needed Minogue along because he, Kilmartin, was frightened. This was not Kilmartin's Ireland any more than it was Minogue's.

"I can tell you that there were no witnesses to the shooting, sir. He was shot once, it appears, in the chest. We haven't turned up a shell yet, so we don't know if it's an automatic. It looks like a fairly large calibre, sir."

The detective took a step back, glancing at Kilmartin and then at Minogue.

"Is one of these lads from the Branch?" asked Kilmartin. The detective frowned in puzzlement.

"The Special Branch. They're the ones who'd know who Connors was tailing. They borrowed him from me."

"Oh yes, sir." The detective turned and tapped one of the group on the shoulder. The man turned and looked at Kilmartin. The detective stood back, eying Kilmartin.

"Kelly, sir. You're Inspector Kilmartin?"

"Yes."

"We're looking for the fellow. You know him, McCarthy, that bloody playwright. He's not in his flat."

"Kelly, Tell me why a man seconded from my department was on a surveillance assignment on such a dangerous suspect."

Minogue saw Kilmartin's hands fist in his pockets.

"Sir, with respect, it's not like that. That McCarthy is the last fella to do this. It had to be something else, sir. He wouldn't have done that, sir."

"My arse for a yarn, Kelly," Kilmartin snapped.

Minogue heard the chatter from a handset the sergeant was carrying. Kelly looked down at the ground, then back at the rigid Kilmartin.

"Understand this, Kelly: when we finish our job, there'll be ructions. Unarmed Gardai are paying the bill with their lives for what's going on. I won't stand for that. Inspectors in other departments won't. Neither will the public. This is Dublin, the capital of Ireland, for fucks' sakes, not New York."

Minogue watched Kilmartin stalk away. He turned to look around and watch the men securing the plastic rail.

Kelly glanced at Minogue.

"He's right, you know. That fella in Blackrock and now this? Where's it all going to end."

"Are we talking about an organised series of killings here?" Minogue asked.

Kelly shook his head and looked over at Kilmartin, now holding a handset. What a place to die, Minogue was thinking.

The plastic-covered ID had slipped from the man's fingers. It lay face up on his chest. The tanned man saw the polaroid with some print to the left side. He felt suddenly seized, unable to move. A cop. *Jesus.*

The tanned man rolled off the silencer and buttoned his jacket. He walked to a path nearby and within two minutes was leaving the Green by an entrance which faced onto a taxi rank. He decided against taking a taxi. His back prickled in a sweat, vulnerable. Still he heard no shouts or sirens. Mentally he counted the people he had met as he left. An old woman who had fallen asleep in a chair. Two teenagers entwined, trying to walk on a path.

The rush hour had eased to the degree that cars were moving into third gear between traffic lights. He walked across to the College of Surgeons and turned right toward Grafton Street. He had to work hard at not running. He knew that he had to get in the hotel and then out as soon as possible. They'd find McCarthy.

The tanned man stepped into a pub and went to the Gents. In the remaining fraction of a mirror, he saw his own face, strange and wide-eyed. He could not stop his hands from shaking. He did some belly breathing. Then he combed his hair and straightened his tie. He checked for any mud on the sides of his shoes. He went back outside and bought a newspaper. He tucked it under his arm and, taking a deep breath, strolled toward the Shelbourne Hotel. And still there was no sign that anyone but he knew that there was a body lying under the trees not two hundred yards from where he was walking.

"Picked him up then?" Kilmartin said into the microphone. "Pearse Street station?"

"Well, tell them I'll be there. I want in on this."

The sergeant jammed the car into the traffic and headed down Kildare Street. Kilmartin turned to Minogue.

"Yes. They found what's-his-face, McCarthy, him in a pub. O'Neill's. So they took him in for questioning in Pearse Street."

Minogue still found it hard to believe where he was and what he was doing. He should be phoning home. What was for tea? Did he have to buy sausages? Connors was dead, dead.

"That was quick," Minogue said, trying to fan away the fear.

"He'd better have something for us quick. Those boyos from the Branch may be full of fancy footwork, counter-terrorist this and counter-terrorist that, but I'll wager they won't know how to make do with this fella."

Minogue knew that the Special Branch could be extra-legal and they could get away with it. They'd be all the more urgent because it looked as if they hadn't looked after a policeman who had been on loan to them: faulty intelligence had occluded the danger, bad work.

Kilmartin's fear and anger were not abating. They had grasped his guts, squeezed and held. A vast indigestion had control of him. He couldn't fathom what had happened, no more than Minogue. His neck and shoulders were knotted. He wanted to shout, to hit someone. For an instant he recalled a mannerism of Connors and it tightened his chest. In desperation, he turned to the sergeant driving.

"Coincidence be damned, hah?"

The sergeant looked over and said gruffly,

"That's too much to swallow, sir. I know that fella Kehoe out in Blackrock. I know his parents too. I'm thinking we have to decide who's running the bloody country, them or us?"

Kilmartin wasn't listening. The sergeant's eyes sought Minogue in the mirror.

Speeding and braking along Pearse Street, Minogue saw a dirty, heartless city. The sergeant swore aloud and bullied the engine, himself a countryman trying to wrestle with this brooding dump.

Minogue recognised the playwright. He looked younger than his years, preserved by a fanatic's purity. He didn't look in the least intimidated. A knot of policemen cluttered the corridor, a mixture of Special Branch, uniformed and hard chaws from the Technical Bureau. Minogue saw the door close on the playwright and two plain clothes.

"This way men," a desk sergeant said. "Come on now, it's set up for sound so ye can listen over beyond."

Minogue saw resentment burning in Kilmartin's face. They sat in the briefing room along with three others who nodded and produced notebooks.

"Tea, lads?" the genial desk sergeant said.

They listened to preliminaries. McCarthy was not going to be manhandled in this session with the mikes on.

"You're obliged to tell me under what Section I'm being held," the playwright said.

"You'll be told sometime during the next forty-eight hours. Where were you this afternoon?"

"Where you found me. In a pub."

"How long?"

"How long does it take to drink two pints of ale?" the playwright asked.

He's enjoying this, Minogue realised. A threshold hiss came across the speakers. The men in the room looked at one another. The sergeant stepped in with a tray of tea.

"Technical problems, lads?" he said and smiled.

No one replied.

The hiss stopped and they heard the playwright's voice again.

"You shouldn't have done that. That'll show. This isn't Guatemala you know. Or Belfast," the playwright said. The men in the room heard him breathing out of turn.

"What time did you get in?"

"About a quarter past four."

"Anybody see you come in?"

"I was with friends. You can ask them."

"Where were you before that?"

"I was in another pub."

"Where?"

"The Bailey."

"With who?"

"With anybody, is who. No one specific. I do the rounds."

"Name any of them."

"Ah, they're regulars, I hardly know their surnames. What am I supposed to have done?"

"How long were you in the Bailey?"

"I don't know. A half hour, three quarters. Since after the Holy Hour. I moved on. There was no one there of any interest."

"You know the barmen there?"

"Yes."

"Who was on?"

"I don't know their names."

"He saw you come in?"

"Well, he said hello."

"Who did you talk to?"

"There was no one there really. The regulars had moved on. I caught up with them in O'Neill's. It's a moveable feast."

"Nobody?"

The playwright didn't answer for a moment. Then he said,

"I know what you want. You want to know about that Garda that was killed the other day in Blackrock. You're going at in a roundabout way, aren't you?"

"Shut up and answer the question."

"I hadn't planned on meeting anyone specifically. Is that the right answer?" Minogue stood up and left the room. He dialled home from a phone on the front desk.

"I'll be kind of late, sorry."

"What's up, Matt?" Kathleen asked.

"Well. You'll find out sooner or later. A Garda was shot. Another one. I'm with Jimmy Kilmartin. We're sort of observing right now. He'll be wanting me for something, I'm sure."

Minogue's ear prickled against the phone. He listened to the

173

sound of his wife breathing. He could hear the radio in the background.

Barely audible, she said, "All right so."

"I'll be all right now. Don't worry. Leave it in the oven for me, whatever it is."

By the time they reached Swords, Allen noticed that Agnes had relaxed into the seat.

"Let the seat back if you want," he said.

She smiled.

Allen thought that this must be what a honeymoon couple felt, the man at least. He wanted to believe that they belonged like this, she sitting beside him in the car, not needing to talk. If his instincts were right, soon they'd be laughing about it. She would laugh and say, 'And I thought it was only me.' Or would she?

Sleepily, Agnes said, "You don't have to drive me to Belfast you know. I can get the bus from Newry. What's the point, you have to drive back to Newry again. Really."

"It's nothing, Agnes," Allen said, relishing the echoed name in his memory. "I'm a day early. I'll probably stay over in Belfast anyway."

"I write plays and articles. Didn't you read my file? I talk to anyone and everyone."

Minogue sat down again. Over the speaker he heard someone walking, opening a door and then closing it. Minogue recognised one of the two plain clothes who had been in the room with the playwright.

Without being asked, one of the men at the table said,

"Can't tell. He knows the routine, that's the thing."

The other at the table nodded. Kilmartin folded his arms.

"Check with the barmen and his pals anyway."

Kilmartin cleared his throat and said in a quiet voice,

"Tell him why he's here. He won't be expecting that. Just tell him."

"I don't think he did it either," Kilmartin continued, "but I'll

174

bet that our patriotic bloody playwright will see he's in over his head with this. The man is a complete hypocrite. He's probably never been in on a shooting or the like in his life. Tell him. Put the fear of God in him and stop farting around. We don't have too much time if whoever did it is on the move."

Plain clothes left the room. They heard him returning to the interview room.

"We're holding you on suspicion of murder. A Garda officer was murdered today in the middle of Dublin. Murder of a Garda, who's in the course of his duty, is a capital offence in this state. You'll be tested for evidence that you discharged a firearm recently—"

"You'll find out then that I didn't," the playwright interrupted.

"You won't be able to worm out of being an accomplice. Same thing in the end and you'll not find the climate too sympathetic when it comes to sentencing. Judges don't like policemen being shot dead."

"You're out of your mind," the playwright said slowly.

There was a minute's silence over the speaker.

"Anything to add, McCarthy?"

Minogue listened keenly. When the playwright spoke, Minogue felt a mixture of relief and loathing. McCarthy had lived up to Kilmartin's expectations. He had realised that the rules had changed. Like Kilmartin and Minogue, this was suddenly not his Ireland either.

"Look. I meet all kinds of people. I didn't know I was being followed. There's plenty of lunatics out there. There's this fellow who started to tell me his story. He's an American. Said he knew of me and wanted to get in touch with republicans or something. I tried to give him the brush. Who knows what kind of a nutcase he might be?"

Minogue's sixth sense told him this was only part of it. McCarthy was parcelling out bits to sell off.

"I don't know the first thing about him."

"How did you meet him?"

"He came over to me in the pub."

175

Minogue saw Kilmartin shaking his head slowly. He wondered what infinitesimal signs had brought Kilmartin to the same conclusion as himself that McCarthy was lying. There was something else to it.

"Just walked over? Never saw him before?"

"Never."

"Describe him."

"Youngish, I'd say. He'd be in his late thirties. He dresses fancy, sort of."

"A man with no name?"

"Never told me a name. I didn't ask. I could care less what his name is."

Kilmartin turned to the detectives listening to the speaker.

"What's the story on the business in Blackrock?" he asked.

"We've picked up more suspects off the lists anyway. No sign of the actual killers, but they have to turn up somewhere. They might steal a car or turn up at a house under surveillance," one of the detectives replied cagily.

"See any links with today?" Kilmartin murmured.

No one answered. This is the belief, Minogue thought, that is why nobody can say it.

"The place is full of Yanks, that's the thing. It'd be like McCarthy to work up an imaginary Yank to explain everything," the Special Branch man said.

"Yes, but what kind of a Yank would pull a stunt like this? Assuming this Yank really exists at all and McCarthy isn't spinning out rope for someone else's neck . . . ?"

Kilmartin's belly ached. It was like someone had stabbed him. He stole a glance at Minogue. No awkwardness rubbed against them now. They listened again to the speaker.

"How do you know he was American?"

"Accent."

"Drawl? New York maybe?"

"I don't know anything about that. He didn't sound like a cowboy."

"Where is he staying?"

176

"Jases, I don't know. He just came up to me out of the blue," the playwright replied.

"How did he know to go to you?"

"How would I know? Maybe I have fans out there and they put him my way."

"What did he talk to you about? You said he wanted to meet republicans."

"Said he wanted to write a piece on the Troubles here. Wanted to get 'the real story,' he says. I told him to shag off but he kept on yapping and asking me things."

"What things?"

"It's hard to know where to start . . . "

The playwright was back in role now, Minogue thought. The confidence was returning to him. He was off acting again. The wall between his inner landscape and the real world had collapsed years ago. Maybe he wanted drama, anything on the blade edge of life whether it was to do with guns or props. But this man sounded normal, even witty. As sane as the next man. Yet he didn't keep budgies or go along with superstitions or worship the sun: he was part of an organisation that killed people. Is that what mad means, when you can't tell the difference anymore?

Minogue's chest leadened when he felt the truth of this. He thought of Dublin in the fifties, moribund and discoloured. No wonder there was so much emigration. This fool had emigrated all right, but inwardly: he had willed his life away to The Cause.

"What exactly did he say, then?"

"I don't remember his exact words."

"Try."

"Like I said, he said he wanted to meet republicans."

"Why?"

"Just to meet them. To do a story on them, I suppose."

"What were his interests?"

"I don't know. Maybe a tourist looking for excitement."

"Married?"

"How would I know?"

"A ring?"

177

"Didn't look."

This could go on for hours and it would. He was lying, probably buying some time for this fellow. Give away a little so they believe the big lies.

Kilmartin leaned back, balancing on the back legs of the chair and said, "Well, are ye out looking?"

"Hotels, airports and ferries, sir. The whole bit," a Special Branch man answered.

"So. It appears to me that a) there's enough truth in this business about an American to allow us to bugger up by wasting time; b) there's some element of betrayal here. McCarthy would like to spill all the beans, but then he'd be a marked man if he sold someone out. McCarthy understands the business about being implicated in a capital offence so he'll let go stuff a bit at a time."

"Time's the thing," the Special Branch man echoed.

"I'm thinking," Kilmartin said slowly, "that you fellas charged with pursuing this investigation in the murder of one of my men should find some way to eliminate this time factor. This would effect a speedy resolution, I'm thinking."

No one answered. Although the interrogation went on over the speaker, Minogue believed that no one was listening anymore. Pencils were being fingered and shoes observed.

"Go over your description again."

"Medium height. He wore a suit," the playwright answered. He was talking too readily, Minogue understood. A command performance.

"And . . . ?"

"There was nothing special about him. In his thirties."

"Eyes?"

"I dunno. I suppose they were blue."

"Balding?"

"No he had a full head of hair. Trimmed, looked after."

Kilmartin seemed to be examining his fingernails minutely. Minogue wondered how many Americans would be in the country at this time of year. Thousands?

CHAPTER FIFTEEN

He slipped the Canadian passport into the inside pocket of his jacket. Again he checked his recall on the dates and events of his new self. He didn't need an inbound airline ticket stub because Professor Levesque had come across as a foot passenger from Holyhead and he had one-wayed it to London from New York on a cheap flight.

He looked at himself in the mirror. Above the glasses, his hair was parted more to the centre now. The light Gore Tex jacket and the lumberjack shirt added to a stereotype. Behind him, he noticed the suitcase he'd be leaving. Inside, neatly folded, was his suit. Everything else had fitted into the shoulder bag. For a few seconds he wondered if he had omitted anything from the routine. Yes, he had gone over the bathroom fixtures; the television, the suitcase. O.K. He turned and allowed his eyes to take in the room. The window? Yes. Door? Yes. Glasses or bottles? Gone.

He couldn't afford to worry about things like a hair in the

bathroom. He zipped the bag. As he bent over, he felt the gun detach itself slightly from his chest. That'd have to go too but after he was on the boat. They could bellyache all they wanted about the trouble it was to get one for him and then him just dumping it. Bellyache, he thought, snared for a moment on memory. His father had used that word often. When he had cried on their first visit to his boarding school, his father had grabbed him by the arm:

"Don't bellyache. You'll look back and thank us."

When he got clear, he'd find a way to do for McCarthy.

Kilmartin stood up.

"Gentlemen, I'll be staying in the station here while you listen on to this drivel. If you have any news for me, kindly relay it to me within the next half hour. Anything after that will be all but useless, I'm thinking."

Minogue saw embarrassment on the men's faces. They nodded. Minogue joined Kilmartin as he turned and walked through the door. As he closed the door behind him, Kilmartin murmured:

"Well, do you think they have the idea?"

Minogue didn't answer. Their driver, the sergeant, was leaning on the back of a chair in the canteen, smoking. The desk sergeant, who had come off duty but was hanging around for news, sat opposite.

"More tea, men?" he said

Minogue and Kilmartin declined.

"The back of the neck is what it is," their driver continued, putting out smoke as he talked.

"'Yank' my arse. Leading us up the garden path, he is," he muttered.

The off-duty sergeant nodded.

The talk dried up. Other policemen came and went in the canteen. When Minogue looked at his watch, twenty minutes had passed. He had thought of asking the driver for one of his cigarettes. Before he did, one of the three men who had sat with them listening to the questioning came in. He walked to their table. Kilmartin looked up sardonically.

"Well? Has the cow calved?"

"Sir. If you could step into the room beyond, we can brief you."

Kilmartin and Minogue returned. No sounds came over the speaker. So that was what they'd done, Minogue thought.

"The suspect has informed us that he believes this American may have more, er, significance than was first thought, sir."

"Go on," said Kilmartin.

"McCarthy stresses his minimal knowledge and involvement."

"And all the rest of it," Kilmartin said grimly.

"But he understands that the American is here to do with some transporting of something or other to the North."

"What exactly does that mean?" Kilmartin's voice rose.

"His guess is that this man is involved in weapons."

Kilmartin snorted and headed for the door.

"Let me talk to Mr Shakespeare and we'll have it out in detail. I know how to deal with the likes of him," he hissed.

The Special Branch officer moved to stop him and Minogue heard the man call out:

"That isn't possible right now, sir."

Kilmartin wheeled around and looked at him, then to Minogue.

"McCarthy is indisposed at the moment, sir. Fainted."

Kilmartin stared at the nervous officer blocking his way.

"But we have a better description of this Yank, sir."

"This hypothetical Yank, you mean. My money's on some gun-happy slug down from the North and Connors came on him."

"And thinks the Yank mentioned something about the Shelbourne Hotel, sir."

Kilmartin stepped back and looked to Minogue. Minogue noted the glimmer in Kilmartin's surly gaze now.

"Maybe there is something to this Yank then . . . " Kilmartin said.

"They'll know him at the Shelbourne, sir, if he's staying there. Nothing as sharp as a good desk-man in a fancy hotel, is there,

181

sir?" the detective said, mollifying. His efforts did not break the cast of skepticism on Kilmartin's face.

Just before they reached Drogheda, a glaring sun appeared from between the evening clouds. It flooded the car with gold. It ran along beside the car, through the trees and the bushes, full on Agnes when they had fields to the west of them. Allen knew they wouldn't meet the sea again until close to Dundalk. By then it would be dark. Agnes' eyes were closed. He smelled a faint perfume in the car. The light set her hair a-dazzle.

Under the trees and in the ditches the shadows were broadening out. Already the sun couldn't get over a hedge here, the roof of a house there. Where the sun still hit fields, the green was luminous. They passed a tinker camp, the men on hunkers next to a fire. Every second or third vehicle was a lorry. The edges of the road were greyed by their passing. Sometimes Allen would find the mirror filled with the dinosaur front of an eighteen-wheeler, out of nowhere. When they stopped for petrol, the boy stood by the car looking over the inside, curious about Agnes.

"A good evening for travelling now," he said. "There'll be no rain."

"How do you know?" Allen said.

"Oh sure we've had our ration for the week. Sure wasn't it a terrible week? Wasn't I drownded myself here several times in the one day," the boy answered.

Allen heard Michael Jackson coming through the half open door beyond the pumps.

"I suppose," said Allen, "you might have something there."

When Allen sat back in the car, Agnes said:

"Where are we?"

"Near Drogheda. It'll be dark soon," Allen replied. "God," Agnes said yawning "Drogheda. This is the longest road in Ireland so it is."

Agnes looked out at the town. Already some streetlights were glowing purple, a prelude to the glare of yellowy light which disfigured towns all over Ireland. The sun was gone now. Overhead, puff carpets of grey clouds showed pink edges. The world was straining toward the west. As the car passed pubs, she saw shadows and soft lights in the windows. The shops and super-markets were busy. Cars parked up on the kerb. Agnes thought of what Jarlath would have done tonight. He'd have suggested a foreign film probably. Reluctantly, Agnes would have agreed to go along. His callowness would make her feel guilty. Then she remembered that she had arranged to avoid a date with him by going to a friend's flat. She didn't want to go there, but she didn't want to encourage Jarlath either. An icy breath ran through her chest. To think that this could have happened. Was it only sinking in now?

She forced herself to think of Tuscany. A moon would be up. The stone walls would be warm. The sky would be full of stars. She could sleep in a barn or in the fields to be awakened at dawn. That was the way to live, sleeping from dusk to dawn. None of those noises at night, the sirens or the floodlights. *La Luna, mi amore.*

"Daydreaming, Agnes?" said Allen.

She glanced at him. What was different about him? She was too used to seeing him deliver lectures.

"A bit, I suppose."

"You think being restless is exclusively the preserve of persons under twenty-five? Or perhaps a sign of early senility?"

"Aye. We all could do with a break," she said.

Agnes thought of the city waiting for her, her bedroom, the telly with the news blaring out one more miserable day for the city. She had trouble remembering her father's face, seeing only the crumbling face of her mother. With no warning, her mother could be stricken helpless with crying. Watching T.V., reading a book or eating, her mother's face would suddenly contort. Agnes understood it was the commonplace things that could upset her, the vertiginous understanding that her husband was dead. No shaving soap in the bathroom, no other person in bed, no need to make sure the toast wasn't underdone. Agnes could comfort her mother again and again, but the weight seemed to increase.

Sometimes she felt that she was nothing, neither young or old. When would it all end?

The sergeant started up the car. Minogue sat in the front passenger seat. He felt Kilmartin's impatience as a palpable weight in the car. Minogue noticed that the sergeant's uniform was spotted with cigarette ash. His breath came across stale, penetrating.

"Well, the Branch didn't so much say it as let it be known," Kilmartin began. "They got a phone call. Somebody claiming that there's going to be a car going north with weapons aboard. Tomorrow. They think it might have to do with that other car or cars in that garage."

Minogue contented himself with looking out at the dusk over College Green.

"They know the heat's on. I don't doubt they want results fast," Kilmartin murmured.

"Yes," Minogue allowed. He was tired. Drifting through the traffic made him sleepy.

"They've bought into McCarthy's Yank business anyway. I still have me doubts. Yank or not, you can't persuade me there isn't a connection though," Kilmartin said.

"What?" Minogue said reflexively.

"The shooting in Blackrock. The place is gone to hell in a wheelbarrow. I can see the news tonight and the bloody headlines: *'Murderers still at large,' 'Armed men on the rampage in Dublin,' 'Gardai draw a blank in search for killers.'*"

"You think the same people are involved," Minogue said.

"Maybe not the actual same people. Did I tell you we got a rocket about being alert for new types of weapons and a new network for getting them in? That's what has the Branch looking for this mysterious Yank and taking crank calls seriously. The fella who called described a car that sounds like the one in the garage. And the way McCarthy was hinting about arms smuggling got them going in a big way," Kilmartin said.

"Well in anyhow: the other thing is a no-go. Those two fellas have gone to ground. Between me and you and the wall—" Kilmartin nodded in the direction of the sergeant's head, "—those shaggers are back in the North by now."

"Signs on," Minogue said.

"And as for the thing about the garage, well I'm sure we closed it down before anything became operational. I say it was a mistake to raid it," Kilmartin said.

Minogue elbowed onto the seat and turned to Kilmartin. He was wary of the sergeant driving because he would be all ears, like anyone else, for an inspector's candour. Minogue imagined the sergeant going home to his wife: 'Wait 'til I tell you what I heard today . . .'

Minogue was surprised to find himself alert. He noticed that Kilmartin was frowning at him. The front gate of Trinity College fell away behind the car, as the sergeant wheeled the car around into Dame Street.

Minogue's knees began to itch. He strained further to look out the back window at Trinity College receding behind them. It looked magical, a place apart. The lights gave it an air of churchiness. Students emerged from the archway, out onto the centre of a city which Minogue believed had gone mad. They could always go back in to the squares and the classic proportions, to the insulated clarity of that island. Stone buildings and edged lawns answered the bullydom of Ireland. But no: that was false, too facile. Minogue was thinking as a peasant. In the week he had been in and out of the university, he had felt it had a vulnerability, despite the intellectual and physical architecture which held it in place. No amount of pretty young girls with baskets on the handlebars of their old bikes could stop history. No amount of paintings hanging down over the dining tables could exempt this place from the present.

Agnes McGuire carrying her terrible burdens. Mick Roche trying to work through the place, not cynical enough to give up on the well-to-do students there. And Allen, for all his academic manner, he was trying in his own way to change things. Was he jealous of Allen? Minogue recalled Agnes smiling briefly as she went off in Allen's car, under his care. Maybe it was that he,

Minogue, had felt stuck on the sidelines again, a spectator to events, with Allen's swanky car hissing away to the funeral in the rain. Allen's car: Jesus, Mary and Joseph . . .

"Pull over here, if you please, Sergeant," Minogue said.

Kilmartin was staring at Minogue.

"That other car in that garage. You said whoever called gave a description which might match that one in the garage."

"The Mercedes, the canary yoke," Kilmartin said.

"No. The other one,"

"We don't know. A Japanese car, fancy, was the best we got on the one in the garage."

"And the one in the tip-off?"

"I don't know. A Branch man just told me it was awful like the description of the other one," replied Kilmartin.

"Are there any reports of stolen cars of that type?"

"Now, Matt, you know as well as I do . . . "

"But it was checked against the reported stolens, wasn't it?"

"No doubt. But, here, hold on a minute Matt. The one in the garage might have been legit anyway, a fella fixing a car. Anything. It was only that oul lad thinking he saw one. Let the Branch worry about it."

The sergeant was assiduously trying to prove he was deaf. Minogue opened the door.

"Sergeant, could I ask you a favour, please."

The driver's head shifted around.

"Anything I can do, Detective Sergeant."

"Would you find out what you can on the radio about this car business. Inspector Kilmartin here will furnish details."

"But Matt," Kilmartin leaned over to look under the roof as Minogue stepped out onto the kerb.

"That can wait. We have this thing on the boil."

"Sure what can we do about this evening, Jimmy, except, kill time waiting for something?" Minogue said.

He had actually been reprimanding in his tone, the driver realised. Now if he himself tried that with an Inspector . . .

186

"I'll be back in a few minutes," Minogue said. He began striding down the footpath toward Trinity.

As if Minogue's new-found vigour had by default led him to lassitude, Kilmartin slouched in the back seat listening to the driver. He was becoming aware that Minogue was more than merely contrary. Because Minogue did what he had just done so rarely, it appeared almost aggressive. Kilmartin decided he needed some time in the near future to sort out how to deal with Minogue. The sergeant was stroking his neck in anticipation of a reply on the radio.

"Takes 'em long enough," the sergeant muttered.

Kilmartin idly watched two drunken men staggering arm-in-arm down Dame Street. They didn't even notice the police car.

Then Minogue was climbing into the front seat, breathing heavily.

"'A magenta Toyota Cressida,' he said."

"What?" said Kilmartin.

"It's a magenta Toyota Cressida. It's on its way north tonight."

"What are you saying?" asked Kilmartin.

"All this talk of a big Japanese car. I was thinking about that McGuire girl, the Walsh boy's girlfriend. Allen gave her a lift to the funeral in a fancy car, I'm sure it was a Toyota, and I think it was a magenta colour. You know, the one you don't know if it's crimson or purple. I could kick meself, so I could."

"But how in the name of Jas—" Kilmartin began.

"—I asked one of the porters, one of the fellas who works in the college. He checked the parking passes off a list."

A voice yowled on the radio.

"No reported thefts of that type. A magnet . . . a magan— a magenta Toyota Cressida or Datsun. Over."

"Tell them," Minogue said. His wide eyes bored into Kilmartin's.

"Hold on a minute," Kilmartin leaned over. "Tell them what?"

"The suspect car is heading for the border."

"But the tip-off was for tomorrow, Matt."

The driver looked to Kilmartin.

"Over," the radio said.

"Allen has a car like that. He's gone up north to deliver a lecture. He left a day early. He's the one."

Kilmartin's frown bit deep into his forehead.

"The professor fella who does the peace lectures?"

"Allen. Dublin registration. A Professor Allen."

He ate in McDonalds in Grafton Street. His throat was still tight, barely letting food down. The restaurant was full. He looked around and realised that almost all the customers were young people. The older folks didn't trust hamburgers. So this was freedom and progress. He looked down at the shoulder bag under the table and he thought back to his exit from the hotel. The shift had changed for the evening and he hadn't been noticed. He had peeled off the moustache in an alley. The glasses irritated the bridge of his nose. He could discard them later.

The food tasted the same as stateside. Near the bottom of his coffee cup, he decided that he should try to get out tonight from Dun Laoghaire. There was nothing else for it. Either he left tonight or he waited for a week or two. His disguise was foolproof up to the point of someone checking when he had entered the country. They'd never go that far.

He stepped back out onto Grafton Street and crossed onto the footpath which led to the Front Gate of Trinity College. Busses and cars swept by him. The lights of shops spilled out over the path opposite. He remembered that the ferry left at nine o'clock.

He felt quite alone for the first time since he had landed. This bothered him all the more when he wondered as he passed people if they knew he was carrying a gun or that he had killed someone. There was no one he could phone or say goodbye to. This is absurd, he thought: get some control. Nothing would be served by an attack of nostalgia on top of the fear. As he passed the front of the college, he noticed a police car turning into Dame Street. The doubts began to creep in again. What could McCarthy tell them if he was picked up? His thoughts turned to wondering how much surveillance there would be at the dock in Dun Laoghaire. Had they installed a metal detector there since he got the O.K.?

Ahead of him, the bustle of O'Connell Street lit up the bridge. A tinker woman with a baby shawled next to her breast sat by a cardboard box on O'Connell Bridge.

"A few ha'pence, sir, to feed the child," she said.

He walked by her thinking of O'Connell, the Liberator, with beggars in his liberated land. In the distance he heard a siren. It came from behind him, from College Green and it faded quickly.

As the police car sped up Dame Street, Minogue watched the red light spilling and wiping along the buildings. The siren seemed to vibrate inside the car. For a few moments he wondered if this was real at all. In five minutes he'd be aloft in a helicopter from Dublin Castle on the way to the border. Ridiculous, to be sure. Was that him who shouted at Kilmartin to get him a place on it with the Special Branch men? And why had he insisted so? He wanted to see Allen's face, to tell him something, not to ask him questions. Minogue didn't know what it was that he should tell Allen. His mind struggled, looking for a grip on some words.

"Have you ever been up in one of those things before?" Kilmartin asked.

"Never in my life," replied Minogue.

The car shuddered over the kerb and stopped abruptly at the gate to Dublin Castle. Walls loomed over the car. A uniformed Garda walked over to the car. The driver knew him. The Garda nodded his head and returned to the booth. The barrier lifted soundlessly.

"Who owns it?" Minogue asked.

"Who else but the bloody army. They can get what they want these days."

Minogue stepped stiffly from the car. He was excited and nervous at the prospect of being whisked away into the night in this contraption. Kilmartin called out to him and he paused. Kilmartin half lay on the seat looking out under the window at Minogue. Looked like a child, Minogue thought.

"Matt. Don't bite any of your company in that whirlygig thing. Remember you're on the trip on sufferance. I'm a bit out of order insisting on you going along so don't poison the well for me. The Branch men will make the arrest and have him driven back to Dundalk most likely. I'll be arranging from this end that they give you a few minutes with him. You know this fella better than I do."

"So: observe," Minogue said

"Now you have it."

Minogue recognised one of the men who had sat with him in Pearse Street listening to McCarthy. He walked over to Minogue.

"Are you the one who hit the button on this?" he said.

"Sort of, " said Minogue, anticipating trouble.

"Be the living jases you must be some kind of magician. Would a bit of it rub off on me now?" he said.

Minogue smiled despite the excitement. It felt like he hadn't smiled for days. He fleetingly recalled the moments in Bewley's, the talk around the tea-table at home: worlds away.

He followed the Special Branch men out through the building to a tarmacadam pad. Eerily, a light helicopter sat there. To Minogue it looked like a big insect. Its blades were claws, its Plexiglass screen a giant eye. Two men in jogging suits stood next to it, smoking. In the floodlights the smoke writhed Hallowe'enish toward the machine. Both men looked up when Minogue and his companion neared the helicopter. Just like that, Minogue was thinking. We're going to walk into this thing, like a bus. One of the two eased into the seat and switched on what sounded like a ventilator fan.

"Are we right?" the other said.

"As right as we'll ever be," the Special Branch said. He looked at Minogue and said,

"It'll be cold, er . . . "

"Minogue. Matt Minogue. I'll be all right. How long will this yoke take?"

"We'll be landed and sitting in the customs post within fifty minutes. Less even."

190

"Be the hokey fly," Minogue marvelled. What was that expression? 'I have seen the future and . . . ?'

As the craft lifted and bowed away over the city, Minogue was again stunned. It was incomprehensible that no wires held this thing up. The city was completely changed from here. It fell away under the belly of the helicopter like glowing embers of a coal fire. To the east the sea was in blue darkness. Ahead of them, then veering away, he saw runway lights at the airport. Minute moving lights of cars pulsed along the veins of this thing below. The lights petered out as they tended to the mountains. Minogue sat between the pilot and the Special Branch man. It felt as if he were in their care. The helmeted pilot was shockingly casual about it all, drawing lightly on the stick, commenting into the stalk microphone which stuck out from the gladiator helmet. Over the rotor noise, the Special Branch man shouted.

"I'm Scully, Pat Scully. I forgot."

Minogue nodded vigorously. This was like a carnival. He tried to identify the constellation of lights ahead of him. Swords? It occurred to him that he wasn't exactly sure what would be happening when they landed. Would they pick up Allen along the road or would they wait until the border? They had time, just about though. The porter at the Pearse Street Gate in Trinity said that Allen had taken his car about an hour ago. He couldn't have made it by then. He'd know better than to try an unapproved road especially after dark. Roving patrols of the British Army and SAS were on the move after dark.

"What's the story up ahead?" Minogue shouted into Scully's ear.

"We're all set up," Scully replied.

What did that mean? Minogue returned to thinking out the possible outcomes. Did Allen know? Allen would not hand over his car like that. It hadn't been stolen so Allen must have voluntarily given it over. Could it all be a coincidence though? What was there in it for Allen?

The pilot reached over and tipped Scully on the knee, then he pointed to a headset. Scully put it on. Minogue lip read the pilot saying 'go ahead.' Scully searched for a volume control but giving up, cupped hands over his ears. As he listened, he nodded several times. Then he said O.K. He looked over at the pilot who nodded once. Minogue noticed the pilot glancing quickly at him and then back to Scully.

"The car has been spotted. This side of Castlebellingham. Plenty of time," Scully shouted.

Minogue looked out over a town, marooned in light. A slash in the sky to the west was flooding a scarlet ribbon in the grey.

"Drogheda," the pilot said, pointing.

"There's someone else in the car."

"What?" said Minogue, leaning.

"There's someone else in the car. A woman," Scully shouted.

"What's the plan?" Minogue asked.

"We'll stick to the original," Scully announced and turned to look at the town passing below. Minogue looked out too. He followed car lights on the outskirts of town. They looked like a video game. A woman. Minogue's heart stopped, then a cold wash fell down through his chest. No, it couldn't be.

Minogue nudged Scully.

"Where will they be picked up?" he shouted. Scully paused before answering.

"At the border."

Minogue felt an alarm, like waking in the night to a strange sound. He stared at the side of Scully's face. Scully turned again.

"The situation on the ground," Scully shouted. "It may change. We have to be ready," he added, and returned to looking out over the Belfast road. Any minute now, they'd be overtaking the car.

The cold was biting into Minogue's shoes and under his chin. He no longer noticed the noise. He began to count but his heart was racing. He thought of Ravel and the tea at home in the oven waiting for him. Allen's face kept interrupting his images. Then he saw Agnes McGuire's face clearly in the darkness below.

CHAPTER SIXTEEN

Agnes sat up on the seat as they slowed, entering Dundalk.

"They called it El Paso, the locals," she murmured.

"I shouldn't wonder," Allen replied.

"Doesn't look bad at night, does it?" Agnes said.

Allen guessed it was eight miles from the border, give or take.

"Tell me, Agnes, do you get nervous crossing the border? Going North, I mean."

"I'm going home, so I am. What's to be nervous about?"

Touché, thought Allen. Stop treating her like she's wounded. As they pulled away from a traffic light, Allen noticed a car parked in a sidestreet. It was half up on the kerb. A double yellow line ran under the car. Briefly he noted the outline of two figures in it. He caught a momentary glint of an antenna as he accelerated through the junction.

"I suppose 'irritated' is the word. I don't like men with guns and costumes or uniforms looking at me. It's all so silly. Sometimes you forget it's serious. I find myself laughing, then crying," Agnes said.

Part of Allen's mind discounted what he had seen. Dundalk was a border town so you'd expect police.

"It's like a game, isn't it?" Agnes murmured.

That had to be routine here. He looked in the mirror but no car emerged from the street.

"Yes. I suppose," Allen replied.

That was the way it had been those years ago, a game. At least that was how he looked at it. In an instant he had felt the full weight of an adult world when the girl's parents opened the door to the garage. He had run, but he knew that he could run nowhere but home. Despite admitting it to the policeman who sat in the kitchen chair where his father used to sit, his mother kept saying it was impossible, that she knew her own son. She didn't listen at all.

Allen felt the beginnings of a headache grasping the back of his neck. Of course he was nervous, he couldn't deny that. Which was he more nervous about, asking her, or facing these soldiers and RUC at the border?

"Are you O.K?" Agnes was asking.

"Oh. Yes. Just tired, that's all," he replied.

Minogue followed Scully over to an unmarked car. Behind him the blades were slowing and the monster was bathed in light. His legs felt like pieces of wood. The blower was on in the car. The driver reminded Minogue of Connors. A creased coat, the shirt half out of his pants probably.

"I'm Scully. Sergeant Minogue here is along for the ride. He's investigating a link here."

"Geraghty, sir. I'm to take yous to the customs post."

So they were going to wait, Minogue thought. That was odd.

"Away, so, Geraghty. What kind of time do we have?" Scully asked.

"The suspects are in Dundalk, sir. They're probably ten minutes back the road."

"Timing, hah?" Scully said, rubbing his hands.

"Were they waiting for us before they make the pick up?" Minogue tried.

Scully didn't answer. Minogue felt his tension edge into anger.

"Who's the other suspect?" he said.

"A woman, sir," Geraghty answered, suddenly aware of a brittle atmosphere.

"Reddish hair, young?"

"We don't know, sir," Geraghty said cautiously.

Traffic was light as they passed the sign for the border. Minogue remembered Kilmartin's injunction to him about meddling. Scully turned to him and said:

"Not to worry, Sergeant, everything will go well."

The mention of his rank skittered away in Minogue's mind. A warning? The floodlights at the customs post ahead filled up the windscreen. A lorry was parked off to the side, facing south. Minogue could see figures in the shed through the screens. They pulled up on the gravel behind the shed. Minogue noticed two cars and a Land Rover in the shadows. It'd be the same up the road, he guessed, on the Northern side. RUC armed and some soldiers off to the side of the road; invisible from within the arena of floodlights. Minogue stepped out of the car. He felt ropey.

Scully walked over to the car and began talking in the window. Minogue heard a man laugh. The car creaked on its suspension. The lorry which had been parked drove off. No other vehicles could be heard. Minogue saw a movement in the shadows behind the customs shed, then another. He recognised the outlines of soldiers carrying automatic rifles.

Headlights appeared, coming from the south. It was a van. It slowed and a hand waved toward the customs shed. Probably a local who made the crossing every day. It accelerated slowly away to the North. Minogue stood at the side of the road. He saw a group of lights on the northern side which filtered dimly through the yellow-white glare of the customs post. He heard a car door open behind him. A big man climbed out awkwardly. In the weak light which shone from the car's interior, Minogue saw the man heft a strap on his shoulder inside his coat. He was carrying a submachine gun, Minogue realised. More cowboys.

Scully walked over to Minogue.

"Any minute now," Scully said.

"I don't see all your lads, is there more of them?" Minogue asked.

"Ah we don't need an army now," Scully said smoothly.

"Are they obliged to stop here? Heading north?"

"Not obliged. But people slow down."

"Do you put down some barrier?" Minogue persisted.

Scully shook his head.

"You're making a lot out of this now. Leave the details to me. Everything's in place. We're here to just see that everything goes smoothly. Don't be worrying," Scully soothed.

Minogue could smell the sea. It was mixed in with the smell of turned soil. He looked to the north again, at the lights of their customs post. A few hundred yards away were British soldiers like on the telly, with real guns and real uniforms.

"Oi," said Scully behind him. Minogue turned. The lights of one vehicle were approaching from Dundalk.

"Over here," Scully said. Minogue followed him to the customs post and stood next to him in the shadows. The big detective joined them. A radio squawked under his anorak and he reached in to turn it down. Minogue caught a few words before the volume went.

"Car's through, maintaining speed. Roadblock in place—"

"What roadblock?" Minogue whispered.

Allen had the road to himself. Only one lorry passed him going south. No lights appeared in his mirror. He felt some relief that he wasn't being followed. He wondered why there were so few vehicles on the road. Ahead of him the lights of the Irish customs post formed an island in the darkness. The place looked deserted. Allen knew that this post here at Killeen had been blown up a half dozen times in the past. Often it was closed down at night.

He could see lights on the far side of the border now. He slowed

196

the car and let it coast up to the light. He knew he didn't have to stop. There was someone on duty in the office. Yellow glare filled the car interior. Agnes was squinting. Allen noticed an army Land Rover and several cars parked some distance behind the customs post. For a moment he felt a bolt of panic, but nobody was out on the road. There was no barrier. He drew abreast of the shed and looked in.

A customs officer looked out at the car through the grid of wire. Should he stop? The customs man made no gesture but continued looking dully out at the car. Allen's eyes were straining to see better.

"God, what a pack of iijits," Agnes said. "They don't know whether they're coming or going."

Allen was almost at a standstill.

"Go ahead" she said, "you don't have to stop, so you don't. It's just that everybody slows down to a crawl. If they want you, they wave."

Allen clutched into second gear.

"What roadblock? I don't see a roadblock," Minogue hissed. The car was pulling away from the customs post. Minogue saw a profile of the driver, yellow light on his shoulder. There was someone else too. Agnes. Minogue felt an aching in his shins and knees. His mouth was dry. The night was suddenly lurid to him with the lights and the evasions. He fixed his eyes on the red lights of the car drawing away.

The detective took out his portable, squelched it and handed it to Scully.

"Gone through now. Over," Scully said.

"What's going on?" Minogue said, louder.

"A success. That's what's going on. What do you want?" Scully said. Minogue looked at Scully's shadowed face. It confirmed what Minogue had felt from the voice: a changed man.

"Who's going to stop them?" Minogue said.

"The other crowd. The Brits," Scully replied. He turned and

nodded to the others who began heading for the door of the customs post. Minogue overheard one of them saying 'big deal.'

Minogue grabbed Scully's arm. Scully's head darted around.

"It's a set-up, isn't it?"

Scully looked disparagingly at the hand holding him. He shook himself free.

"Your superiors didn't burden you with too much info. Leave well enough alone, now. Your job's done, so's ours."

"What's going to happen?"

"Look Minogue. There's reasons."

Minogue stood in front of Scully.

"I want to know, Scully. I'm involved."

Scully stared a hole in Minogue before replying.

"We have to give the Brits something. They're moaning about security this side. They're expecting this. We had that tip-off about the car and we passed the ball to them. It's a token. They get the credit and so do we for delivering. We'd have a job convicting them in the South probably. Trade, tit for tat," Scully said.

"But you would have missed the car if I hadn't come up with Allen," Minogue protested.

"If, if," Scully repeated, looking out into the darkness. "Fair dues to you, we would have missed him all right. I'm not saying we're not beholden to you for it. That's why you get to be here, sitting next to me," Scully murmured.

He turned abruptly to Minogue.

"A day here, a day there, what does it matter in the end? We're all on the same side, Minogue."

Panic ran up from Minogue's knees and prickled his scalp. He looked at the red lights of the car. He heard the engine pick up speed. Scully ignored Minogue and looked at the car too.

When Minogue heard himself speak, the voice seemed to belong to someone else. Scully's frown had eased as he stared at the small bowl of light in the distance.

"What if he tries to run it, Scully?"

"He'd want to be a terrible stupid gobshite to try that class of

198

a stunt, I'm thinking," murmured Scully. "Their border lads are sharp little thugs."

Scully hadn't taken his gaze from the car lights ahead. Doesn't care, Minogue realised dully.

"The girl," Minogue said. "The girl in the car with him, she's—"

"The girl in the car is the girl in the fucking car, Minogue. For all you know, she's in cahoots with him somewhare along the line," Scully snapped. "Maybe you didn't twig to her."

"She's not, I tell you," said Minogue hoarsely. "I know she's not."

"We'll find that out then, won't we? Let them sort it out."

Minogue grasped Scully's arm. He felt the muscle tense. Scully turned to him.

"Get your shagging hand offa me or I'll drop you, Minogue."

"These are cowboys, these border patrols, Scully. You know that. They're trigger-men. They're volunteers, they're just itching to take the law—"

"Get back in the car, Minogue. I've had enough of this rubbish. I'm going to lodge a slip on you for this. Shut up and get—"

Then Minogue ran.

He heard Scully's shout hang in the air behind him as the night air brushed over his face. With the glare ahead, Minogue was running blind. The road thumped the soles of his leather brogues. His coat flapped behind him. The raised voices behind him mixed with the sounds of air rushing into his nostrils. His shins cracked with each slap of his feet on the tar. Beneath him was darkness and all around darkness, just the glow of light ahead, like a magnet drawing him. It occurred to Minogue that he might well be shot at. The night seemed full of his breathing and flapping. Ahead of him the tail-lights glowed stronger as the brakes were applied.

Minogue prayed for the brake lights to stay on. He saw a figure step into the light ahead. It looked like the figure was carrying a stick, a hurley maybe. Minogue's chest was bursting, his legs jellying. *Old, old.* He was slowing. Spots of light danced all around him, a crazy swirl swarming around the lights ahead too. As though floating, Minogue took note of the low hedge running along beside him. For an instant Minogue thought the dream would end. He was getting no nearer the lights. It was an endless treadmill where he lost ground quicker than he gained it. He hoped he wouldn't trip. He knew he wouldn't be able to talk if he caught up to the car and that could be dangerous. The thing was, he must get her out of the car.

Allen felt as if his chest was being squeezed. From the recesses of his mind, he observed himself there in the car, slowing. He saw the soldier bulked with a flak jacket step into the light. Allen wondered where the RUC were. The soldier was holding the automatic rifle almost level. Off to his left Allen caught a glimpse of a vehicle in the ditch, a Land Rover. Where were the RUC?

Agnes turned around and looked out the back window.

"Do you see it?" she said.

Allen was rolling down the window. She looked at him and he turned to her. He saw her frown and her face go loose. Now she knows, he thought. This is it, all of it. She tried to say something but couldn't. Her back pressed into the door, looking across at Allen.

There was no traffic. The car was rolling to a halt, endlessly. Allen felt blood rush around his head. He looked out at the soldier who was not moving toward the car. Allen could see the kid's face clearly. He was no more than twenty-five. He wore his beret low on his forehead. Allen grasped the slicked wheel with both hands. His upper arms began to tremble. He thought something passed behind the car, a flicker in the mirror. The car stopped and rocked back slightly as the suspension returned it level after the braking. All Allen could hear was the regular infuriating tick over of a well-tuned car.

"Switch off the engine. Then step out of the car," the soldier said. Allen couldn't take his eyes off the rifle.

"Surely—" he began.

The soldier looked over the roof of the car. He glanced at Allen again.

"Out."

"Really," Allen said. "Is this neccessary? Don't you —"

"There's something out there," Agnes whispered.

The soldier backed away from the car and levelled the rifle.

"Out of the car!" he shouted.

Allen saw the soldier look behind the car again, frowning. Time stopped for him. A rush of understanding settled on him. He felt a finality, close. Something was wrong. He could feel Agnes' alarm. It was dark outside this bowl of light. Was there nothing outside this terrifying oasis? He laid his hand slowly on the gearshift and looked to his right.

Minogue wondered why nobody had stopped him. Each of his feet was landing flat and heavy now. His breath was in hoarse gasps. Maybe if he shouted, they'd hear him from there. A stitch like a cold knife was slicing under his ribs, jabbing. He saw the man with the stick move back from the car. Another two men came up behind the car, sticks raised to their shoulders. Minogue stopped. He was within a hundred yards of the car. He saw the back of the car dip. The tires squealed. Minogue shouted with all the wind he could hold. The light was pulsing in front of him. He swayed with the effort.

"Wait! Police!" he shouted. "Wait!"

The soldiers turned and crouched. Minogue shouted again. One of the soldiers turned back and Minogue heard the *pop pop*, a staccato. Minogue dropped to the ground. Seconds ticked by. He heard more shots. The car lights were moving from side to side. Then, lazily, the tail-lights straightened out their course. Minogue heard shouting. The lights leaned to the left and followed, shuddering, the grass highlighted by the beams ahead of the car. Floodlights froze the slowing car in their glare. Minogue leaned on his elbows in the road, dumbfounded. The red lights leaned more as the car mounted the ditch and came to a standstill.

201

Figures ran to the doors and pulled them open. Minogue saw them pull the two passengers out to the ground. He heard more shouting. Suddenly he was blinded by light.

"Stay where you are," he heard the English accent through the loudspeakers. "Do not move or you will be fired on."

Minogue heard the siren warbling stronger from behind. He felt completely vulnerable, spreadeagled on the road. He waited for the *whack* of a bullet. Minogue thought of all the minute indentations in the tar. It smelled of petrol and rubber and farms. He closed his eyes. A car pulled up behind him.

"Police!" someone shouted, an Irish voice. "One of ours! Police!" Minogue heard footsteps in the ditch next to him.

Again the voice, "Police, don't shoot!"

A faint blue light swept around in the glare. To his left Minogue saw a British soldier. He looked around and saw Scully cupping hands to shout again. The soldier's face was blackened. He was squinting down the sights of the rifle. Under his eyes, the small black hole of the muzzle seemed to rest on his hand. Minogue wondered if this boy was going to shoot him. He couldn't miss. Minogue could hear the boy's breathing.

The soldier said, "O.K." and lowered his rifle. "O.K."

"He's one of ours. He's O.K."

"O.K.," the soldier said. "Just get the bastard out of here. Just get him out of here."

Minogue elbowed onto his knees. The soldier was shaking his head. Another soldier appeared from outside the glare.

"Get up, Minogue," Scully's voice, thickly.

"John fuckin' Wayne," the soldier said.

The boat train to Dun Laoghaire was only three minutes late. It emerged from between the houses and gardens by Merrion Gates at a rush, rumbled over the level crossing and seemed to relax as the bay opened up to to east. Howth with its necklace of lights shouldered out into the sea across the bay from the swaying train.

Three men sat ahead of him. They looked like navvies on their way back to England. They smoked constantly and spoke little.

He tried to maintain the appearance of a tired tourist. He had held off the bouts of panic, but the effort left him jittery. He tried to block out images which were coming to him constantly now. He saw the playwright, that expression of disdain on his face, talking to a policeman. Then he saw that cop's hands reaching for his chest as he lay on the ground. It looked like he was trying to pull the slug out. The cop's head arching back, digging into the ground and then falling back as the hands went limp.

"That's the end of the holidays now, hah?" a navvy said. "Back to the grind, hah?" he added, and returned to staring out through the grass.

The tanned man tried to smile and he nodded. He was relieved to have escaped wordless from this. Then it occurred to him that he might be passing up something. In his caution he might be losing out on an advantage. If he got in with these men, it might help him. They might adopt him if he bought them some drink. It would take effort, but it would be worth it.

"Excuse me but are we close to Dun-Dunleery?" he said.

"I'm telling you now, Minogue. When we go over you better mind your p's and q's. You're bloody lucky you didn't collect another hole in your arse off those fellas," Scully said.

Minogue's legs were cramping, but his breath was back. He felt like an errant schoolboy sitting in the back of the car with the big detective eying him.

"Seems to me it's your arse is in the sling, Scully," Minogue said quietly. Scully turned to look at Minogue. His eyes flickered to the detective and then back to Minogue.

"You've said enough, Minogue. You're a loose cannon. Bloody iijit, you nearly banjaxed the whole thing."

"You're forgetting something, Scully. I have a mouth on me. You're just the pot-boy with the piss-bucket here along with these cowboys. The arrest should have been made here. You know and I know that the Brits are trigger-happy. They've been given the green light. They're just itching to have a go at anyone. You threw those two to them," Minogue said.

"Watch who you're calling a piss-boy, Minogue. We heard about you." Scully's voice rose.

"This was a planned operation—"

"—And you're just here to execute it. Or them," Minogue said.

"—so get it through your head!" Scully shouted.

"So what are you going to say to them? You don't even know yet if Allen was shot or what happened," Minogue retorted.

"Was that the deal? You throw them to the wolves for public relations and the Brits let you question him for ten minutes. If he's still alive. And the passenger?" Minogue continued.

"You don't get holy on me, Minogue. I'm doing this stuff every day of my working life and more besides. Don't give me the innocent bystander bit. They're all at it."

"I'm telling you that she's not involved!"

Was that himself shouting, Minogue wondered. How long since he had shouted at someone?

"Look, Minogue. All I know about you is that I'm to assist in you getting an interview with this Allen fella. I don't know or care who your mother is or whether you're the full shilling or even whether you got your arse shot off or not. If I have to revoke this because you've gone off the deep end, I will, and I can live with the bloody consequences."

Before Minogue could reply, headlights flashed twice ahead. The driver flashed back and accelerated toward the light. Minogue looked behind as the car started off. He saw men in battle dress in the ditch. Back at the customs post, blue lights whirled.

Ahead of them, Minogue saw three vehicles blocking the road. One was an ambulance. As they slowed, the ambulance moved off. A soldier waved them down. Scully rolled down the window.

"We're to see a Sergeant Davies," said Scully.

The magenta Cressida stood like an abandoned toy. The doors hung open and the lights were still on. The back window had been shot out. Minogue saw a half-dozen holes in the boot and a ding in the bumper. Scully stepped out of the car and Minogue followed him. Minogue realised there were people standing off in shadows, soldiers. Two cars started up almost simultaneously beyond the floodlights. A Land Rover equipped with a crane drove slowly toward them. It turned away from them and began reversing into the ditch behind Allen's car. More soldiers and men in plain clothes appeared out of the darkness. Minogue thought that there must be a lot more of them out in the fields too. Behind them, their car with the two detectives still in it, backed slowly to the side of the road, followed by the soldier who had waved them down, cradling a rifle.

Two men in plain clothes approached Allen's car and looked inside. One of them walked to the back of it. He bent over, his face inches from the back lights, examining the boot lid. Then he closed the doors slowly. He guided the Land Rover in. The other man walked over to Scully and Minogue. Minogue felt nervous and exposed.

Sergeant Davies was a slight man with pale features which were whitened further by the glare off the lights. His hair was neatly trimmed. He wore a v-necked jumper over a collar and tie. Minogue guessed him to be in his early forties. Looked like he had just put down the paper after tea and come out for a stroll. His face suggested a minimum of surprise at guesting these coppers from the Free State.

"Davies," he said.

Minogue wondered why he had not learned to distinguish regional accents in the North. For an instant he was back watching the news at home, listening to the inquiring and querulous tones of the North. Another shooting, more condemnation, more bile. Why did he feel they were so foreign?

"Detective Sergeants Scully and Minogue," Scully said. Minogue nodded. There were no handshakes. No love lost here.

"In the van here," Davies said.

Minogue's heart was pounding. He had restrained himself from asking about the ambulance. He noticed his hands were in fists.

"What was that little problem ye had there with some fellow running along the road?" Davies asked.

Scully paused a moment before answering:

"Nothing to it. It's settled now."

"Uh," Davies said. He stopped at the back of a Sherpa van. "Ten minutes or so. We have to get out of here. Too much lights, do ye know. It's not the safest of places," Davies said.

Allen's face was white. Minogue crouched for a few seconds, paralysed, at the door. Allen's shirt hung out over his pants. He was shivering. Looking at Allen's strained and damp face, Minogue doubted that he was the same man he had spoken to recently.

Davies leaned in the doorway. Scully sat down opposite Allen. Minogue noticed flecks of blood on Allen's face. There were cuts on the back of his hands. He looked out under his eyebrows and the toss of hair at Minogue, then at Scully.

"I'm Detective Sergeant Scully. Sergeant Minogue here will be asking you questions. If you make things awkward, there'll be trouble. Just tell what you know."

Allen's pupils were tiny. His eyes seemed to bulge wider. He didn't know what to do with his handcuffed hands.

When Allen spoke, Minogue was shocked at the voice. It was a high, child-like register, with none of the assurance Minogue had expected.

"I might have known," Allen said.

"What about the girl?" Minogue whispered. Allen didn't answer but looked at Scully and Davies instead.

"What about the girl? Agnes," Minogue hissed. Again, all they heard were the engines outside. He's in shock, Minogue realised. He's out of it.

"She's gone in the ambulance," Davies said. Minogue reeled inwardly. He turned to Davies.

"Is she badly hurt?"

Before Davies could reply, Allen said:

"Agnes is taken away. They took her away, you see." His voice trailed off. Then he stared at Minogue.

"She was hit," Davies said. Minogue concentrated on the accent: '*hot*' for hit.

"Minogue," Scully said.

Minogue heard the reprimand in Scully's voice.

"Loftus. I know I don't have to tell you anything. You know Loftus? Yes. Loftus. You could say he is . . . very, resourceful. He is quite without any . . . " Allen whispered.

He looked up at Minogue.

"No. You needn't ask. It wasn't voluntary on my part . . . Not at all, I can assure you."

"Who else?" Minogue asked

"People on the phone. I don't know"

"Was there an American?" Minogue asked

Allen's brow knitted over.

"An American," Minogue repeated.

"I'm not sure. I don't know."

"What's in the car?" Minogue said

Allen grinned but his eyes held the fright, unchanged. Minogue saw that Allen's eyes were blinking rapidly.

"I don't know. I really don't," he whispered.

Minogue looked at Scully. Davies was pushing back the cuticle on a nail.

"But there was something."

"I suppose. They said—"

"Who?"

"On the phone . . . that's all."

Minogue waited before asking. Then he spoke slowly.

"Where does Jailath Walsh fit in?"

Allen stared at his handcuffs. Minogue asked again.

Allen looked up at Minogue. His eyes were wet, blinking.

"That wasn't my decision at all. You should understand that," he whispered hoarsely. "I had no hand, act or part in it."

"In concealing evidence you did."

Allen stared at him for a moment. Minogue saw some defiance in the stare before the eyes slipped out of focus again.

"You don't know half of it, Minogue. Nothing," he said.

"Tell me then," Minogue said, "You've nothing to lose now."

207

CHAPTER SEVENTEEN

The train jolted to a halt with the rattle of couplings.

The older man stood and stretched.

"Canadian? Are they fond of their beer there, tell me."

"Fairly."

The tanned man followed them out onto the platform. Groups of people were wrestling luggage down toward the rear of the platform.

He looked at some of the others walking down the platform. A couple with a sleeping child and too many bags. A heavy-set man, his suitcase tied with a belt, walking unsteadily.

"Is there a big line-up here?" he asked the red-faced navvy.

"Ah no. Nothing to it. Sure they know the half of us going across."

"What about a ticket?"

"Go round the corner there. There's a sweet shop and a ticket office at that gate in. Here, hold on, I'm going meself."

He saw no police. He couldn't ask the navvies about the police. The red-faced navvy was paying for his ticket ahead of him.

"Cabins?" The red-faced man was saying to the woman behind the counter.

"Do I look like Jack Tar or something, like Moby Dick? What would I want a cabin for? Here look after your man here, he's a Canadian. He's a long way from home."

The tanned man grinned, but he felt an icy touch. He didn't want any attention drawn to himself.

After he bought the ticket, they rejoined the other two. They were now leaning against the wall at the end of the passageway leading to the passenger entrance to the ship. He smelled the pungent air, a mix of fish and engine oil. Through the window he saw Dun Laoghaire pier and the waving masts of moored yachts. Isolated figures walked from light to light along the pier.

"Me belly thinks me throat is cut," the short navvy said.

"Give over bellyaching, Joey. There's plenty of gargle on the bloody boat. We'll be on in a minute," the older navvy said.

A uniformed member of the crew opened the doors leading to the gangplank. Two men in grey overalls stood next to the gangplank, idly looking at the waiting passengers. The line began to move.

The tanned man practised his breathing to ease his tension.

"No big deal, is it," he said. "They don't make a fuss, do they?"

"Why would they? Sure aren't they glad to be sending us back? There's no jobs here," the older navvy remarked wryly.

Another member of the crew walked down the gangplank. Still, the tanned man saw no one that looked like the police. He shuffled along beside the red-faced navvy. They were within a dozen people of the doors. Then he saw a stocky man standing to the side of the doors, outside. He looked to the other side of the door, but he could not yet see far enough around the jamb.

"Aye, aye Captain!" the red-faced man called out to the two crew-members. Both looked over at him. One of them grinned.

"Here, look it," he said to the other one.

"Well lads, did you fix the hole in the boat?" the older navvy asked loudly.

Both crew members were grinning now.

"Where would a fella get a bit of refreshment here, Admiral?" the small navvy called out.

"Yiz could try a swim. That's very refreshing," one of the crewmen said.

"Very funny. Pass the chicken, the feather's worn out. We'll see yiz later, hah?" the small navvy said.

The tanned man had lost the breathing routine. His neck felt as if it were in a vice grip. As he stepped through the door jamb he saw the other cop, his hands in his pockets, looking over the faces. He cursed the wit of the three navvies for drawing attention to themselves. Better not try to avoid their eyes. Look surprised, a bit puzzled. The cop on the left was looking at him. Without thinking about it, the tanned man had drawn his elbow in so that he could feel the gun under his arm. He couldn't see any metal detector. He stopped breathing.

Minogue did not speak on the way back to Dundalk. Agnes McGuire's face kept pushing his thoughts aside. Occasionally he noticed that the detective beside him was watching him. Scully sat in the front looking ahead. The most that Minogue knew about her came from Davies, who reminded him somehow of a stale room. Davies was making little of it, as an object lesson for what he saw as Free State clodhoppers who needed instruction in the violent ways of the North. Davies probably wouldn't admit that the whole thing was out of his hands anyway, that he was dragged in to front the operation for the British Army.

Minogue had stood beside the customs post back on the Republic side while Scully radioed in a report to be passed on to Dublin. He watched as the vehicles drove out of the aura of light back up the Belfast road. The floodlights turned off all at once. There were more troops and police on the Republic side than when they'd crossed. They had stood around, not sure what to do. Then they began dispersing.

Allen had asked him what he could do. Minogue told him he'd try to get news of Agnes to him but that he, Allen, was going North. As Davies slammed the door he said to Minogue:

"There ye hove it. For a perfesser he's a torrable stypud mon."

Minogue's loathing for the broken man in the back of the van broke through his own numbness and threatened to overwhelm him. For a few moments, Allen's face had communicated the strain he had been under, but then Minogue's mind reddened with anger. He might be a step closer to Walsh's murderer, but who paid in the end?

When the car stopped, Scully got out and walked over to Minogue.

"You got what you wanted, Minogue. So far as I'm concerned that episode is over. There's no need for it to be written into the record. It was quite understandable when you think about it. I mean, you had your priorities. The word from on high was to pass the ball. That's hard to live with these days, I know."

Minogue looked beyond Scully to the helicopter.

"What with policemen being shot in the streets. I put two and two together you know, even if nobody told me all the ins and outs of it. It's connected with the things in Dublin, isn't it, the murders? You don't have to tell me," Scully continued.

Minogue began to walk off. Scully walked alongside.

"Just ask yourself this: if it helped to find the killers of those lads in Dublin and if it helps stop more police being killed, shouldn't you weigh that in the balance?"

Minogue stopped and faced Scully.

"You know, Scully, you sound exactly like a brother of mine. He talks the exact same way. The same kind of logic, but he's on the other side. Does that bother you at all? Allen and the girl were thrown to the wolves just so the various custodians of this bloody island can tell all of us to sleep soundly. You know and I know that car should never have crossed the border. But you're just doing what you're told to do, same as the rest of us. That stuff doesn't work in the long run you know. Our kids can see through that rubbish as easy as kiss hands."

211

Scully frowned.

"Nice speech Minogue. Except it doesn't fit in this world."

As the helicopter lifted off, Minogue reflected that Scully was right, but it shouldn't be Scully saying it. It was after nine now. As they came in sight of the northern suburbs of Dublin, the message was relayed from Kilmartin that the Special Branch were outside Loftus' flat, waiting for the word to go in.

He felt claustrophobic as the passengers crowded closer at the door. He met the cop's gaze for a few seconds. The cop's gaze rested briefly on the tanned man and then it moved on. He began walking toward the gangplank railing. The other cop had not looked at him.

The first cop glanced at him again. He felt the skin at the back of his neck prickle. He patted his jacket to make sure it was zipped. As his feet started up the metal tongue of the gangplank, he risked a look at the cop. Unbelievably, the other cop was stepping onto the gangplank as well, timing it to match his arrival. The tanned man froze as the two cops met on the gangplank directly in front of him. He realised he had left it too late. He looked directly into the face of the cop who was blocking his way. The cop flicked a glance at him but looked over his shoulder. The passengers had come to a standstill. The two cops edged around the tanned man and one grasped the arm of a teenager behind.

"Will you step aside for a moment, please," the cop said.

The tanned man turned to see the teenager dart a look from one cop to the other. Then he shook his head and stepped off the gangplank. The tanned man resumed his climb. The navvies looked behind.

"What's with your man there. Is he mitching from school or what?" red-face said.

"Maybe he did in the budgie at home," the older navvy replied.

The tanned man realised he was breathing heavily through his nose. His legs were lazy springs that barely carried him onto the ship.

"Here lookit, where's the gargle?" the short navvy yawned.

"Jases, you're a divil," the older one replied. "It's a wonder those fellas didn't take you aside. You're not out on bail for something, are you?"

"Out on bail is right. It's baling out is what I'm doing. Bloody place."

"What was all that about?" the tanned man managed to ask.

"Your man? The young fella?" red-face said. "I don't know. Maybe he was skipping the country or something. Looks like they were waiting for him."

"Here, do you miss the place already?" the red-faced navvy said. "Come on up and I'll stand you a drink. You have to have something to puke up if it gets choppy."

The tanned man forced a smile.

"Do they let Canadians buy drinks on this boat?" he asked. The older navvy laughed.

It had begun to rain in Dublin. Kilmartin's face was streaked with the shadows of rain which clung like eyelashes to the windows of the car. The constant hush of rain washing up under the car made Minogue sleepy. Kilmartin's face brightened and darkened alternately with the passage of the streetlights as he talked.

Minogue turned to him.

"I want to ask you something about that business earlier on," Minogue said.

Kilmartin returned Minogue's steady gaze.

"I want to know if you knew it would turn out like that."

Kilmartin blinked and said:

"You mean the girl being shot? Of course I didn't—"

"Not that," Minogue interrupted. "I mean dumping them with the Brits."

Kilmartin paused. He took in Minogue's darkened face, the tiredness and the wariness gathered around his eyes.

"No I didn't, Matt."

Kilmartin let his eyes go out of focus as he gazed out beyond the driver and the squeaking wipers.

213

"They don't tell me that stuff. They're a law unto themseves, so that's that," Kilmartin said softly. He wondered if Minogue believed him. Kilmartin's unease impelled him into talking.

"Our mystery man stayed at the Shelbourne. One of the porters put a good face on him, right down to the shoes he was wearing. 'Looks a bit like a bank manager,' says he. Between what McCarthy told us and what the nosey staff up above in the Shelbourne say, we have a rough-and-ready Identikit of this fella. There were clothes left in a room and there's no sign of the man who stayed. No visitors. He was there for a while," Kilmartin was saying.

"What will he do?" Minogue asked.

"I don't know. Something tells me he is a very polished performer entirely. The Branch are quite up in a dander about him. They don't know anything about him. Came out of nowhere. I'd say he'll lie low here. I wouldn't put it past him to have other passports and things."

Minogue imagined a well-groomed, confident American. He'd have good teeth anyway, probably aftershave, one of those diver's watches on an expandable strap. Hairs would poke out under the strap. He might chew gum. What was he doing here though?

"Irish American. A true son of Erin," Minogue murmured.

"Seems likely, doesn't it?"

"If he's so well set up, then why would he shoot someone?" Minogue wondered aloud.

"Strictly speaking, we don't know that he did," Kilmartin answered. "It's a lead."

"Hardly coincidence then about Walsh," Minogue said.

"Well what do you think, Matt?"

Minogue didn't answer immediately. Then he said;

"I'd better fill you in on Allen."

After he had finished, Kilmartin said:

"God, isn't that the back of the neck? Great oaks from little acorns grow. How long ago was this?"

"Well, Allen is getting on fifty. So let's say nearly forty years ago."

"And what happened?"

"Took psychiatric treatment. Made to. And it worked, he says."

"So he changed his name . . . "

" . . . and turned out to be a model. Got interested in the psychology and took it up. He's a very smart fella, Allen."

Kilmartin harrumphed.

"—Not smart enough to deal with Loftus I'll warrant. He had nothing to fear. Jesus God in heaven, people are nearly getting credit for any kind of perversion these days. Sure what age was he?"

"Thirteen," Minogue said.

"And didn't he pull himself up by the bootstraps ever since. I can tell you I couldn't hold it against him. He should have skinned Loftus when Loftus put the pressure on."

"Well," Minogue murmured as a bump interrupted him, "he had to gild the lily, or so he thought. He wanted to measure up, you see. His father was dead these years, probably the only one who could tone down the mother."

"Go on," Kilmartin said. "A real bloody cop-out. 'It started with me mother' and all the psychology stuff. And he told you this in a van in the middle of nowhere?"

Minogue wondered if he could tell Kilmartin how relieved Allen had been to let out with the intolerable stresses he had endured. He had said it all in a matter of minutes. Minogue had felt less disgust than some vague and frightening acceptance of Allen's story. He didn't need to tell Kilmartin the real, the simple and the quite absurd truth which Allen had communicated to him. Allen, elbows on his knees and looking at the handcuffs, had told him in so economical a way as to be devastating, that he could not have Agnes McGuire know about his past. Ordinary, like the rest of us, Minogue had understood, he wanted deliverance and love too. There had been no accounting for that.

On the way back to Dublin, Minogue shivered and spent most

215

of the time wondering how it would come out, how much damage would be done to Allen's work for peace. All come to nothing, probably.

"Pressure," Minogue said, "You never know what people'll do."

Kilmartin did not miss the tone of Minogue's remark. Had Minogue known all along that everyone was watching him to see if he was the full shilling? Maybe he even played on it, controlling it in his own way. Kilmartin gathered himself in the seat.

"Anyway. Allen is small fry. I want Connors' killer and you want whoever killed that lad in Trinity. We may well be talking about the same character, hah? We'll root him out in short order and there'll be no bones about it."

Loftus looked quite different without a tie, Minogue observed. Still, he retained the appearance of confidence mixed in with a knowingness and a contempt. He had not ranted and raved but slipped on a coat and gone to Donnybrook Station with the three Special Branch detectives. He appeared almost relaxed. His hair had been oiled by the rain. He sat in his coat some six feet from the table. When Minogue entered, an amused glance of recognition came from Loftus. Then he returned to observing the desk and walls. Minogue nodded to the Branch man standing outside the door as he closed the door gently. He stood next to the desk looking at Loftus' face. Loftus smiled.

"Unorthodox. And melodramatic too," Loftus said.

"These are dramatic times, Captain Loftus. Less comedy though, I'm thinking."

"You're wrong there. I was at home watching the television and now I'm here. It's fairly comic, wouldn't you agree?"

"Do you want the rigmarole about what you're doing here and what you're being held under?"

Loftus didn't answer.

"I requested to interview you alone."

"I recall you doing that in my office last week, Sergeant. Am

I supposed to be disoriented and confess to something now that I've been dragged down here?"

"You'd know about that stuff, Captain. I mean you've been trained. How long were you in the States on your training?"

Loftus raised his eyebrows.

"Really now, you haven't brought me down here to get me to start an autobiography. I've been out of the army for eleven years."

"When did it all turn sour for you?" Minogue asked.

Loftus laughed briefly.

"Get someone in here to get on with whatever I'm supposed to be here for. And make it good. After I get amused, I'll be none too pleased and heads will roll about this."

"Is that so, now? I have convinced the Special Branch crowd and even my superiors, who are all waiting to talk to you, that I can get you to help us. Now I don't mind telling you that they think I'm cracked. I don't even want to tell you that they are in a fierce hurry to talk to you. Pressure, you see. We're all under pressure. So I'm here to pass on some pressure to you."

Loftus' bemused look had changed to one of curiosity.

"Everyone seems to believe that systems can be designed to rule out human weakness. Perversity, maybe I should call it. I mean nothing is ever watertight. People don't behave according to plan. Isn't that really banal, Captain?"

"You're putting it mildly."

"The best-laid plans and all that. You think you can depend on people. Especially if you control their motivations. I mean, young people are called cynical the way they scorn the carrots dangling in front of them—the job, the car, that stuff. What happens when the incentive isn't there though?"

"You're nearly as entertaining as the programme I'm missing at home," Loftus said.

"Weakness, though. Some people can live with it and some can't. Some despise weakness, don't they? They fall in love with efficiency, action. Any action if it comes to that. Looking for to be heroes of some description."

Loftus drew in a breath and expelled it noisily through his nose.

217

"Or was it Captain Loftus, the great nationalist, who has all the ready solutions at hand . . . ?"

Loftus' eyes glittered with contempt but he said nothing.

" . . . If I had to place my bet, though, I'd not put money on your brand of patriotism, Loftus. Not even your love affair with the problem-solving know-how that you learned off the Yanks when you were there . . . Oh no, I see the dark horse as the one for this course. You're a good, upright lad who probably still goes to Mass and visits his mother, are you? But every day in the college you rub up against what's left of the Anglo Irish. And you find that you're not really their equal, no matter what the job description says . . . You're just not a college boy, are you? A Catholic lad, up from Cork, you have your wits about you, but you find it's not quite enough to be acc—"

Minogue saw Loftus' nostrils flare. Loftus leaned forward in the chair.

"Easy does it now, like a good man, Loftus. There are men outside here who have had friends killed by the types of people you favour with your politics. Do you follow the gist of what I'm saying?"

What would have been a sneer had Loftus not controlled it eased into a strained grimace of a smile. He sat back stiffly in the chair.

"I'm getting tired of this ramble, Minogue. I've been patient. I have an idea how things work for security organisations. The more you talk, the bigger a stink I'm going to make about this. I'm not your common or garden-variety citizen who has to put up with this. I maintain enough links through the college with people who can have you on the carpet—"

"So Murphy's Law of Damage is true again," Minogue continued.

"What?"

"You know. If there's a one percent chance of something going wrong, it'll go wrong ninety-nine percent of the time and cause one hundred percent damage."

"That's rich all right. I'll remember that. Now—"

"Now we'll talk about Allen, Captain."

"Who?" asked Loftus.

"Allen, the one who's putting the finger on you. You don't have a lever on him anymore. Something else came up. Didn't you know? I'm sure you did. Agnes McGuire? Well she was in the car with him, but he didn't make it this time. Someone tipped off the Brits. They were waiting for him. Yes. Allen tried to make a run for it, but they shot up the car. Yes. Don't know if she'll live or not."

Minogue stood up and crossed his arms. He began to stroll slowly around the room, watching Loftus out of the corner of his eye. Minogue felt the day would never end. He had an ache like a kick in his belly. The tea would be burned by now and he'd reneged on one of his resolutions. Kathleen would be worried. As he paced the room, he recalled the blades beating the air as he bent to walk to the cockpit of the helicopter. Rust-coloured blood on Allen's face and shirt, but not Allen's blood. He stopped and sat on the desktop.

"He has nothing to lose now, you see," Minogue murmured.

Inspector Colm Quigley arrived at a run from the car which had raced through Dun Laoghaire. Even before he stepped from the car, he had been breathing heavily. The drizzle came as a relief to him. Somehow the smell of the sea calmed him. He reminded himself to be more regular with his exercise as he approached the van.

Other policemen were jealous of what they thought was glamorous stuff that Quigley's Emergency Response Team did: hostages, shoot-outs, surveillance. Often arriving unannounced, Quigley walked heavily on many toes. His teams were called cowboys. At meetings, Quigley spent a lot of time returning the gazes of senior uniformed Gardai whose looks indicted his forty-three years as well as the paramilitary operations he reported on.

Three other cars stood next to the van, their engines running. He tapped on the window of the van. A face behind the drops widened in recognition.

"They're ninety percent sure," the driver of the van said, rolling down the window. "Come in outa the rain, sir," Sergeant O'Rourke added.

Quigley declined.

"He was in the crowd getting on," O'Rourke said.

"And how did it get this far?"

"Came out on the train, sir. We don't have anyone actually on the train."

"Are the two detectives down there armed?" O'Rourke asked quickly, nodding toward the ferry lights, half hidden in the trees which lay below the carpark on Marine Road.

"No, sir. A fair crowd on the boat tonight," O'Rourke said.

Quigley recognised the tact and he privately admonished himself.

"Right. How many are we?" Quigley said.

"Gibbons, Maher and meself here, sir. There's eight more in the cars outside. All the stuff is here."

Quigley thought for a minute. This could be buggered up very easily. If it was the fella, then there might be shooting. There were a lot of confined spaces on the boat. Too many places to cover as well. The drizzle was soaking down his hair now, settling, cool.

"Anybody told the Gardai yet?" Quigley asked.

O'Rourke shook his head.

More trouble, thought Quigley. He'd have to tell them sooner or later. Maybe this fella was standing up on a deck looking around for police. Imagine a crowd of yahoos tearing down here with the lights flashing . . .

The ferry was due to leave at a quarter to nine. They had twenty minutes before having to ask for a delay and arouse the man's suspicions. Now: if they could coax the fella out on a deck alone. No one would be out in this weather.

Quigley could see the beginnings of the pier's lights below. The rest of it hid behind the trees, curling around to meet the East Pier at the mouth of the harbour. Behind him he could hear music coming from the lounges in the seafront hotels. The idling engines reminded him that time was running out fast.

"O'Rourke, listen. This fella may have the same gun on him. It's a 45 Calibre, an automatic, so it'll put out a lot in a hurry. Under no circumstances are you or any of these lads to challenge him if there is another party present. Bystanders and it's out, completely. That doesn't leave us much leverage. No one is to take submachine guns on board."

O'Rourke raised his eyebrows, then he nodded twice, slowly. "Moloney, you get a call through to the bridge for the captain or first officer only. Tell them we're coming on board. Don't tell them why. Tell him I'll go directly to him so have someone meet me and tell any crew at the entrance."

O'Rourke paused. He was aware of a slight tremor in his voice.

"Then you'll wait for ten minutes and you'll radio in for Garda assistance. If there's any questions asked of you later, you'll refer them to me, and me only. Gibbons, I want a vest. You and O'Rourke and myself are going to go ahead, one by one at a half minute apiece. I'll go first. The two lads at the gangplank say he might be with a crowd of navvies, but I don't get it. He has a red outdoor jacket, like an anorak, like something for climbing mountains. One bag. When you get on, just disperse, move around. We don't have much time. He'll be suspicious if the boat is late. If you spot him and there's none of us near, then use the radio. If he's clearly on his own and you've got the space, well and good. Assume he is armed so follow procedures. I repeat: assume he is armed."

Quigley paused before continuing. He looked from face to face and worried lest the men see his own fear.

"Have you some kind of duffle bags to carry? Something casual . . . ?"

"What about the other lads, sir?" Gibbons said.

"Too much. We can't take that chance. Moloney: tell'em to scatter around the dock and maintain radio silence. We'll be wired up, but we can't use an earpiece. We'll only use it if we have to. Just be ready to get on board in a hurry if you hear anything on your set."

O'Rourke was looking down at the gauges on the dashboard. He's not happy, thought Quigley, but he won't say anything. This was the worst kind of operation. A not-so-hot description, a boat half full of people, a million cubby-holes to get lost in. They hadn't even got a plan of the decks. The suspect wouldn't hesitate to use a gun. In a small space the jacket wouldn't mean much. He could even go for a head shot. There'd be ricochets.

Quigley hunkered into the back of the van and slipped off his anorak. He undid the strap and elbowed out of the harness. Where the leather had warmed, now felt exposed. He banged his head off the panel as he got into the Kevlar vest. Before he put on his anorak, he unclipped the Browning and checked the magazine. He remembered O'Rourke looking at it one day.

"They let you have one of those things? That's a very all-or-nothing yoke if it's the one I'm thinking of, sir. Bit of a whack to it for a nine millimetre."

Quigley hadn't had to use the standard automatic off the firing range, but the double action had never jammed yet. He took a deep breath. He zippered his anorak right to the neck to cover the vest beneath.

He closed the van door behind him. Men were getting out of the parked cars. Two he recognised, Lacey and Doyle, strolled over to take over the van when Gibbons and O'Rourke left. As O'Rourke stepped lightly onto the tarmacadam, Quigley noticed the sergeant was blowing air around his tightly closed lips, running bulges around his gums. Nervous. Quigley touched O'Rourke on the shoulder.

"All right Donal, give me a half minute. No radio contact until we need to, all right?"

O'Rourke nodded. He shifted from foot to foot as if winding up for a race. Quigley felt a slippery warmth like pins and needles at his knees as he descended the glistening steps toward Marine

222

Road. As he got under the trees, more of the ferry came into view. Its gaping maw, beak upturned, seemed to draw the cars into its yellowed belly. He looked up at the decks and railings but could see no one there. The floodlights floated above triangles of light, misted by the drizzle.

CHAPTER EIGHTEEN

Minogue's eyes roved around the room. The worn green and white lino tiles stretched to a wall painted yellow. The wall gleamed dully with the oil paint. The room contained two chairs and a desk. Innumerable hieroglyphics were etched onto the desktop. They had been done with some care though, Minogue realised. Probably the work of a civil servant, one of many who had occupied the desk. Funny the things you do and you don't notice, like dancing around the place when you're talking on the phone. Minogue glanced at Loftus. Loftus was looking straight ahead, but Minogue knew that he was alert.

Minogue thought of Iseult on the phone at home, twirling the wire, poking at a picture on the wall, pulling on strands of her hair. Sometimes she scribbled things on the phone book, strange signs left behind after a conversation. Nerves? Daithi fiddling with something when he was talking to him: irritation, concealment? As if Minogue had something terribly important to say and that he should sit up and listen? But it wasn't that, ever. It was merely a furious desire to see these strangers' faces, grown people. Genes my arse, Minogue thought. He was different from the children. A whisper would have woken him in the night and Kathleen awake beside him too; to tiptoe as best as a size ten countryman's feet can, to the little room over the stairs. An ammoniacal smell of piss, but even stronger was the curious baby breath warm air; a struggle to turn over, a frown; lips licked, maybe a grunt. He'd wait to hear the rhythm of breathing start up again. 'All right?' Kathleen would whisper, neither awake or asleep herself. 'Yes,' and back into the bed: will I sleep now? It's hormones is what it is, Minogue thought, time of life to be lusting after girls. Five minutes gone now, he realised. He was wrong about Loftus. Maybe Loftus didn't have a blind side.

"It's a matter of time really, Loftus. We know you're not going to open your heart to us. Don't forget Allen. He'll testify and you won't be able to get at him. Know a fella by the name of McCarthy, one of our playwrights?"

Loftus seemed to smile faintly at the mention of the name.

"Can't stop that man from yapping, I can tell you. I'll bet you a fiver he'll stick another needle into you. Ah, if only they were all as perfect as yourself, Captain Loftus," Minogue said. "But you can't deny me. They'll trip you yet. You know I was going to begin our interview here by getting right down to brass tacks, straight from the word go. I was going to ask you directly, 'Captain Loftus, did you murder Jarlath Walsh?' And I expected you to give me an honest answer, just like in one of those melodramas on the telly. You know, a burst of violins after it, the case solved. But I'm not going to ask you that at all, because I know you didn't do it. All I will ask you is who you gave the key to."

"What key?" Loftus asked.

"Whoever did it had to get out of the college at night after the gates were locked. Only higher-ups have keys to the sidegates. Whoever did in young Walsh could slip in and out when he wanted," Minogue replied. Loftus laughed.

"You know, Captain, I have this picture in my head of the fella we want. We've started calling him the mystery man, but we know what he looks like. You met him or at least you've talked to him on the phone. He is a Yank, we think. The fella who killed the guard in St. Stephen's Green. In a sense I think he's like you. Went to the States, didn't you, and fell in love with the efficiency thing? They call everything 'problem solving' over there, don't they? Still I bet you came back a convert. Am I right? But what I don't get is when it all turned bad for you here, when you decided to get into this from the other side. What was it?"

Loftus' gaze rested on the wall behind Minogue. Thinking about it later, Minogue believed that Loftus was about to speak when Kilmartin stuck his head in the door and motioned Minogue out.

The four of them sat at a plastic-topped table bolted to the floor facing the bar. Underfoot he could feel the hum of the ship's engine. The three were anxious for the screen to come up from the counter.

"And what do they drink in Canada now?" the older navvy asked.

"Oh, beer and lager. I'm not much on them myself—"

"—No more than myself," the smaller navvy added.

"—but I can toss a few back in the summer," the tanned man continued.

"'Toss a few.' Hah, that's a good one. We say 'sink a few' so we do. Same thing only different. All goes the same way, amn't I right? I hear the pubs do be open until all hours in America, I mean Canada."

"Longer than they should, people say," the tanned man parried. He ached for some sign that the ship was preparing to go. A blast of the siren, a rumble below, maybe. He looked around at the passengers who had come straight to the lounge. Altogether about twenty-five people. Sitting opposite one another over a table by a window too big to be called a porthole, a young couple was the only exception to the general air of brooding tiredness which the men in the lounge had brought with them. Some sat on their own, watching the steward, yawning. The train from

226

Holyhead would get the passengers into Euston Station in London by seven the next morning. A sense of loneliness gathered itself at the edges of his thoughts, surprising him. That Irish people have to do this, that the country is so bathed in this habit, he thought.

"Any minute now," the older navvy said, nodding toward the bar.

"Are there delays on this trip fairly often?" the tanned man asked.

"The weather can slow you down, that's a fact. It can speed you up too though. I was on this a few times, and I'm not joking you, I was the only one not spewing me lights up all over the place. Even your man, the barman or the steward or whatever you call him, officers, the whole lot. All puking goodo all over the place. We were three hours late getting into Dun Laoghaire. Wait 'til I tell you, they wanted to close down the bloody bar. 'Hold on there a minute, brother,' I says. 'I'm a paying customer and I can guarantee you that yous won't need to be mopping up after me. I was well reared. So hand me a pint of stout there and keep the oul flag flying.' Not a bother on me." The older navvy fisted gently on the tabletop and wagged his head with pride.

"Jack Tar," the red-faced navvy said.

"Yeah. Mutiny on the what-che-me-call-it," echoed the smaller one.

"Ah go on, yous are only jealous," the older man derided them.

The four men fell silent as if each knew that the talk only served to distract them from waiting. Another few passengers—again all men—trickled into the lounge. The tanned man felt his radar sense ease with each arrival. Then the sound of the screen sliding up returned him to the present.

"Aha. What'll you have," the old navvy said to him.

"Hold on, it's my twist" said the red-face.

"You buy later. I'm flush. A pint of beer?"

The tanned man wasn't listening. He was trying to supress any outward signs of the alarm that was yammering in his head.

The man had walked in just as the screen was going up.

227

Instantly, the tanned man was aroused. He felt his pulse push at his collar. The man had glanced at his group and then affected to look around. He was a tallish man with a full head of hair. His gait suggested an attempt to look slovenly, but it didn't come off. The face was a little too impassive, his glance a little too neutral. The man's coat was darkened at the shoulders by rain and his hair was stringing. His duffle bag should have bit into his shoulder but it didn't: it was probably half empty. Who would travel with a half-empty duffle bag?

"Beer. You can have Smithwicks, though personally I wouldn't drown a cat in it. How about Harp? That's a lager . . . "

"Yes."

"The Harp?"

"Yes. Please."

It was as if there was a stage director in his head pointing out all the moves. *See how he is being too casual? Walking so slow? He's trying to look sloppy but look at the shoulders. Face is too bland by far, because he's not tired. He's trying so hard not to look . . . excited.*

The red-faced man leaned over.

"Oi. We haven't got going yet. Don't look so thrilled."

"Pardon?" said the tanned man. He watched the man disappear round the corner, back out toward the stairway.

"You look a bit peeky so you do. Go out and stick your finger down your neck. Honest to God it works."

The tanned man looked directly at the red face. He saw a dissolute, loose face. Written on it were evasions and self-pity. The shallow banter was a poor attempt to mask the weakness. Instantly he loathed these men and the inanity which formed their lives. They were caricatures and they didn't know it, half-alcoholic, petulant children. Their humour had a manic, follow-on quality. The red-rimmed eyes above the bristles, puzzled and wary, the very pith of the simian Irish peasant in Punch. He looked at the smaller navvy, whose face showed a mix of cowed agreement and resentment at the world, tempered with anticipation for the drinks on the way. He felt a rage against them. All he had risked and hoped and: not for these.

He left the table without a word. He didn't turn to the "Oi" from the older navvy who was carrying pint glasses of beer and stout to the table. He felt himself walking almost on his toes, ready to break into a run. The cop was not there. He unzipped his jacket three-quarters of the way and he opened the door which led out on deck. Immediately a spume of drizzle came in out of the night at him. Dun Laoghaire pier ran out alongside the boat.

He looked over the railing. The gangplank was still down. It was the only way off the ferry unless he was to jump into the water. He began walking toward the steps which, he supposed, led to the back of the boat. There was no one on deck. He passed portholes and windows where he saw passengers settling listlessly into chairs. A seagull flew through the lights and into the darkness overhead. Above the back of the ferry, he saw the lights of the hotels half hidden by the trees. Stepping closer to the railings, he looked down at the dock. Several porters and men in overalls stood around, sheltered by the roof of the railway terminal. A faint cloud of drizzle hung over the rail tracks in the light which came out under the roof. Two men appeared from a doorway and walked hurriedly to the end of the platform.

He thought about the lifeboats or storage, but they'd search them. The ship's engine droned up through his feet. Maybe the car decks, there might be a car open. Or a truck. They'd want to isolate him in a set-up like this. Dump the gun and brazen it out with the Canadian passport: the playwright . . . *Trust in no one. Well, father, what would you do?*

"Here come on. Is the job done?" he heard behind him. The older navvy stood at the door.

"In a while," he managed to say. Turning around again, he noticed a movement behind the navvy. The navvy made to step aside and let the person pass. The tanned man called out:

"Come on over for a second, would you?"

The navvy stepped over the jamb, scratching the back of his

229

neck. As he began walking , the tanned man realised he might not have the time to put the silencer on.

"I'm a bit groggy," he said.

The navvy came over reluctantly. Whoever had been about to come out the door had not appeared.

With the navvy between him and the door, the tanned man turned back to looking at the town and reached into his jacket. He felt, rather than heard, the navvy's footsteps approaching him reluctantly across the deck.

"What's the story?" the navvy began.

The tanned man turned and brought the gun away from his chest.

"We're getting off the boat. Don't say anything, just listen to me."

Quigley saw the older man freeze, with his arm out a little from his sides. He heard Gibbons breathing close to his ear. Quigley's finger pushed out at the trigger guard, the muzzle touching the side of his knee. His arm felt heavy as if the gun were hanging from it.

"He has a gun on him," whispered Gibbons.

"He'll probably bring him down on the stairs outside as much as he can. There's no one on deck," Quigley murmured. Quigley tried to guess the distance from the door to the railing. Probably the best part of fifty feet. The door opened out and there was a jamb to jump over too. The Yank was right-handed. Quigley watched the Yank's hand come down on the navvy's shoulder, the navvy's arms go up almost horizontal. Must be an instinct, to raise your hands like that, he thought. Anything could happen here. This was what they had feared, a hostage. For a second he remembered the stoicism on O'Rourke's face, well in control of the skepticism. Even in broad daylight you couldn't shoot accurately at fifty feet with only one chance. So: the Yank had copped on when he had walked into the bar. Quigley leaned back against the wall, flattening his back.

"Which deck is the ramp on again?"

"For passengers on and off, sir?" Gibbons asked. Quigley nodded.

"Two decks down. If he's going to try and get off the boat, he'll have to take at least one stairs inside the boat, sir. The deck right below us is the last one with a promenade outside . . . "

Would he jump to the dock? Quigley wondered. Fifteen . . . eighteen feet; bad light . . . hardly.

"Fuck it, fuck it!" Quigley hissed. "Go down one deck you, Gibbons. Wait by the door there. That's where he'll make his move to come inside if he's really headed off the boat."

"Right."

"Now listen, man. I'm going to get behind him from here, so's I can take him at that door if I have any safe angle at all. I'll call out to him. You see him turn around, grab the oul lad he has with him. Through the door, if you can. By the hair if you have to. Just get him to the deck as fast as you can, I don't care. We'll have a clear take-down on the gunman if it works."

"Lookit, you have the wrong man. Where's the cameras? Is this 'Kojak?'" the older navvy said.

"Shut up. Walk slowly. You'll know it's for real if I have to use it."

The navvy turned and began walking slowly to the pier side of the boat. The tanned man stared at the door and then to the stairs ahead. Had he been mistaken?

When the navvy reached the stairs, he grasped the rail and stopped.

"Look, mister, it's none of my . . . "

The tanned man nudged him with the gun and stepped down after him.

"Slow down." The navvy stopped at the bottom of the stairs.

"We have to go inside now," the navvy said quietly. "It's the only way off without breaking your neck. If me mates see me, what'm I going to say to them?"

"Tell them you're looking after me."

The two men stood four steps from the door. The tanned man

looked around and listened. He looked toward the stairs they had come down.

"The door opens out, so no funny stuff," he said to the navvy. As the navvy grasped the handle, the tanned man hid his gunhand under the left side of his jacket. The navvy yanked the door open with ease and lifted his leg over the jamb. The smell of cigarettes and the *opep-opep* of a video game came through the door. And something else: the tanned man turned and looked back up the stairs. He knew instinctively that he had to hold out his hand to stay the closing door, but it would have to be his left hand. The sound from inside drowned out the voice from the top of the stairs.

Someone had knocked the navvy over inside. The heavy door had snapped almost shut. It was hissing slightly in the closing gap. The tanned man stepped back from the door and fired up the stairs. More shouting inside, the door clicking shut and the huge *daanng* as the bullet hit off a rail, whining off into the dark. The figure at the top of the stairs stayed flattened against the wall. The tanned man began backing away on his toes. A face appeared in a window next to him and reflexively he squeezed off a shot. The glass webbed instantly. Someone screamed. He watched the door where the navvy had been swallowed up. Overhead he heard footsteps running along the upper deck. Things were happening too fast, at least three men. Turning, he ran.

Quigley waved O'Rourke on toward the stairway forward of the ship. He heard O'Rourke's crêpe soles squeak softly as he began running down the wet promenade. Quigley started down the stairway slowly. Three steps down he saw the two men at the doorway below. Quigley shouted as the navvy opened the door. The Yank turned toward the stairway as the door closed abruptly ahead of him. Quigley heard muffled shouting from indoors. He saw the flash as his back pressed into the plate which formed a wall section to the upper stairway. The second shot was from further away, Quigley guessed.

He eased himself down one step, then another and took aim

232

at the doorway. Outside the door at the bottom of the stairway, the promenade deck was empty. Drizzle had gathered into droplets at the rims of the overhang, and they fell off slowly onto the railing beside him. Quigley strained to listen: the hush of sea, a breeze, drizzle. His arms were hurting. Images of passengers walking into a line of fire flashed on and off in his mind. He crouched near the railings, still pointing the gun at the doorway.

"Gibbons?" he called out, still pointing.

"Sir!"

"You got your man in?" he shouted.

"I have him here!" Gibbons shouted back.

"Where's the target?" Quigley didn't care that the edge of panic in his voice was quite plain now. He looked down the promenade. He thought he saw a flicker of movement, a shadow in the dimness beyond the lifeboats. Running? Gibbons' head appeared in the doorway. Quigley looked in at the navvy still sprawled on the floor, pale.

"Looks like he's headed for the stairs up ahead. Go inside, now and quick. O'Rourke's up there, maybe ahead of him, up above. Don't let the Yank inside!"

Quigley went forward in a crouch, his left hand on top of his right to keep the barrel down when he fired. He felt the beginnings of a cramp grasp the palm of his right hand. As he passed a window, a glance showed him some passengers on their knees, others running for doors from the lounge. The ship swayed very slightly from side to side. Faintly, a siren, two. Quigley swore aloud.

The tanned man stopped abruptly. Ahead of him was the other stairway descending from the deck above. It ran against him. A perfect spot to command entry to the doorway at the foot of the stairs. He strained to hear footsteps above him. Nothing. He looked behind. There was someone or something moving quickly around the lifeboat stanchions. He felt the ship's engine at idle, resonating underfoot. And something else, he sensed: the slightest tick, a vibration nearby. A footstep on the stairway? Through

233

a window he glimpsed a figure running inside. Another one. Had to move now.

He stepped abruptly to the foot of the stairway and aimed up. The figure had one foot tentatively on the step down and he was already turning sideways. The first shot staggered O'Rourke. The tanned man saw something fly up from the head with his second shot, as the head jerked. The arms flopped and O'Rourke fell, as a puppet dropped. He tumbled down the stairway flopping loosely, without any attempt to slow. O'Rourke's pistol clanged, fell down a step, then another, and lodged. His leg caught in a support and the rest of him fanned bumpily against metal, pivoting around head first.

The tanned man had three steps to the doorway. He was through the second and reaching for the handle when a blow to his left side danced him sideways. Shot, he thought remotely. Must be the one coming up behind me. This is what it is like to be shot? No pain yet, why? He almost lost his balance.

The shout from behind seemed to be coming from the far end of a playing field. Must have been the guy behind. The other one inside would have reached the door by now too . . . yes. He felt himself swaying. Dizzy a little, but things were clear, not like being drunk even.

He turned and fired, wondering. He heard the shot ricocheting angrily off metal. The ejected shell *pinged* and rolled lazily along the deck toward the door. He felt hot, things were loud. Can't even try to go up the stairs, he thought. He wondered if he had spoken aloud. He tried to grasp a railing again, but he couldn't feel it. Another shot, but this didn't hit. He strained to see where the one who had shot him was. The after-image of the flash wavered as his eyes scanned dully along the deck. Someone crouched by that big box near the stanchion . . . ? Not sure, keep looking, a movement . . . For a moment the tanned man was back in the water again, a child, listening to the voices of people on the beach, so far away, a plane droning overhead in the blue Florida sky. *Ah, shot. Mistakes but tried, tried hard.* Yes, there was someone crouched down there . . . The tanned man levelled his

234

pistol. A chance, he thought. Done tougher shots on the range a couple of times anyway . . . He thought of his father's face turning back to the newspaper, tight lips: his mother kneading her hands at the door, always defending *"He couldn't help it Seamus, he's only a boy."*

Out of the corner of his eye, the tanned man saw the door fly open. He started to draw his gun arm around toward the doorway, knowing he was too late.

Already braced in the doorway, Gibbons fired. The shot caught the man behind the ear and his chin rocked onto his chest as he fell forward. His knees hit first and Gibbons heard the *thunk* of his forehead hitting the deck. A spray of blood flicked onto the deck around the head. The body rolled slightly but then seemed to right itself, face down. Gibbons stared at the gun next to the right hand, and he walked slowly over the jamb of the door. He looked up the stairway at O'Rourke. The side of his head showed purple in the light. A steady stream of blood had run across two steps and was draining onto the last step. Gibbons could see it moving like there was no end to it, edging and pouring over onto the deck now, mixing with the wet gleam left by the rain. Quigley was running toward him, shouting. How could people have so much blood?

"Jesus, Mary and Joseph," Gibbons whispered. He remembered something out of his youth, long gone now, and not knowing what else to do for O'Rourke, he started on the Act of Contrition.

CHAPTER NINETEEN

On Wednesday, Kilmartin had met him for dinner in the Civil Service Club in St. Stephen's Green. After the soup, Kilmartin winked at Minogue.

"Will you take a glass of whisky with me beyond in Dwyers pub afterwards?"

"No thanks, Jimmy," Minogue murmured.

Kilmartin nodded slightly and toyed with his fork.

"It'd put me to sleep for the afternoon, so it would. Thanks anyway," Minogue offered.

"I see, I see," said Kilmartin, still observing the fork studiously. "To be sure, I understand."

The waitress clumped a plate in front of Kilmartin.

"Cod?" she said to Minogue. Kilmartin forked a piece of stringy beef.

"He flared up only the once yesterday, Loftus. But then he shut up very quickly," said Kilmartin. Minogue worked on the batter around the cod.

"Something about 'duty.' I asked him if he thought it was the duty of an officer in the Irish Army to resign his commission and work against the laws of a democratic state just because he didn't agree with the way the country was being run. I thought he was going to spit at me, so I did. But he clammed up then after a dirty big sneer at me. That's as far as we've got with that boyo."

Minogue nodded but stayed silent. By unspoken agreement, they had given up on Loftus. They had tried to lever him with news that the Yank had been caught and that he was telling all. Loftus, it seems, knew better. He said nothing. He had withdrawn, leaving a composed expression. It struck Minogue that Loftus seemed relieved now that he had done his duty.

"Some duty," Kilmartin said. "Ah, but something will turn up on this Yank, you'll see. Then Loftus'll say his piece."

Kilmartin had been wrong to date. The most that Loftus said in the days after his arrest was couched in a mixture of disdain and a half-hearted effort to explain by allusion. He soon stopped that, even, apparently sure in his mind that the audience of interrogators would never understand. That left Kilmartin to wonder if the Irish Army really would have gone into Derry in '69 like Loftus said. They had field hospitals and vehicles gathered up near the border, everyone had known that. Should they have gone in? Against the British Army, could they? Loftus had resigned within the year.

"I think maybe his trip to the States is what turned the corner for him," Minogue said finally.

"You mean all the hardware and blather they have over there? And where did it get them in Vietnam I ask you, Matt?" Kilmartin replied.

"America is a country full of savages. They don't know what they're at half the time. Look at the telly, I mean. Or should I say, don't look at the telly," Kilmartin said indignantly.

"'*Dulce et decorum est pro patria mori*,'" Minogue murmured.

"What?"

"It's about dying for your country."

"I have a brother out in the States. The wife is always at me to go over and have a look at the place. What about yourself, Matt?"

"I don't think so. I don't think I could manage over there at all. It's a different life entirely," Minogue replied.

Kilmartin affected to be considering some other matter and attacked the limp broccoli. Minogue waited. After several minutes' silence, Kilmartin looked up from the wreckage of his dinner. Minogue met his gravely gentle look reluctantly. Kilmartin's voice was barely above a whisper.

"Matt. What did you tell the Walshes out beyond?"

Minogue remembered Mrs Walsh dropping cup and saucer on the fireplace. A stain started in the carpet, her shaking hands reaching under cuffs for a hanky. Walsh had changed. No speech from him. He sat across from his broken wife, not wishing to be involved in weakness before a visitor. He told his wife she mustn't upset herself and she stopped. Minogue told them the truth. No, he couldn't be sure, but it was the most likely turn of events.

"How did they react, I mean," Kilmartin probed.

Minogue's anger turned the potato quite tasteless, an obstruction in his mouth. He waited, disguised in eating.

"I don't know how they reacted, Jimmy."

And he didn't. His thoughts went back to the Walshs' sterile living room, his attempt to explain the run of events to them . . . How Jarlath Walsh's knock on the door had probably not been heard by Allen because he was on the phone. The door was ajar, visualise. Jarlath puts two and two together and sees several things. Your son Jarlath sees credibility, a scoop if he can bring Allen to admit things out in the open. He doesn't know Allen is being blackmailed. Jarlath seems to have wanted to keep this all to himself. An exclusive. He tells nobody. He drops hints at Agnes. It's his secret, he's working on it. It's something he'll be proud of. Jarlath brings a tape recorder with him to talk with Allen, but Allen says nothing directly. Jarlath may have tried to wear him down probably, hints, winks. Allen is under terrible pressure and tells Loftus. Loftus tells him it'll be looked after.

Loftus is the one who has checked into Allen. Allen's original name is O'Donohue and Loftus trips him up on what happened a long, long time ago. So, Mr and Mrs Walsh, these people severally and individually have helped to have your son murdered. Outburst of tears from Mrs, glares from Mr: did you have to be like this, Minogue?

"And did Loftus murder Jarlath?" Mr had asked then.

Minogue can't pick careful enough words.

"We know he didn't actually kill him. He has an alibi for that night. But in law, he did, because he helped arrange it. Allen will be on the stand to testify to that."

"Who killed him . . . ?"

"We don't know. Loftus is saying nothing at all. We doubt he'll even be induced to tell, if indeed he knows, at his own trial for capital murder. We think your son was killed by the same person who killed two Gardai within the last week."

Mrs Walsh, perking up: "And who's he?"

"We're trying to find out. We think he's American."

Minogue, leaving, had felt the cold stare on his back all the way down the driveway.

"Well, you let them know we're continuing on the case. Doing our best," Kilmartin said. Minogue shook his head. The case was technically open, but Minogue's papers had been removed, the office was being painted. Minogue wondered if Garda inspectors spent more than half their time worrying about the management of impressions for the public.

"Yes," Minogue offered. Kilmartin was suspicious again.

"Doesn't that beat Banagher though," Kilmartin went on. "His prints are not on file with the Yanks. We're going through the airline lists now. My bet is he'll turn up to be a dud as regards the passport he came in on too. We have the pictures sent out, that's all we can do. Some of the lads thought he looked familiar, but they couldn't put a finger on it. Looked kind of Irish they all said."

Minogue tried the stewed apple but turned it away after one spoon.

239

"Think he did it, do you?" Kilmartin said.

"Yesterday, yes. Today, I don't know. There's the temptation to shove all the pieces together, to tidy up, I suppose," Minogue said in a conciliatory tone.

Minogue wanted to allow the unspoken intimacy to drift back to them. He made an effort to leave clear answers and comments for Kilmartin. The waitress banged their plates onto the trolley. She returned and plonked two cups of tea down. Minogue looked up at her, but she had turned and gone. Kilmartin offered his packet.

"Do you want a smoke?"

"No thanks, Jimmy. I'll try and steer clear of them."

"And Allen, how long ago was it . . . ?"

"He was thirteen at the time," Minogue answered. "He was babysitting and the parents walked in on him. I don't fully understand the wording from then, but I think it amounted to an aggravated rape on the child."

"Jesus, Mary and Joseph," Kilmartin whispered with a grimace.

"So he went to juvenile court, but they didn't send him to reformatory. Took counselling afterward and never looked back since. That's where he got the interest in psychology."

"That's not one bit funny at all," said Kilmartin.

"It caught up with him," Minogue speculated. "The whole thing."

"Like . . . ?"

"His mother. Nothing he did was ever good enough for her. He couldn't be Irish enough for her. No wonder his Da died young. Allen, or O'Donohue, was left to her mercy more or less. It's no wonder he did what he did."

"You don't believe that stuff about Irish mothers or parents in general, Matt, do you?"

Minogue didn't answer.

"What possessed that fella to be like that? I ask you. Couldn't he leave things well enough alone. I mean to say this hop-off-me-thumb helped to get people killed, do you follow me?" asked Kathleen.

Minogue was following a lorry on the road into Tulla. The hedges and trees almost met over the road. The ditch was full of grass and brambles. Small fields, stonewalled, secretive patching over hillocks. Clare: fields like a quilt.

They had passed the holy tree on the Limerick road, coins jammed into the bark, pieces of cloth tied to its branches. Minogue was daydreaming, waking, daydreaming. Words and verses had stayed circling in his head since he had woken up, thinking of his own parents.

> Will you come out tonight,love
> The moon is shining bright, love

His mother hanging clothes across the bushes from the haggard, air sweet and close on a May morning, the birds filling the air with sound.

"I mean. All this lu-la would never have happened. He must be a twisted man entirely. In Trinity College Dublin with them nobs. There one in the eye for that crowd. I'm glad Daithi and Iseult go to UCD, I don't care what they say. Where's your man from? Loftus is it?"

"He's Cork. Well-to-do, I suppose. A career soldier who should have stayed in," Minogue murmured.

"They all want power, isn't that the be-all and end-all," Kathleen asseverated.

"I suppose. Some notion of duty mixed in with an inferiority thing, I'd wager. A powerful mixture, that . . . "

"And he didn't budge," Kathleen added.

"Even after your man being shot out in Dun Laoghaire," Minogue said.

"Go on. Tell us a bit," Kathleen said.

"Well. There was a watch on for this fella. Very brash he was, brazening it out by trying to get on the boat to Holyhead. It's not that he was stupid or anything. He calculated things, that's my feeling. But he got annoyed at some point."

"How do you mean?" Kathleen asked

"Well, frustrated maybe. He shot that Garda Connors. Maybe they were hounding him."

"Who's 'they?'" Kathleen asked.

"The likes of that gangster, McCarthy. The old crowd. Maybe he just imagined it though."

"Isn't it the strangest thing?" Kathleen said.

Minogue was half driving, half looking around, half thinking. There were cars behind now. One had a Clare flag stuck out the window. No sign of the Kilkenny mob; the Kilkenny Cats, a sharper crowd of hurlers hadn't been let on the face of the carth. The Clare goalie would have to do Trojan work today.

Minogue had smelled deep from a cattle lorry on the way into Portlaoise. They had been unable to pass for ten minutes. The smell was still with him. It had left a lingering unease which surprised him. He wondered if he had detected a fear in the animals, perhaps knowing they were on the way to be slaughtered. Minogue tried to laugh off the persistent memory still locked in his nostrils. Middle age, dotage—he tried all the sneers to keep himself in line.

By the time they turned off the Limerick road to Killaloe and the Shannon, he had let his efforts slide. Though rested and jockeying a desk for a week, he felt the strangeness flood through him again. He had the baffling notion that things had changed again, that old things had faded and been eclipsed by something new. It was like waking up to know something was gone but that something else was imminent, a rejoinder. Without looking at her, Minogue sensed that Kathleen's thoughts had gone elsewhere too. She stared out the side window at the drumlins, the hedges, the tight and secret fields. Worrying still, Minogue knew.

Within ten minutes, Minogue and Kathleen were in sight of the village of Tulla, home of the resurgent Clare hurling team. The overcast sky hung still over streets glutted with cars. Men with caps down over their eyes, dogs, children with ice cream. The pubs had just closed. Sunday hours. They'd have to go out the Ennis road to get parking.

"You should do this more often so you should," Kathleen said. "The rest is a tonic, isn't it? Does for the both of us."

Minogue's thoughts edged onto irritation. He didn't want reassurance this way, people circumspect as if he were an invalid again. He couldn't even think of the questions he wanted to ask. The words fled away on him like pigeons disturbed off a roof. He fought off the resentment.

"Well now, if I'd known you were a fan, I'd have brought you here a long time ago, wouldn't I?" he said.

"I'm getting pointers for the Dublin team so we can leather ye when we get the chance," Kathleen replied with a laugh.

The traffic had been stopped for nearly five minutes. Minogue switched off the engine in the middle of Tulla. People walked around between the stranded cars on their way to the pitch. Then the cars ahead began to move. Stop again, wait.

"Look," Kathleen said "It's Mick. Maura—and Eoin."

Minogue looked out and saw his brother about to walk beyond the car.

"Mick. Maura!" Kathleen called out.

Mick turned, recognition dawning on him. He looked beyond Kathleen to Minogue. Maura came over too. Eoin, their oldest, looked on.

"Off to the match, so we are," Kathleen said.

"God bless ye," from hearty, pious Maura. Minogue imagined Maura tying bits of cloth onto the twigs over the holy well, polishing statues of the Blessed Virgin around the house. He watched his brother's face.

"Aye, aye," Mick said.

The wives began talking. Mick strolled around the driver's side. Minogue listened to Maura and Kathleen laughing. Eoin stood away. Like his Da, Minogue thought.

"How'ya Matt?" and his arm resting on the door of the car.

"Struggling," Minogue said, protected in ritual.

"Great goings on above in Dublin I hear," Mick said.

Minogue nodded and looked ahead. Maura and Kathleen were

243

touching each other, laughing. Eoin stood like a sentry, frowning off into the distance, his arms folded.

"Hard to know these days, isn't it? Who's who, I mean?" Mick said.

Minogue nodded.

"I saw your name in the paper, Matt, in connection with it."

"Marginal, Mick. Very marginal."

"We all do what we can, I suppose. Or do what we must?"

Minogue saw cars moving ahead.

"A bit of both, I'm thinking," Minogue said.

Mick nodded his head slowly and studied the chrome rim on the gutter.

Minogue started up the engine.

"That's the way of it, isn't it now? There's always another day, so there is," Mick said.

"God bless ye! " Maura waved.

That day, Clare beat the socks off Kilkenny thereby overcoming a superstition about losing vital games on their home ground of Tulla.

To Minogue the land, the hills, the hedges, the clouds were as parts of a stage. Kathleen had done more cheering than he had. Minogue began reciting "The Ballad of Tommy Daly":

On the windswept hill of Tulla
Where the Claremen lay their dead,
Three solemn yews stand sentinel
Above a hurler's head . . .

The crowds began to disperse. The pubs were opening, cars starting up. Only once during the game did he feel himself falling away, but he recovered quickly. His chest felt like a damp house for a while afterward.

He bought Kathleen and himself a steak in Portlaoise and he was picky about the wine. Kathleen was excited.

During the meal she told him she wanted to find a job and would he mind, bearing in mind that Iseult and Daithi would be gone soon. And speaking of which, Daithi was too embarrassed to broach the subject, but could we see our way to paying his fare to the States in the summer. If he gets the visa that is. He could visit his cousins up in Canada. It'd do him good so it would. And why not, because everyone else was going there these days and he'd learn to look after himself and couldn't be worrying about every little thing that might happen to him. Good experience for him.

Kathleen drew him out. He said let's go to France and why the hell not. She laughed and blamed it on the wine when she couldn't stop laughing. Oh didn't I marry the right one, she laughed, romantic nights in gay Paree, go on you're joking me. He said he wasn't. She laughed against her breath. Spluttering, laughing again. He said look at the Dublin crowd making a show of themselves down the country with drink. You can do what you like in Paris, she croaked in reply, even see the Follies but don't tell anyone.

In the valley after the wine, they were crossing the Curragh in darkness. Like the plains or the Prairies, Minogue thought. His throat was dry. He did not resist when the memory changed tense for him again that day. He knew this might be the last time it erupted over him before he could finally house it and think about it without the anger or the desperate urge to be forgiven, to try again. He wondered if he could bear to look at Allen again as he would probably have to during Loftus' trial.

CHAPTER TWENTY

Herlighy showed no surprise at Minogue's request. He followed Minogue out of the office.

"I'll be back within the hour, Mrs Sullivan," Herlighy said as he passed the receptionist. There was no one in the waiting-room.

"You're sure I'm not inconveniencing you, now," Minogue said as he grasped the hall door handle.

"Not a bit of it," Herlighy replied lightly. "I've been cooped up inside all day. Pardon the expression. Glad of a bit of fresh air, such as it is here."

Minogue pulled the heavy door open. The brass plaque on the door caught his eye as the wan afternoon light moved across it. Dr Sean Herlighy in black, the brass clear and polished. No mention of Herlighy's stock-in-trade, psychiatry, Minogue mused again.

Minogue paused before descending the half-dozen steps to the footpath. He looked out on Merrion Square ahead. Two days of wind and rain had left the trees bare of leaves.

"Hold on a minute," he heard Herlighy from behind. "I forgot my cigarettes."

Minogue leaned against the railing and looked down the terrace. Merrion Square was still a showpiece of Georgian architecture. Railings everywhere, granite edges to the steps, the wide doors with fanlights above. The rain had left the tree-trunks blackened. Cars hissed by on the roadway. The grass inside the Square would be completely sodden, Minogue calculated vacantly. Stick to the paths.

Herlighy had a lighted cigarette in his hand when he opened the door. The two men crossed the street and headed for the pedestrian gate. Minogue felt his nervousness as something unnecessary, a leftover from the anticipation which still clung to his thoughts even now beside Herlighy. They entered the Square. They had the place to themselves.

"I half thought of slipping into the National Gallery beyond and having a cup of coffee or the like," said Minogue.

"That'd be grand too," Herlighy said neutrally.

"Ah but I'd spend the day there looking at the pictures, I don't doubt."

Herlighy smiled tightly and blew out a thin stream of smoke. They walked slowly on the gravel path. Herlighy seemed to be studying the path ahead of him. Minogue knew it was up to him to start.

"So I was thinking I'd like to postpone things awhile," he began. "Wait and see what way the cat jumps, do you see "

"The sessions we have?" said Herlighy.

"Yes. What I mean is that . . . I think I'd like to try out things for myself now," Minogue added quietly.

"I understand," Herlighy said after a pause. "If you say you are ready, that's fine by me."

"You're not going to be idle now that I'm taking a break from the sessions, I hope," said Minogue.

247

"There's always plenty of work in my line," replied Herlighy.

"It's not that I didn't get a great deal of value out of our . . . you know," Minogue looked to Herlighy.

"Our chats."

"Our chats. I got a great deal of good out of them, yes indeed . . . "

"Are you staying on in the job, so?"

"If you had have asked me that two weeks ago, I would have said no. I don't think I would have even gone back to Vehicles."

Herlighy stopped and glanced at Minogue.

"You had offers of doing something away from the front-line, I remember. Crime prevention, a bit of training for in-service or new recruits . . . ?"

"Ah, I'd be bored stiff with that stuff, I have to admit," Minogue shrugged.

"Tell me why you're staying on, then."

Minogue blinked. He looked beyond Herlighy to the dripping trees. Were psychiatrists supposed to be this direct? A test?

"I haven't quite worked it out completely but . . . I didn't want to throw in the towel because of what happened. What you explained about trauma was very good, you see. I got so as I knew what was happening better. It's more like I don't want to be sitting at home watching the news, being able to switch off the telly or change the station if I don't like what I see . . . It's hard to express, you see . . . "

Herlighy nodded once and began walking again.

"I don't want something like this happening again, I suppose you could say," Minogue added. "I wish I could . . . "

"About Agnes McGuire, you mean?" asked Herlighy without slowing his stride.

Minogue felt the tightness close on his chest again. he drew a deep breath. The air was full of the dank smell of rotting leaves.

"Yes," said Minogue hoarsely.

He stopped walking. Herlighy sensed he was walking on alone now and he turned. Minogue was standing with his hands deep in his coat pockets, staring out over the wet lawns. Herlighy took a long drag on his cigarette. He thought of some of the comments he had written in Minogue's file after the first sessions. An overly sensitive cop, caretaker personality quite dominant. Herlighy had been pessimistic at the start. A bogman, this cop, plainly out of place in this fraying city.

He walked over to Minogue.

"You'll be trying again then, Matt. Is that how I should write it in me file?"

Minogue searched Herlighy's face for any humour.

"You know that I can sign you for the full disability. There'd be no problem in the world in you getting the full salary until you qualify for the pension at retirement age," Herlighy added. "Have you considered that aspect?"

Minogue didn't reply immediately.

"I'd still like to keep on at the job," Minogue murmured. "If they'll let me."

It was Minogue who started down the path first this time. Herlighy flicked the cigarette butt into the grass and followed him. Minogue seemed to be more relaxed now as he walked next to the psychiatrist.

"I don't need to tell you that you're welcome to stop by anytime," said Herlighy.

"Thanks very much."

Herlighy reached for the packet of cigarettes again. Minogue stopped when he heard the scratch of Herlighy's lighter. Herlighy eyed his patient over his cupped hands as he flicked at the lighter again. Minogue's gaze was straying out over the acres of grass again. Gone already, thought Herlighy. The gas ignited this time and Herlighy tasted the first papery burn of the smoke. He caught up with Minogue.

"Did I tell you that Kathleen and myself are going to steal away to Paris for a little holiday?"

"Paris?" asked Herlighy. "Why Paris?"

Minogue smiled and scratched behind one ear.

"Oh there's a sort of a story to it . . . do you want to . . . ?"

249

Herlighy said he did. They walked on under the trees, Herlighy silent, listening to Minogue.

When tired, Herlighy often had an image of himself sitting in his office here in a country on the periphery of Europe, trying to sort out the Byzantine web of sophistry and evasion. Sometimes he had to remind himself that he, Herlighy, was searching, himself. He wondered if Minogue would visit again. Herlighy put the packet of cigarettes back in his pocket. So Minogue was ready for more. More what? Another drag on the cigarette reminded him of his envy.

EPILOGUE

Minogue had walked around Dublin on Friday, from church to church, museum to gallery. He had sat in the chill caves of cathedrals for a rest, unable to pray.

There had been nothing in Allen's car. It had been taken apart: nothing at all. They didn't want to charge him with anything, just dump him. All a mess, dump it back on Dublin.

Agnes McGuire had died early on Friday morning, letting go and casting off for where she'd not be let down again, Minogue thought. Did Allen know yet? And Loftus, now silent and remote, the little Napoleon, the one-eyed king, did he care? Minogue had not run fast enough or far enough. Again and again he saw the soldiers pulling two out of the car that night, then Allen's grey face in the back of the van.

Instead of a Mass Card, Minogue bought a card with a copy of Walter Osborne's 'Scene in the Phoenix Park' on it. He got them to use it as a Mass Card in Clarendon Street. He thought about going to visit Mick Roche, but he felt he should wait.

Walking through Trinity College, nothing had changed except the film of suspicion and resentment which had come across his vision. Gowned lecturers billowed past him in Front Square. Minogue turned away from his path and wondered if he should tear up the card.